ALSO BY JUDITH A. BARRETT

Maggie Sloan Thriller Series

Grid Down Survival Series

Riley Malloy Thriller Series

Donut Lady Cozy Mystery Series

SEE BEYOND THE FOG

Maggie Sloan Thriller Series

Book 5

Judith A. Barrett

SEE BEYOND THE FOG

MAGGIE SLOAN THRILLER SERIES BOOK 5

Published in the United States of America by Wobbly Creek, LLC

2023 Georgia

wobblycreek.com

SEE BEYOND THE FOG is a work of fiction. Names, characters, businesses, places, events, locales, and incidents either are the products of the author's imagination or used in a fictitious manner. Any resemblance to actual persons, living or dead, or actual events is purely coincidental.

Cover by Wobbly Creek, LLC

ISBN 978-1-953-870-17-9

PREVIOUSLY . . .

My name is Maggie Sloan Ewing, but most people call me Gray Lady, like the undercover gray man who blends in; my tall, blue-eyed husband is Larry Ewing; his original name was Kevin, but he's become so accustomed to being called Larry that he claims Kevin is his undercover name.

We moved to be near Larry's first Georgia Bureau of Investigation assignment at the regional office in Columbus, Georgia; of course, Lucy, our sweet, old, brown German short-haired pointer and the imaginary men, Palace Guard and Spike, went with us.

You might have noticed I mentioned "imaginary men." There's a long story behind that, but the short version is I was severely injured several years ago by a massive explosion in the library where I worked; the force of the blast tossed me across the lawn, almost to the parking lot.

Palace Guard and Spike helped me when I struggled with physical therapy then stayed with me after I left the hospital. Palace Guard ran with me to build up my strength and taught me how to throw a knife; Spike toughened me up and taught me how to cheat.

Setbacks happen, right? When I caught a senior center's custodian in the act of replacing valuable jewelry with fake, the jewel thief sprayed my face with a powerful alkaline cleaning solution. The surgeon couldn't save my left eye but has hopes that the second surgery on my right eye will eventually result in at least partial sight. My sense of hearing has become extremely sensitive, probably to compensate for my sight limitations, so there is that.

Heather, Spike's favorite undercover officer, gave me a 'jo,' a shorter version of an ancient Japanese weapon, to use as a cane and a weapon, and Palace Guard helped me renew my knife-throwing skills. It was a huge boost to my confidence that I could still protect myself.

A killer ambushed me after my second eye surgery; evidently the coward was confident that I would be blind and vulnerable. He was only half right because I had anticipated an attack, and with Palace Guard's eyes to guide me, I stopped him permanently.

When Larry told me we'd be leaving in a week for his crime scene specialist training in Tennessee, I was more excited than when I stopped the killer because it's what Larry has always wanted to do. What do I want? Just a normal life. Are you laughing along with Spike and Palace Guard?

CHAPTER ONE

When I tapped down the hallway with my jo from the guest bedroom to the faint light in the Coyles' living room, Palace Guard tapped my shoulder then guided me into the kitchen.

"Good morning, lazy bones. I'll pour you a cup of coffee," Kate said.

She must be getting soft; she didn't ambush me in the hall.

I sat at the kitchen table, and Kate continued, "You're getting pretty good with your jo, or did Palace Guard guide you? Your cup is in front of you. Dad, Lucy, and Spike went out back. Did the cinnamon rolls wake you?"

"The coffee did." I yawned then wrapped my hands around the cup. "Thanks for the coffee. Before I had the second surgery, I could see light and people-blobs. This morning, I was happy when I saw the light from the living room because I was afraid I'd never get away from the dark. The doctor said my sight might improve in my right eye to near normal or at least correctable with glasses, but it will take a while."

Kate joined me at the table and slurped her coffee. "Mom and Ella expected to have your things unpacked and organized in three days at your new place, but they ran into a sudden change in plans. You know about that, right?"

I cringed at the high-pitched screech of the baking pan as it scraped across the oven rack when Kate pulled it out.

"I don't know about any changes. What are they? Good or bad?"

"You'll hear, and it's good."

She's enjoying this; I need to ignore her. After I inhaled the clean, sweet, yeasty aroma of the cinnamon rolls, I sipped my cooled coffee.

"Any requests for what we can do today other than an ambush?" Kate asked. "Dad told me Mom made him responsible for enforcing the truce, and I promised him we wouldn't be the reason Mom divorces him."

"That's right." Glenn came into the kitchen. "Good morning, Maggie. Ready for breakfast?"

I smelled Lucy's doggy aroma and heard her as she padded toward me; when she nudged my elbow, I reached out, and she gave my fingers a quick lick. I giggled when I heard her flop onto the floor.

"Are you rubbing her belly, Spike?" Glenn asked. "Because if you aren't, Lucy has gone into a trance over the cinnamon rolls."

Kate snickered. "Wasn't hard to guess, was it, Dad?"

"I don't understand why you can see Spike, and I can't," Glenn grumbled.

Kate spoke in a haughty voice. "It takes a certain, typically unobtainable level of intellectual—"

I interrupted, "Immaturity."

Kate growled, "You want eggs and sausage, or not?"

Glenn cleared his throat. "Yes, Kate, we'd like eggs and sausage."

Kate slammed the frying pan on the stove then while the sausage sizzled, she said, "Just a friendly reminder, Maggie: you're the one who's blind, not me. I saw that smirk."

When she dropped my plate onto the table in front of me with a thud, I imagined Glenn's glare and pursed my lips to hold back another smirk as I reached for my fork.

While we ate, I said, "There are two things I'd like to do today: run and shoot."

"We can do that. I poured you more coffee, Dad," Kate said.

She's trying to smooth things over with Glenn.

Glenn's phone rang. "I'll take this on the patio."

"What's our running plan?" Kate asked. "More coffee?"

"Sure." I set my cup on the table for the refill. "Larry, Palace Guard, and I ran when no one else was on the track. Larry walked and ran with Palace Guard and me; my pace was slow, but I still wore out after a few times around the track."

"That's easy then. You can meditate while I run at my pace a few more laps, and we can go to the range. We can shoot, clean guns, or both. I always told 'em you could clean a gun blindfolded."

I smiled at the memory of the times Kate and I spent together in the back office of the range while we cleaned guns. "I didn't think about cleaning guns. That would be fun."

Glenn returned from the patio. "I need more coffee. Sarge called, Maggie. He told me one of your mother's friends called her and told her about a murder near the training center in Tennessee. Sarge said your mother wants you to stay with us until they return. They're preparing to leave Arizona to come back."

"I'm going to Tennessee to be with Larry," I growled.

"That's what I told Sarge, and he agrees with you. He's taking his time getting their RV ready to move until after you talk to your mother. She'll call you. I'd ask if you needed any backup, but you'll be fine."

"I'm going to make a call," Kate said. I heard the sliding glass door to the patio open then close.

"She stuck us with the dishes, didn't she?" I asked.

Glenn chuckled. "She tried that when she was a teenager too. We'll leave them; she won't be able to stand the sight and will take care of them when she comes back to the kitchen. Want to go with me to the grocery store? We need more steaks if Jennifer and Ella will be here tonight. Ella will want to invite Moe to have dinner with us."

I shuddered. "I'm not sure I'm ready for a big crowd."

"You aren't," Kate said, as she came inside from the patio. "We have plans tonight."

"Right," I said. *I wonder what they are.*

Glenn rose from the table. "While you two get your story straight, I'll be at the grocery store. Just let me know if I'm included, and I'll turn over the grill to Ella."

My phone rang before Glenn left.

"Your mother," Kate said, and the front door clicked.

When I answered, Mother said, "Margaret, Tennessee isn't safe. We can be home in two weeks, then you can stay with us. I'm sure you can stay with the Coyles until we get there. Big D said we don't want to spend too many hours on the road without taking a break, and he has a list of people he has plans to visit on our way back. He told me I could fly home, but I don't want him to travel by himself because he'd hurry to get home and drive all day and half the night to get back, and I know he wouldn't eat right. Big D would eat salty snack foods right out of the bag for dinner if he had his way, and I know he wouldn't take his medicine if I wasn't right there to remind him. Big D told me police officers are notorious for not eating what they should. I suppose that's why you don't want to leave Larry alone. I'll bet Larry's the same way, isn't he?"

When Mother took a breath, I said, "You're exactly right, Mother. Friends and eating right are very important."

"This is our first trip this far west, and we're meeting with Big D's contacts in every town we pass through. My friends told me that marriage would change you. I'm glad you agree; it's settled. Big D can meet up with his friends, and I'll make sure he takes his medicine, and you'll make sure Larry takes his medicine. I'm glad we had this talk."

Mother hung up, and I smiled.

"I heard the entire conversation, and I hate to admit it, but you were amazing," Kate said. "I wouldn't have guessed that she just needed to get it out of her system."

"When I was a kid, I'd argue with Mother, but she was so hard of hearing that she never heard me. I finally realized she'd loop around and agree with what I already said, but she didn't hear. Time for me to get dressed."

After I returned to the kitchen, Kate asked, "Do you just grab a random shirt?"

I nodded. "I usually do unless I feel like a certain color, then I ask Larry for help. If I have a special occasion, I grab one of the plastic bags with the coordinated outfits that Heather put together for me. Did you talk to someone about Tennessee?"

"Sure did. So, want to go to your fancy apartment for the evening? Dad has the key."

I sighed. "I'm not sure I'm up to going anywhere. Couldn't I just hide in my bedroom, and you could sneak me my steak?"

"Go sit on the patio while I make a batch of spicy sausage for Mom. The fresh air will do you good, and you can decide if you want to stay here and be polite to people or leave and be grumpy. I'm okay either way, but those are your two choices."

Lucy followed me while I made my way to the patio. I grumbled, "Wasn't that a version of an ambush?"

"Sure was," Kate cackled from the kitchen, "and Dad wasn't here to witness it."

Lucy whined, and the door from the patio to the backyard squeaked open. I smiled. *Lucy and Spike went out to the yard.*

After I sat on my chair and propped up my feet on the footstool that Glenn had put on the patio for me, I picked up my phone and said, "Text Larry: 'See you tomorrow. Can't wait.'"

Palace Guard patted my shoulder.

I relaxed and leaned back. "Thanks."

The nearby birds serenaded me while I listened to Lucy join in with the dogs that barked as they spread what sounded like the canine version of neighborhood gossip.

When the sliding glass door groaned, Kate joined me on the patio.

"You smell like sausage," I said.

"No surprise there. I brought you one of your sippy cups with sweet tea. Ready to hear what I found out about Tennessee, or do you want to sulk some more?"

"You're all heart, Kate. I'm done pouting, and thanks for the tea."

Kate's chair scraped against the concrete floor as she moved it closer to the table, and I clenched my jaw.

I need to adjust to annoying sounds or get some earplugs.

"The murder in Tennessee has all the earmarks of a domestic homicide. Witnesses reported that a man shot a woman in the parking lot of a fancy bed-and-breakfast. When the police detective went to the woman's home to notify her husband, he was not there and was nowhere to be found. The owner of the B&B said the woman and her companion, who was inside the door waiting for her, were frequent guests, but the companion left abruptly by the back door at the sound of the single shot. The neighbors on both sides of the married couple's house said the pair argued loudly and regularly, and the neighbor across the street said a man frequently stayed overnight when the husband was out of town. When the neighbor asked the wife about the man, the wife said her brother kept her company because she was afraid to stay alone. Snoopy neighbors are my favorite."

"Doesn't sound like anything to keep me from going to Tennessee."

Kate snorted. "I agree, as long as you don't dig into it and find something the local investigators missed. So, what are you having for dinner tonight? Steak or pizza?"

I sighed. "Steak."

"Good." Kate's chair scraped again when she rose. "Don't be too perky, though. If you're mopey enough, Mom will take pity on you and bake a big batch of cookies for you to take to Tennessee, and I'll snag some for my trip."

I giggled. "I'll work on it."

Lucy and Spike joined me on the patio after their backyard time. Lucy padded past me on her way to the kitchen then noisily slurped water from her bowl.

"I'll leave the sliding glass door open. Holler if you need anything," Kate said.

After she left, I sighed. *I need Larry.*

My phone buzzed, then the automated voice read the text. "From Larry. On the road. Save me a seat at supper."

When I whooped, Kate shouted from the kitchen. "Are you okay?"

Palace Guard pulled away the footstool then helped me to my feet. With his guidance, I hurried to the kitchen. "Larry's on his way and will be here for supper. We can have a party."

"Unfortunately, you missed the full impact of my rolling eyes and my morose glare because Larry just messed up my brilliant cookie plan, but it makes sense and might work anyway. Mom will be glad that Dad won't be taking you to Tennessee and traveling back by himself after all. We'll work it from that angle, and Larry can help make it work. Now, aren't you glad I ambushed you?"

"You did not have a successful ambush because Larry was my preferred choice all along. He actually helped me ambush you, but I'll be pitiful enough for cookies as long as Larry doesn't catch me."

I listened while Kate hummed and wrapped the sausage to put in Jennifer's freezer.

Kate sounds happy. What's up with that?

Glenn's truck pulled into the driveway, then he grunted as he came inside. "Here's the ice chest. I made a mistake and asked your mother to send me a shopping list; there's more in the truck." The heavy ice chest banged on the table when he set it down.

"I'll put away the groceries, Dad," Kate said.

After he returned with his third load of groceries, Glenn said, "I assume you've heard from Larry. Any bets on who gets here first?"

"That's a hard one. Ella is a total speed demon. I think it depends on who left town first," I said.

"I'll bet Mom and Ella were on the road long before sunrise because Mom would want enough time to cook this afternoon," Kate said. "Didn't Larry say to save him a seat for supper? I'll go with Ella and Mom."

"I'll go with Larry," I said. "He won't be here for lunch, but he may have left early too, and his breaks will be shorter."

"You want to be the tiebreaker, Dad?" Kate asked.

"Thanks, but no thanks." Glenn chuckled. "It would be like trying to pick my favorite daughter."

"Me," Kate and I said in unison, and she smacked my hand when I held it up for a high five.

"Exactly." I heard the smile in Glenn's voice. "Maggie, since you didn't want to be around a big crowd, you'll be interested in hearing that Jennifer invited Paul and his wife to eat with us this evening because she said it was only right to have all the office together. She claims you never resigned your position with the Coyle Detective Agency."

"A small crowd?" I giggled.

"Has your hearing improved with your loss of sight?" Kate asked. "I'll give you a set of remarkable earplugs; today should be an excellent test of them for you."

"Thanks, my hearing has become extremely sensitive. The surgeon warned us it might, but she said I may adjust and become less reactive to sound after a while."

"How about the track and range? Still interested?" Kate asked.

"Let's go to the range first, so I won't wear out before we get there."

"Are you going to shoot at the range?" Glenn asked.

"Don't look so surprised, Dad. Of course, she is, then she'll clean guns. Blind girl needs the practice. She can wear the all-powerful earplugs and muff hearing protection together. If the noise still hurts her ears, we'll leave."

I raised my hand. "She's right here."

Kate laughed. "Palace Guard, tell her to grab her gun and hat, so we can go."

I stuck out my tongue toward her voice, then with Palace Guard's help, I made my regal exit as I princess-waved, and Glenn guffawed.

Must have been effective. I smiled.

"I need my Texas Tech cap," I whispered after Palace Guard and I were in my room. He guided me with taps to my cap, my holster with the pistol snugged inside, and a box of ammunition. I put on my cap then placed my holstered gun and ammunition into my backpack.

I shivered in anticipation then picked up my backpack and jo. Palace Guard followed me to the living room, and we waited. When I caught a whiff of sausage behind me, I turned. "About time you were ready. Your fancy, high-up FBI position has spoiled you and slowed you down, hasn't it?"

Kate snorted. "Glad your spirits have improved, even if your temperament has not. You better wipe away that cheerful face before Mom shows up, or we'll both leave town without cookies."

"I can do that."

After Kate pulled away from the house, I said, "I don't ever remember hearing you hum before. What's up?"

Kate exhaled then growled, "Nothing."

I cleared my throat and pretended to watch the scenery as we headed toward the range.

Kate parked, and I waited.

"Fine, we'll talk later. Hold out your hand, and I'll give you the earplugs. You'll still be able to hear conversations and even soft sounds, but the earplugs will soften the loud and screechy sounds."

I felt the earplugs in my palm and picked one up.

"Either ear. They mold to your ear canal after you insert them, and they won't be visible."

After I put in the earplugs, I said, "Comfortable."

"Good. Let's go."

On the way to the range store, Kate asked, "How did you shoot Eric Stephens?"

"Palace Guard and I took advantage of my hearing, and I practiced by throwing my knife at a target. He tossed a rock at the target then adjusted my position with a tap on my arm. When Eric Stephens came around the corner to the backyard, Palace Guard threw a small rock that told me where Eric was standing. After I tossed my knife and hit Eric, I pulled out my pistol. Palace Guard tapped my arm for a slight correction, and I fired."

"How did you judge the distance?" Kate asked.

"We planned in advance where I'd stand as he came around the corner."

"Genius. You're amazing, Palace Guard, and you're no slouch yourself, O Sightless Wonder."

After she parked, Kate said, "Give me your gun."

I listened while she checked it. "It's clear. I'll load it for you on the range."

When we reached the door, Kate paused before she opened it. "The sound of your shots didn't bother you?"

"I hadn't thought about that before, but I think I was too wired."

"Good to know. That means you can wear your earplugs during the day without having to pull out earmuff hearing protection when you shoot a bad guy."

"Don't say that in front of Larry. He thinks my days of shooting bad guys are behind me."

"Gotcha." Kate opened the door, and we went inside.

Kate went into the office while I pretended to be interested in whatever was in the case in front of me.

When someone came into the store, Palace Guard tapped my arm to move, and I shifted to a different display.

"We're set," Kate said, and I followed her out the door with Palace Guard's guidance. On our way to the range, Kate said, "The range is closed for our private session. The owner, Skip, wants to observe, and I told him we didn't mind, but he had to be quiet. He's working on a class for people with disabilities and hoped he could pick up some tips. After we finish on the range, he has some rentals we can clean."

"Perfect. How do we start?"

"Let's figure out distances, so Palace Guard can give you an idea of where your target is if there's no time to find a rock."

Palace Guard laid his hand on my forearm. "Can we go with long, medium, short range?"

"Let's see how that would work." Kate walked away from me, and I turned toward her voice, then Palace Guard adjusted my position.

"This is long," she said, and I held out my arm. Palace Guard tapped my wrist; I tapped my wrist and said, "Long range."

Kate moved then said, "Medium." Palace Guard tapped the middle of my forearm, and I said, "Medium."

She moved closer to me. "Short." Palace Guard tapped my elbow, and I said, "Short."

Kate returned to me and said, "I'm within range to grab you."

Palace Guard tapped the side of my knee, and I said, "Jo. Knife." I swung my jo then reached down for my knife as Kate yelled from the ground, "Truce."

I heard a low quiet whistle behind me, and I smiled. "You were supposed to be quiet, Skip."

Kate chuckled. "At least you called it, so I could drop before you hit me."

"I knew you would."

"I'm going to move targets to different ranges, then we'll go down the line. Shoot each target once then move, but don't worry about speed. Right now we're looking for any corrections," she said.

After Kate returned, she handed me the muff hearing protection and loaded my gun. Palace Guard and I moved down the line while he marked the range on my arm then corrected my position, and I shot. We had a good rhythm by the time we were midway.

After the last target, I placed my gun on the table, removed my muffs, and rubbed my forehead; Kate asked, "How are you doing?"

"I'm fine; just a little headache."

"Thought so."

"I could clean a few guns." I tried not to sound whiny because that would prove Kate's point.

"Skip," Kate said, "We're going to have to call it a day. We won't have time to clean guns."

"I'm sorry I won't see that, but I learned from you, Kate. Keep it simple and pay attention to what your trainee says."

"One gun?" I asked.

"We'll clean one gun, Skip. Got a nice dirty one for us?" Kate asked.

"Sure do."

While Kate unloaded my gun and packed everything else up, she said, "Clean two guns: your own, and one for Skip."

"Perfect, thank you." Palace Guard and I followed Kate into the store to the back room.

"Okay, Maggie. Kate asked for my dirtiest gun," Skip said. "I have a gun that we found shoved under some rags in one of our rental lockers after we broke the lock to get in. I contacted the owner, and he was pretty curt and said he didn't want it back. I was ready to salvage parts from it because it doesn't look like anyone has ever cleaned it."

"Awesome." I shivered in excitement, and Kate and Skip laughed.

After I sat at the table, Kate said, "Let me know what tool you need, and I'll hand it to you."

"No, lay them out in front of me, so I can reach them. I'll select them by feel."

"Okay, but I'm close if you need anything," Kate said.

As I took the gun apart, I shook my head. "Poor thing."

I hummed one of the fairy tunes as I cleaned each piece then stopped. "Skip, this part needs to be replaced; it's defective."

When Skip leaned over my shoulder, I smelled gunpowder. "Dang, now I see it. This gun would probably have misfired or completely missed the target every time the owner shot it. No wonder he didn't want it back, and no one would have bought it, as filthy as it is."

"I'll finish cleaning the rest of the parts, so it will be ready to be put together. This will make a great rental gun for beginners to use."

While I cleaned each part, Skip placed them into a box.

"Shall I put it together for you as much as I can without that piece?" I asked.

"Go ahead, Pistol Girl," Kate said. "I think Skip lost his voice."

Skip cleared his throat. "I did; I'd like to see that."

I hummed another fairy tune while I put together as many pieces as I could. "Well, that's the best I can do." I sighed.

"Well done; your talent is still there," Kate said. "Clean your gun, then we'll go home."

After I took it apart, cleaned it, then put it back together, Kate said, "I've seen you do it faster."

"I know, but this time I wasn't trying to beat you."

"I've never seen anyone like you, Maggie," Skip said. "If you and Lieutenant Ewing ever come back here, you have a guaranteed job. Heck, I'll give you a fifty percent partnership."

I felt my face grow warm.

"Not much makes Maggie blush, but you did it, Skip. It's like offering a kid a fifty percent partnership in a candy store," Kate said.

Skip hugged me before we left.

On our way to Glenn's, Kate said, "You've got a friend for life, Maggie. I didn't notice that defective part, and I was sitting next to you. There's a lot to be said for knowing what a functioning part feels like. How are you feeling?"

"Much more confident; I loved cleaning the guns and fitting together the pieces of Skip's gun. That was great therapy, Kate, thank you, but the sound of a gunshot is too loud for me. I don't want to shoot again for a while."

"You hit every target, so you'll be fine if you have to shoot. Just remember the sound of the gunshot, so you'll be mopey when we're back at Mom's house. We're skipping the track; if you're worn out, Mom will blame me, and we won't get any cookies. What were those tunes you were humming? They were very relaxing."

"Some tunes I learned from Mother when I was growing up, but I'd forgotten them for quite a while. They're the tunes the fairies sang to her when she was young."

When Kate parked in front of the house, she asked, "Fairies?"

"Yep, we're here, right? I'm starved. Is it close to lunchtime?" I climbed out of her SUV with the assistance of my jo to find the curb. Palace Guard and I headed to the house, and Kate slammed her door then caught up with me.

CHAPTER TWO

"Besides real imaginary men and fairies, what else do I need to know?" Kate asked.

I paused and stood in the doorway. "Why were you humming?"

"Don't mess up my cookie plan," Kate hissed.

Palace Guard tapped my arm, and I blocked her way with my jo.

"Fine. I'll go in the back door," Kate huffed as she stomped away.

"That went well, don't you think?" I asked.

Palace Guard patted my back in congratulations as Glenn opened the front door.

"Where's Kate?" Glenn asked as Palace Guard and I went inside the house.

"She went around back; she needed a little time to think. When's lunch?"

"Anytime you're ready. I have ham and turkey. What would you like?"

Should I tell him I can make my own sandwich? Palace Guard put his hand on my shoulder. *Palace Guard's right. I need to pace myself.*

"Turkey sounds good."

"I'll make it," Kate said as she came in through the patio. "What would you like, Dad?"

"Turkey. Want to sit on the patio, Maggie? I'll bring you some sweet tea. I'll bet you're exhausted."

I exhaled. "Thanks."

After we were all on the patio with our sandwiches and tea, Glenn asked, "How was the range?"

I took a bite of my sandwich, so Kate could answer.

"Maggie did really well for her first time after her surgery, but I'm afraid we wore her out," Kate said.

I nodded then listened to a familiar sound outside. "A truck just pulled in front of the house." I knocked over my chair when I jumped up and squealed, "Larry!"

I rushed to the door with my jo; Palace Guard stayed with me and kept me from running into walls. Lucy joined me and yipped, and Spike chased after her. I threw open the door and tore down the driveway and leapt into Larry's arms.

He lifted me up and swung me around, and I giggled with delight.

When he put me down, I said, "You beat Ella, honey. Did you have her stopped for speeding?"

He hugged me and laughed. "No, sweetie, that is what you would do. I skipped the last rest stop and waved at them. They're about five minutes behind me."

"Want some lunch? How was your trip? Do you like the house? Let's go inside."

"I'll grab my gear first."

We strolled into the house with Larry's arm around my waist.

"I guess you won, Maggie," Glenn said. "Have you eaten, Larry? We have ham and turkey."

"Whatever's convenient." Larry hugged me.

"Turkey it is."

"I missed you." Larry kissed me. "Hi, honey. We'll be home soon. I have good news for you."

Lucy whined her hello to Larry, and he held onto my hand as he knelt to greet her. "There's my sweet girl."

When he released my hand, I knew Lucy had flopped over for her belly rub.

A car screeched to a stop in front of the house, and Ella stormed inside. "Dang it, Larry. We were in front of you the whole way until you blew past that rest stop. We'd have done the same thing if we'd have known how close you were, and don't you dare tell Les how fast I was going."

"Hi, Ella," I said.

"Well, aren't you a sight for sore eyes? Mine, not yours." Ella hugged me, and her booming laugh was contagious; I giggled, and Larry chuckled.

"That is one big stick for such a tiny thing to carry. Where'd you get that?"

"Heather gave it to me. It a smaller version of a Japanese fighting stick."

"Nice. I like your hair color; it's light brown with blond and red streaks." Ella lifted my hair with her fingers. "We should have thought of camo hair for you earlier. You'll blend in wherever you go, except for carrying that big stick." Ella chuckled.

"I didn't know I had camo hair. Thanks." I pulled a thick strand of hair in front of my right eye to examine the color, but it just blocked the light.

"Maggie!" Jennifer smashed me into a hug. "Have you and Kate behaved?" she asked.

"Yes, ma'am," I said.

"I don't believe you, but I don't see any bruises on either of you, so it must have been a virtual ambush."

Kate came into the living room and snorted, and I smirked.

"Thought so." Jennifer released me.

Larry put his arm around my shoulder and whispered, "Tell me later?"

"Ready to put away your gear, honey?" I asked. "What's the big news? What time are we leaving in the morning?"

"Whenever you wake up; come supervise me while I carry my gear to our room, and I'll tell you our news." We strolled down the hallway together, then Larry led me to the soft chair and knelt next to me.

"Is all this going to be too much for you?" he asked.

My heart melted at the concern in his voice. "It would be, but you're here. I'll be fine."

I told him about Kate's ambush, the bet, and the cookies.

"I have great news. On my way to Tennessee, the training center called me. They had an opening in two of the apartments for families, and we were first on the list, so I had a choice. I picked the ground level apartment even though it was smaller. Dogs aren't allowed, but the housing director approved a waiver for Lucy because of your sight. I paid the extra fee in advance for the cleaning they will do after we move out. Jennifer diverted the moving truck to a storage unit because the apartments are fully furnished. Ella, Jennifer, and I inspected the apartment, and they approved. While the moving truck crew put our furniture in storage, I rented a small trailer for the day, and Ella and I moved all the boxes with clothes and other things that we'd need while we're at the training center while Jennifer recleaned the apartment. Thanks to Ella's organization and careful cataloging of the boxes, it was very simple to do. It took Jennifer and Ella less than thirty minutes to unpack the boxes with our clothes and belongings that Ella packed."

"So, we'll be living on campus?"

"Sure will. That makes reporting to my next assignment much simpler, and the landlord for the apartment in town was happy to have the apartment available for a longer-term renter."

"What a wonderful surprise," I said.

"I asked Jennifer and Ella to keep it quiet, so I could tell you myself. So, I'll help with the cookie caper. I'll look concerned and hover," he said.

"Cookie caper? I like that." Kate walked into the bedroom. "You've always hovered over Camo Girl, Larry; you're a natural. Mom sent me to tell you two that lunch is ready, and Ella said we're not allowed to call Les by the name we all call him: Moe."

"Moe is Les." I snickered. "Got it."

"Get it out of your system now, sister; Mom will trash the cookies if you make Ella mad," Kate hissed as Larry and I followed her down the hallway toward the dining room.

"Spoilsport; Ella's not that delicate," I grumbled.

"Perfect," Larry whispered. "Remember that grumble and Kate, the spoilsport."

I'll just be mad at Kate until she tells me why she was humming.

When we reached the dining table, Larry asked, "Have you eaten, sweetie? There are enough sandwiches for an army. Did you make the potato salad, Kate?"

Ella chuckled. "Jennifer made it last night before we went to bed, so we'd have something to have with lunch."

"Have you eaten, Glenn?" Jennifer asked.

"I had a small bite with Maggie while she ate, so she wouldn't feel bad about eating alone."

Blame the blind girl. Too bad I can't glare at Glenn.

I sat in my chair next to Larry, put my hands in my lap, and kept my head down. *I sure hope this looks morose enough for cookies.*

"Aren't you having anything, Maggie? Wouldn't you like a little potato salad?" Jennifer asked.

I shook my head.

"Maggie, I stabbed a bite of potato salad for you. Hold out your hand." Larry gave me a fork.

As I ate the tasty morsel of potato salad, I tried not to smile. *He knew I didn't want any because it would embarrass me when I dropped it on my shirt.*

"Maggie, I'm worried about you," Jennifer said. "You look exhausted. Why don't you take a nap this afternoon?"

I nodded.

When we reached our room, Larry's audible yawn was catching, and I yawned with him.

"Let's climb under the sheet; I'm tired too," he said. "I'll hold you while we rest."

After I kicked off my boots and climbed into bed, I sighed and melted against Larry when he pulled me close. I put my hand on his chest and matched the slow rise and fall of his chest then synchronized my breathing with the rhythm of his quiet, even breathing as I floated away wrapped in a cloud of security and total relaxation.

I woke to the click, click of Lucy's toenails when she came into the bedroom. I rolled toward Larry, but he wasn't there. I snorted. *Sneaky. He wasn't holding me; he was holding me down.*

When I sat up and stretched, the chair creaked, then Larry hurried to my side. "Lucy and I were waiting until you woke up, but Ella left to return with Moe, and they will be here soon."

I sat on the edge of the bed. "I need to brush my hair."

"I'll brush it for you," Kate said from the doorway. "I can't fix it fancy like Heather does, but I can get out the tangles, and I promise I'll take it easy. Mom will ground me if you yelp, and that's not a dare."

I stood up, and after Kate quickly and efficiently brushed my hair, I said, "That was fast; thanks."

"Anytime. It was easy; just like untangling a mess of fishing lines."

Larry chuckled. "Now that Kate's put it into perspective, I'm certain I can brush out your tangles too."

I wish I could roll my eye. I need to work on that. "Thanks, I think."

"How up-to-date are you on your eyedrops?" Larry asked as we passed the dining room on our way to the patio.

"Good hovering," Kate whispered.

"I might have missed my lunchtime drops in all the excitement." I sighed. "The drops are in the kitchen." I went to my dining chair and leaned back.

Larry said, "Got them. Ready?"

No.

He held my eyelid open and instilled a drop of the first medication. "Five minutes then the second one."

After he dropped in the second solution, I mumbled, "Thanks."

"We want your eye to heal as fast as it can," he said. "Only three more days, then we'll be down to only one medication three times a day."

I sighed loudly for the cooks in the kitchen who were listening, and Larry kissed my pouty mouth.

"Good job," he whispered as he nibbled on my ear. When I tried to protect my ear with my shoulder to keep from giggling, he kissed the other side of my neck. I swatted at him but missed, and he chuckled as he returned the bottles to the kitchen.

As we walked to the patio, he said, "Jennifer will make sure we have your eye medicine after your evening dose, so we won't miss your morning drops. It might be tricky on the road, but we'll figure it out."

After Ella and her Les arrived, Glenn answered the knock at the front door, and Paul and Julie came inside. The noise level reached a volume that was almost unbearable, and I shuddered.

"Where are your earplugs?" Kate asked.

"I put them in my backpack."

"Larry and Moe are in a big discussion. Let's go for a walk; grab your coat, so you don't get chilled in the night air," Kate said.

As we strolled down the sidewalk with our entourage of Lucy, Spike, and Palace Guard following us, Kate said, "There's this guy. He's really nice."

Ah ha. Thought so.

"Do I know him?" I asked.

"No, but you will. He's one of the instructors at the crime scene investigator program."

"I'll see more of you too then. That's awesome, but I need details. What's his name?"

Lucy slowed down behind us. "Is Lucy okay?" I asked.

"She found something interesting to sniff, and Spike's with her. His name is Dean." Kate's voice became more animated. "He's taller than me, a year younger, muscular, and his hair is graying prematurely at his temples. I told him it makes him look distinguished. He's working on a Virginia case with me; that's how I met him. I've only known him for three months. His wife was in the Army and was murdered a few years ago in a grocery store parking lot near the training center. It's a cold case."

"Are we going to work on her case?" I asked.

"I can't in any official capacity." Kate's pace slowed. "If I send you some public information documents; press releases, stuff like that—"

"I'll read it and let you know what I find, but don't say anything to Larry; he'd blow a gasket." I quickened my pace, and Kate stayed with me.

"I can email you the documents, Maggie," Kate said, "but how are you going to read it?"

"Heather magic: she gave me some text-to-speech software."

When we reached the Coyles' driveway, Kate tapped my arm. "We're back at Mom and Dad's."

"Thanks for telling me and for giving me a project, Kate." I inhaled a cleansing breath then exhaled. "I can't be bubbly because Larry would know something's up."

Palace Guard poked me.

"Don't worry about it; I'll tell him later, Palace Guard."

Kate laughed so hard, she snorted.

"What's so funny?" I asked.

"Spike's doing his wacky dance. I'm not sure anyone believes you, Camo Girl."

"I'm ready for some grill smoke therapy," I said as Kate and I linked arms and walked to the house.

When we walked inside and passed the dining room, Jennifer asked, "What's up? You two look like fast friends."

"Just a little therapy session, Mom," Kate said.

I nodded and headed to the patio with my jo. "Thanks, Kate."

"I'm not buying it," Jennifer said as Kate caught up with me and opened the patio door; the volume of conversations almost knocked me down, and Kate caught me before I fell.

Larry clutched me in his arms. "What's wrong? Are you okay?"

"She's not ready for a crowd yet," Kate said.

Larry put his arm around me and helped me to the living room sofa.

"Hum one of the fairy tunes for me," Larry said.

I slowed my breathing then hummed. When I finished the third tune, he asked, "Were the fairies your mother saw the same fairies Mrs. Martin saw when we were in Columbus?"

"I think so." I told him about Mother as a child sitting under the dining table with the fairies while they told her stories then told him a quick summary of one of the shorter stories she told me.

"I'm really amazed. I don't know what I expected a fairy person to be, but it certainly wouldn't be your mother," he said.

I giggled. "I wouldn't either. From what she said, her mother didn't accept the fairies. I suspect Grandmother was very angry at Mother for naming me after Margarite Flanagan who had introduced Mother to the fairies."

"Can I listen while you tell our babies about the fairies?"

"We're having babies?"

Larry kissed me. "Yep."

"I really wish I could roll my eye. I need it right about now. Are you sure? Do you have any idea how many grandmothers those poor children will have?"

"Oh. I didn't think about that. We'll wait a while, right?"

I nodded. "Good idea. Let's talk about something else."

"Like what?" Larry asked.

"Well, Mother told me about a murder near the training center. She didn't want me to go to Tennessee, but I don't know why. What do you think?"

"I heard about the murder, and it seemed straight-forward to me; the husband shot her then took off." He paused. "It would be interesting to find out why your mother didn't want you to go to Tennessee. If she has a good reason—"

I interrupted, "We'd still go, but at least we'd be forewarned, right? I'll call her tomorrow."

"It's three hours later here than where she is. You could relax in our room and call her now; it's practically the middle of the afternoon in Arizona. I'll come get you when the steaks are ready. Everybody should be calmer by then."

"That's brilliant. I'll do that."

After Larry left our room, I told my phone to call Mother.

She answered on the first ring. "Are you okay, Margaret?"

"I'm fine, Mother. I was wondering why you didn't want me to go to Tennessee. Is there something about the murder that makes it not quite as simple as it seems?"

Mother lowered her voice, and my eye widened in surprise. *I've never heard her speak softly.* "I can get more details for you later, and Big D wouldn't approve of me telling you, but my friends heard the locals think there is a serial killer. I'll send you names in the next day or two; all the victims were women. Big D thinks it's just gossip."

"I'd love to know the names; send me whatever else you learn. I can't go anywhere or do anything while Larry's in class, so I might as well work on a puzzle."

"You were always good at puzzles when you were a child. I could never understand how you could dump out a box of a thousand pieces and a half hour later have a beautiful photo of a snow scene in Montana. I should suggest Montana to Big D. He wants to wander around the western states. I'll get back to you tomorrow."

Mother hung up, and I smiled. *She always hangs up on me because she never wants to hear me say good-bye.*

The door creaked as Larry opened it. "Beer or wine?"

"Beer."

"Good, that's what I brought. Glenn said to put in your fancy earplugs and join him at the grill. He's waiting for you to be at his side when he drops the steaks on the hot grill, so you can hear the sizzle, and Kate said to put on extra hearing protection if you need it, but I don't think you will. When you're at your place at the grill, I'll hand your beer to you."

"You're the best."

"And don't you forget it." Larry set down the bottles, and while he kissed me, I wrapped my arms around his neck and met his kiss with my own passion, and his hands roamed.

"Break it up, kids," Kate said. "Dad's waiting for you, Maggie."

"Spoilsport," Larry whispered as he put my earplugs in my hand, and I giggled as I inserted them.

When I stepped out on the patio, Paul hugged me, and Julie's musical laugh told me she was close too.

"Missed you," I mumbled in Paul's chest.

"Missed you too, Gray Lady; it's been kind of dull without you around. Ella told us your new name is Camo Lady."

I giggled. "Leave it to Ella."

"The Greek goddess Iris carried a winged staff and could change her form," Julie said. "Isn't that a startling coincidence? I think it's very fitting for you with your staff, your right eye, and your new camo name."

"What are you all staring at? I think Julie's brilliant," I said.

"Good guess, camo goddess," Larry whispered.

"I don't get it," Glenn said. "What's the coincidence?"

"It's symbolism at its best," I said. "Iris represents my right eye, the winged staff is my jo, and changing form symbolizes my camouflage hair and new name."

"I didn't get it either," Paul said. "Where do you come up with stuff like this, honey?"

"I read books and know things," Julie said; the laughter on the patio was warm and friendly, and I smiled.

"You coming, Maggie?" Glenn asked. "It's time for you to change into a grill master."

Palace Guard patted my shoulder, and I nodded. Larry released me, and I strode with confidence as I held my jo in front of me while Palace Guard tapped my arm to adjust my direction to Glenn and the grill.

"You are very accomplished with your cane," Ella said, and Kate snorted.

"Palace Guard?" Glenn said in a soft voice when I stood next to him.

"Yep."

"Thought so," Glenn said before he raised his voice. "Quiet in the house for our sizzle."

When everyone hushed, Glenn dropped five steaks in rapid succession onto the grill, and the meat hit the hot grate with the distinctive sizzle. We all applauded, then I moaned when the characteristic iron odor of raw steak transformed to the intoxicating, deeply nutty aroma of seared meat. I inhaled deeply as the smoke from the mesquite chips swirled around me and permeated my hair and clothes.

"I've really missed this," I said.

"I know." Glenn gave me a one-arm dad hug.

As the conversations resumed on the patio, Glenn said in a low voice, "Sarge told me about the murders near the Tennessee training center. Your mother and her friends are actually onto something. Paul has been working on the background for two weeks. We'll email you what we have so far, and Paul thinks he'll have more for you by Monday. Moe told us about the text-to-speech software that Heather installed for you. Pretty slick. Call us after you've read it; it's interesting stuff, and we have a few ideas."

"Please don't tell Larry," I said.

Glenn chuckled. "We haven't even told Kate."

"How are the steaks doing?" I asked when I caught the familiar whiff of Larry's woodsy, fresh-cut pine soap wafting my way.

"I'll let you check. Will Palace Guard guide you, or should I?" Glenn asked.

Lucy leaned against my leg, and I knew Spike was nearby too.

"Don't crowd me," I hissed, and Glenn chuckled.

Palace Guard patted my shoulder, and I said, "We'll do it. Back off, Spike."

I heard the glee in Glenn's voice. "Cool. Here are your tongs."

When I held out my hand, Glenn tapped my palm with the tongs, and Palace Guard guided my right hand to the first steak, and I pushed on it with my fingers.

"It's ready to be turned," I said.

"Turn it and check the next one," Glenn said.

"Maggie, what are you doing?" The tone of fear in Moe's voice startled me.

"It's okay, sugar; Glenn's right there with her," Ella said.

"If you say so, dumpling, but her fingers look too close to the hot rack." Moe spoke in a stage whisper, and I coughed to keep from gagging.

"I hear this lovey-dovey stuff all the time," Glenn said softly. "Welcome to my world."

"She's still the grill master," Kate chuckled.

Moe growled, "Yeah, but—"

Ella interrupted Moe when she called out, "Grilling like a boss, girlfriend."

As I turned the first steak, Glenn said, "Move it slightly to the right then check the next steak."

After I declared that all five steaks were medium rare and ready to come off the grill, I moved them to a platter with Palace Guard's help.

Jennifer said, "I'll take the platter, and I intend to hear how you did this later."

As she walked away from the grill, Jennifer said, "Ella and Julie, grab your men, and we'll go to the dining room. The five of us are the first shift. Paul, we've got a bottle of fancy wine that needs to be opened. Could you take care of that?"

"On it."

Glenn said, "I'll take over now, Maggie. You and Larry sit while I grill; try out my new glider. You've earned a rest."

Larry put his arm around me, and as we walked away from the grill, he said, "You were back in your element. How did it feel?"

"Energizing. Thanks to you, Palace Guard, and Glenn. It was very therapeutic."

Spike poked the middle of my back. "And Spike; he made sure Lucy was happy," I said.

"I appreciate that, Spike. Lucy is a special girl." Glenn dropped four steaks onto the grill, and Larry whispered, "Spike blushed."

CHAPTER THREE

I listened to the chatter from the dining room and Glenn as he mumbled at his grill while Larry held the glider still, so I could sit.

"I was dreading this, but it's very pleasant, after all," I said.

"Thanks to Glenn and Jennifer, it's been very low key, hasn't it?" Larry sat next to me and put his arm around my shoulders, and I snuggled against him.

"Want to glide?" he asked.

I pushed against the floor with my toe to start the glider into motion then slammed down my foot to stop it. "It's too disorienting, probably because I can't see."

"Interesting. Do you think you'll be okay for our long drive tomorrow?"

"Of course, I will. I'll just pretend I can see the sights along the road."

Larry squeezed my hand. "I'll tell you if you see anything interesting."

I smiled. "That will work."

"Steaks are resting," Glenn said.

"Mom planned for us to eat on the patio, Dad; as expected, the dining room is still occupied," Kate said. "She set aside a full complement of food for us on the patio bar, so we could have a buffet. I'll serve your plate for you, Maggie; just don't get used to it."

Larry held the glider still while I stood up, then Palace Guard led me to my seat at the patio table.

"The dining table people have wine and cloth napkins; we have beer and paper towels." The beer bottles clanked as Glen set them on the table. "Patio people are real folks." He chuckled as he opened the bottles.

"Here's your beer, Maggie." I held out my hand and smiled at the paper towel Glenn had wrapped around the bottle for me.

I listened to Kate and Larry argue over how much food to put on my plate, the conversations and occasional loud burst of laughter from the dining room, and Lucy's soft snore after she settled on my feet.

When Larry sat next to me, he said, "Jennifer prepared loaded mashed potatoes with butter, sour cream, chives, and bacon for you. The rest of us have baked potatoes and the fixings set out in a make-your-own-style. You have carrot sticks and asparagus spears with blue cheese dip. I cut a fourth of your steak into Maggie-sized pieces to get you started. Eat what you want, and if you want more, there is plenty left."

Kate and Glenn joined us at the table.

"Mom's been watching us to be sure we're hovering over Maggie. How are we doing, Dad?" Kate asked.

"So far, so good. At least Maggie hasn't told us to back off," Glenn said, and Kate and Larry laughed as I waved my hand around my head to chase away a pesky fly or mosquito.

"Spike did his version of hovering, and you almost swatted him, but he must have expected it because he ducked," Larry said.

"This is a real boon for me, Maggie. The three of you used to laugh, and I never knew what was so funny. I'm enjoying the commentary," Glenn said.

After everyone had eaten, Larry, Glenn, Ella, Julie, and Paul cleared the dining room and patio tables. *I never knew clearing tables took so much discussion.*

Kate loaded the dishwasher, and Jennifer put the leftovers into the refrigerator. I smiled as I listened to the chatter. *All the kitchen tasks seem to require a great deal of discussion.*

I was astonished when I caught a whiff of Moe's shaving cream as he sat down at the patio table with me.

I said, "It was nice getting everyone together."

He must be nodding.

"Maggie, Ella and I will do whatever we can to help you and Kevin," he said. "We're both strong; I have plenty of leave that I need to take, and Ella tells me her hours are flexible, especially when it comes to you."

He rose and cleared his throat. "Just wanted you to know."

I reached out, and he took my hand.

"Thank you. It means a lot to me to hear that," I said.

He patted my hand then released it and walked away.

Isn't that something? I've never seen Moe's nice side before.

Spike poked me, and I said quietly, "I know; I never dreamed I'd ever hear anything like that from Moe either. Almost spooky, wasn't it?"

Palace Guard patted my shoulder.

After everyone came out to the patio and enjoyed the dessert of peach cobbler with homemade peach ice cream, Paul said, "I have some work I'd like to finish up this evening. It was great to see you, Maggie and Larry. Have a safe trip."

Ella, Julie, and Paul hugged me, and Moe shook my hand, then the conversations continued to the front door until the four of them left.

"Ready for your eyedrops?" Larry asked.

"I'll come inside; it's getting chilly out here."

As we walked into the house, I said, "Moe talked to me while you all were doing dishes."

"Really? Were you shocked?" Kate asked.

"I was stunned; he was nice."

"I'm not sure I've ever heard anyone say that about Moe before," Larry said.

"Dumpling must have softened up her crusty sugar," Kate said.

"Excuse me?" Jennifer called out from the kitchen, and I snickered.

"Dining table?" Larry asked, and I trudged to my seat then leaned back.

After he dropped in the first medication, he said, "Jennifer's making coffee. Want some? Or would you rather have hot tea?"

"Tea, please."

"I'll bring it to you in the den," Kate said.

Larry finished instilling my eyedrops before we went to the den.

"Kate's being nice to me. I'm getting nervous," I said as we sat on the sofa together.

"I'm always nice, but tonight was a terrible strain on my psyche," Kate said. "I'll put your tea on the table next to you; Mom is packing up cookies for both of us."

"Oh, good; we have success. Does that mean I'll get back my normal Kate now?"

"Not until I leave tomorrow morning with my cookies on the seat next to me where I can see them."

Kate lingered while I sipped my tea; Larry loaded his truck.

"I have an old friend from the FBI who retired and bought a place in Tennessee," she said. "I talked to her today, and she told me to tell you hello from Grandma D."

"Della? The last time I saw her was when she took that artwork from an old theft off our hands to verify its authenticity. She's a force."

Kate chuckled. "She said the same thing about you. She wanted you to know there were some things going on that might interest you. Call or text her when you get settled. Don't fall asleep; I have a couple of things to carry out to my car that I'd left with Mom and won't be long."

"Glenn and Lucy are in the backyard. Glenn wanted to spend a little time with Lucy before you leave," Jennifer said. "Have you been abandoned?"

I inhaled the familiar, bitter aroma of her cup of hot coffee. "Probably. Your coffee smells good."

"I almost changed to tea when Kate was brewing yours." I heard the smile in her tired voice. "Your mother called me earlier. She was sorry she couldn't be here, but it sounded like they are definitely enjoying their life on the road."

"I'm glad she and Sarge are happy. Both of them deserve it."

"She had a list of names and asked if I'd give them to you. I wrote them down, so I wouldn't have to remember them; it's quite a list. I can give it to you or put the names into an email for you. Are these friends of hers she wants you to look up?"

"You can give it to me, and Larry can read it to me later."

After Jennifer gave me the list, I shoved it into my pocket. "You sound almost as tired as I feel," I said.

"Oh, honey, in that case, you must be ready to drop. When Kate and Larry come in, both of us need to go to bed. I'll be up before 4:00 tomorrow, so I can have breakfast ready at four-thirty for Kate. You and Larry can leave whenever you like, but you have to have a good breakfast in you first."

When I yawned, the front door opened, and I rose from the sofa, but I was too slow; Kate grabbed me in a hug and whispered, "Consider this your ambush."

I stepped on her toe and twisted my foot. "Good night. Be safe."

She pinched my shoulder. "You too, Camo Lady."

I clenched my teeth to keep from flinching; Larry pulled me away before I could deliver a throat punch.

"Good night, everybody," Jennifer yawned. "Now, admit it: wasn't it nice to have an evening with no ambushes?"

"Yes, it was." Larry practically carried me down the hall to our room.

After he closed the door, he whispered, "Were you going to throat-punch Kate?"

"No." I mustered all the indignation I could pull together on such quick notice. *I must be tired. I should have been ready for Larry to question my motives.*

"Ha. Like I believe you. I would have let you except for the cookies." He pulled up my shirt and when I raised my arms, he pulled it over my head. After he tossed it to the floor, he kissed me sweetly then unfastened my bra.

* * *

I woke when the coffeepot in the kitchen gurgled. After I shifted slightly to untangle from Larry, I paused then listened to his soft, even breathing and slipped out of bed. I grabbed my jo and my bathrobe and scooted to the bathroom for a shower. I turned on the shower to warm the water then stepped into the tub. I found the soap and lathered then rinsed and turned off the water. I stopped to listen. *Good; I didn't disturb Larry.*

After I dried off and hung up my damp towel, the door creaked, and Larry stepped into the bathroom.

"Good morning, sweetie. Did you use up all the hot water?" he whispered.

"You know I did."

"Good enough; I probably need a cold shower anyway, naked Maggie." He chuckled, and I giggled as I imagined him leering then sighed. *I want to see him leer.*

I threw on my bathrobe and kissed him in passing before I hurried across the hall to our bedroom. I felt the bed; Larry had already stripped the sheets for Jennifer and set out my clothes for the day. *Definitely a keeper.*

After I dressed, I grabbed my jo and went to the kitchen.

"Good morning, slacker," Kate said. "My cookies are in my car."

Jennifer said, "You can behave for another half hour, Kate. Good morning, Maggie. Your coffee is on the table at your place."

"Good morning. Larry will be here in a second."

"Good morning, everyone," Larry came into the kitchen and kissed me before he sat next to me.

"The cinnamon rolls will be out of the oven in one minute, and your breakfast tacos are almost ready."

"Breakfast was my request for old times: the diner and Galveston," Kate said.

"I ate breakfast at Reggie's a couple of times with Parker," Larry said.

"I remember! In the old days when you were Officer Ewing," Kate said.

"And you were the cook, waitress, and ballerina," Larry added.

"Exactly the impression I intended," Kate said.

I'll bet she flipped her hair for effect.

"That was the same thing I thought when I first saw you," I said, "but I should have known those smooth glides were ninja, not ballerina."

Kate spewed her coffee, and I jumped up, raised my arms, and danced, and Larry laughed.

Kate coughed. "Cut it out, Spike. It wasn't that funny."

Larry tugged on my sleeve, and as I sat, I mumbled, "I win."

"Don't even go there, Maggie. Kate and Spike, you stop it too," Jennifer said. "Oh, look. You woke up Lucy."

Lucy click-clicked from the living room to the den. "I'll go out with her," Larry said.

"That's okay, Larry; I'll go out with Lucy and take my coffee," Glenn said.

"Sorry, Dad," Kate said. "We didn't mean to wake you."

"You two didn't wake me; I was enjoying the morning entertainment and didn't want to interrupt." Glenn chuckled as he headed to the den.

"Maggie, the cinnamon rolls are on a plate in the middle of the table. One breakfast taco for you?" Jennifer asked.

"Yes, please."

Kate snorted, and I smiled sweetly. *Mad because I can be polite?*

Jennifer cleared her throat. "Larry, two? Two for you, Kate?"

Glenn came into the kitchen. "Two breakfast tacos for me too."

After Jennifer turned away from the stove and toward the table, my plate clinked on the table in front of me.

"Your taco is in front of you, Maggie. You can pick it up and hold it while you eat, then it won't fall apart."

"Thanks." I bit my lip then sniffed to keep back the tears. *Jennifer is so thoughtful.*

"Are you okay, Maggie?" Jennifer asked.

"She's just sappy," Kate said.

I guess if I whapped her legs under the table with jo, Jennifer would notice.

"Shake it off," Larry whispered, and I sighed.

After she ate, Kate pushed back her chair. "Okay, I gotta go. Love you, Mom. Love you, Dad. Take care of Crazy Camo Lady, Larry."

She stopped by my chair and hugged my neck; when she tightened her hold, I steeled myself for her to strangle me. "Get well, Maggie."

I heard Larry lightly tap Kate's back, but before she moved away from me, she whispered, "I'll getcha later."

I was certain Jennifer was watching, so I sighed as I nodded.

After Kate left, Jennifer said, "I almost forgot. I made you a camo eye patch last night as a going away present. I hope that's okay."

I giggled. "It's wonderful."

I heard the relief in Jennifer's voice. "I'll help you put it on."

While Jennifer fussed over the proper placement of my patch, Larry said, "Everything's packed. I'll load the truck, then we can hit the road."

"Don't forget your sandwiches, the thermos, and your travel mugs, Larry," Jennifer said.

"I found a collapsible water bowl for Lucy," Glenn said.

"Thank you so much for everything." My voice broke, and my eye overflowed when I heard Jennifer sniffle.

Larry came inside. "Almost forgot your eye drops, sweetie." He brushed away my tears, then I put back my head, so he could instill the drops. After the second set, he said, "Here's your coat. You'll want to wear it until the truck is warmer."

"I'll carry out your lunch sack, thermos, travel mugs, and Lucy's bowl," Glenn said. "You can be responsible for Maggie, Larry."

Larry snorted.

After Lucy and I were in the truck, Larry climbed into the driver's seat. "Glenn and Jennifer are waving to us from the front porch. Wave."

I waved, and Larry chuckled as he pulled away from the Coyles' house. "Spike and Palace Guard waved too, and Lucy grinned. I'm sure Glenn knew the men were waving because he laughed. Here's your Texas Tech ballcap."

He tapped my hand with the brim, and I put it on. "I'm really excited we're all going to Tennessee." I turned to my window. "I'm going to watch for the sun."

Palace Guard patted my back, and I smiled.

As we traveled north, the drone of the tires relaxed me, and I leaned back. I jerked awake when Palace Guard patted my back and turned to look out my window. "It's getting light," I squealed.

I turned to peer at Larry. "You're not a blob yet, but I bet you will be soon."

"I'm looking forward to it," Larry said.

"So am I." I sighed.

Spike tapped my ear then fluttered his fingers on my cheek. "That you, Spike? You want to hear fairy stories?"

Spike patted my shoulder.

"Spike smiled his version of a smile and leaned back, and Palace Guard nodded. I think that's exactly what they want," Larry said.

"Palace Guard isn't very fond of the fairies; maybe fairy stories are okay, though."

Palace Guard patted my back.

"Okay, I'll tell you a story about Mother and the fairy that got her out of trouble."

"We're ready," Larry said.

I leaned back. "Mother was six years old, and the fairy was her best friend, except for her grandmother that we know as Margarite Flanagan. Mother's name is Isolde; she was named after an Irish princess, but I'll tell you the Irish princess's story another time. Mother's favorite fairy was named…" I whistled four different high tones softly between my teeth then finished with a trill. "…but I don't always pronounce it correctly unless I concentrate, so I'll just call her the fairy. My mother, Isolde, and her favorite fairy spent most of their time together under the dining room table, but one warm day, they decided to go outside to explore the world. Isolde wasn't allowed to leave the apartment alone, but she decided she wouldn't be alone because the fairy would be with her. Since the rule no longer applied after all, she spread peanut butter on one piece of bread then smeared apple butter on another slice. Isolde made her sandwich on the counter with haste; she did not have neatness in mind while she stood on a chair. She left the peanut butter and apple butter jars open on the counter. After she cut her sandwich in half, she accidently dropped the knife on the floor and forgot about it in her rush to dump out her bookbag's contents, so she could drop the sticky sandwich, unwrapped, inside."

"I can't imagine your mother making such a mess. Are you sure this story is about Isolde, not Maggie?" Larry asked.

I giggled. "I'm positive. When Isolde and her companion were outside, the fairy led the way to a playground. Isolde had never seen a playground before, and she marveled at the slide, the swings, and most of all, the climbing bars. When the fairy told Isolde the climbing bars were called monkey bars, little Isolde raced to the bars and screamed, 'I'm a monkey!' in fairy language, but I don't know how to say it."

"Your mother spoke fairy?" Larry asked.

"Either evidently or allegedly, your choice." I giggled.

"I'll go with evidently because she did teach you how to say the fairy's name, unless she made that up. Hmm. Did you make that up?"

I snorted then resumed the story. "After Isolde and the fairy became hot and sweaty from playing, they drank from the bubbly water fountain then sat in the shade under the slide and shared the peanut butter and apple butter sandwich. Isolde tugged at the hole in the knee of her pants until she widened it enough to rub some dirt on the still-bleeding abrasion from her fall off the top of the monkey bars because the fairy told her the dirt had magical healing properties. When she finished eating, Isolde wiped her sticky, dirty hands on her white shirt then sat on a swing while the fairy pushed her higher and higher. After they played in the sand box and slid down the slide, the fairy announced it was time to go home. When they reached the apartment's parking lot, Isolde's mother was locking her car door. Isolde gasped, and the fairy led her in a roundabout way out of her mother's sight to the stairs. A neighbor stopped her mother to chat, and Isolde and the fairy scooted inside the apartment door. Isolde froze when she saw the mess in the kitchen and looked down at her dirty and torn clothes. She flopped down on the floor and cried. The fairy sang a short song, and Isolde calmed down; the fairy told Isolde to wash her hands and face, so

Isolde trudged to the bathroom to scrub away the dirt. After Isolde returned to clean the kitchen, the fairy sang a happy tune, and Isolde clapped her hands at the sparkling kitchen. When she glanced down at her clean shirt and her pants with no hole, she laughed as she hurried to sit under the dining table with the fairy. Her mother came into the apartment and went into the kitchen without saying a word, and Isolde and the fairy hugged."

"What? That's it?" Larry asked.

I smiled. "Isolde's mother peeked under the table and said, 'I've never seen the kitchen so clean. Has your grandmother been here?' The fairy spoke quietly then Isolde said, 'I don't think so, but I've been napping.' Her mother shook her head and said, 'I left it cleaner than I thought.' Isolde put her hand over her mouth to cover up her giggle, and the fairy sang Isolde's favorite song: their song of victory."

"We want to hear the song," Larry said.

I sang the song that Mother taught me: the whistles and sounds of unrecognizable fairy words and an inspiring tune of joy and triumph.

"I couldn't understand the words, but I certainly felt like a winner, and the guys agree," Larry said.

I peered at the horizon in the east and smiled at the growing light then turned to Larry. "The light is getting brighter." I squinted my eye. "This is exciting; I think you might be a blob."

"Best news I've had in ages. There's a rest area ahead. Expect a big hug, then we can have lunch."

After we were back on the road, I leaned back, closed my eye, and relaxed. When the truck slowed, I woke and sat up then gazed out my window. *It's not as bright as it was.*

"We're here," Larry said.

I yawned. "I didn't mean to take a nap."

"I'm glad you did." Larry stopped the truck. "We're at the office. I already have our apartment keys, but I'll check the notice board and let the office know we're here. On Monday, our mail will be in our locked mailbox that is inside the office lobby. We'll have a few adjustments to make. A big one is that we're on the ground floor, and there is another apartment over us. It will be more convenient to take Lucy outside because we have a backyard, but I'm worried about you and the sounds from upstairs. Lucy will have to be on a leash when she goes anywhere. I think I forgot to tell you that Ella called Paul yesterday, and Julie made a vest for Lucy because she and Paul looked at all the dog vests including hiking vests but couldn't find one that Julie thought would be comfortable enough for Lucy. I'm amazed by our remarkably talented friends. The vest isn't required, but it would be a nice addition when we're on campus or in town."

"We'll adjust," I said. "It's temporary."

"You're right. I'll have a lot of research to do, but the library is only two blocks away. It's much more convenient than driving across town to go home."

When Larry returned, he drove the short distance to our apartment then backed into a parking spot. "We're here."

He opened the door, and the light aroma of apples and cinnamon greeted us. "Honey, we're home." Larry kissed then hugged me.

"Smells like home," I said.

"I think so too; I'll give you a tour then bring our things inside. The apartment is not new, so it has character, according to Ella. We're standing in the living room, dining room, and kitchen: one big room that Jennifer called a great room. There are two windows in the living room that face the parking lot, and they are covered with horizontal blinds. The front door has a peephole to look outside and has a deadbolt in addition to a lock. The floor is wooden, and the living room has a sofa with a coffee table in front of the sofa and a floor lamp next to it on the right side. The sofa isn't long enough for me to lie down, but no surprise, right? We have a recliner and an overstuffed chair with a small footstool, and each chair has a small table next to it but no lamps. We might want to buy two small lamps. You can decide which chair is yours. There's a ceiling fan in the living room area but no ceiling light."

"The overstuffed chair sounds like one that I could curl up in; I'll try it first."

Larry put his arm around me. "The dining area also has a window that faces the parking lot, and it's covered with blinds too, but it does have a ceiling light. When you come inside the front door, the light switches for the outside light and the dining room light are on your right. The dining table is rectangular and has four chairs. Ella installed a light-sensitive nightlight for us in the dining room. If it's too bright for you, we can unplug it. We can easily set up your computer on the end of the table that is nearest to the window if you need extra light. The kitchen has a bare window that overlooks the back; the kitchen door goes out to the small, fenced backyard, but there's no porch. I hope the yard will be big enough for Lucy. You and the men can take her for walks, but she'll have to be on the leash. There's a dog park five or so miles away, so we could go there on weekends and in the evenings when I don't have to spend extra time at the library if she wants some social time."

"She's content with a backyard, her people, and an occasional trip to the hardware store," I said.

"You're right; I was worried she'd feel too confined here, but she'll be happy as long as she's with you and the men." Larry kissed my forehead. "You're always thinking and setting me straight."

Larry's phone rang. "Hi, Jennifer. Thanks. I'll see what I can do."

After he hung up, he said, "I asked Jennifer to make an eye doctor appointment for you tomorrow, but the doctor doesn't have anything open. You have an appointment on Monday at two. I'll have to see if I can take a couple of hours off."

CHAPTER FOUR

"I don't think it's a good idea to take off a few hours your first day of class," I said. "I'll take a taxi or something; Palace Guard will go with me."

"I'd rather go with you; I'll see what I can work out."

"It's just for me to be established with the doctor, and Palace Guard and I will be fine; please go to class. Tell me more about the apartment: what about the kitchen. Do we have a dishwasher?"

"We have a dishwasher. The refrigerator is similar in size to the one at our house in Barton, and the stove is electric. There's no microwave."

"Kate would ambush me if I touched a microwave," I giggled.

"You're not the microwave type; that's for sure. Lucy and Spike are going out back," he said. "I'll show you the bedroom and bathroom." He led me to the far end of the living room. "There's no hallway."

He stopped then took my hand to touch two door handles. "The door on the left is to the bedroom, and the door to the right is the bathroom. There's also a panel door from the bedroom to the bathroom. I'm thinking we'd want to leave it closed, but we can see what works best."

Larry opened the bedroom door, and we walked inside. "There's another window facing the parking lot, and it's covered with blinds and dark curtains. The large, walk-in closet is near the panel door to the bathroom."

We stepped inside the closet, and I felt the clothes on my left that were hanging nearest the door. "These are mine," I said.

"Jennifer separated your clothes into shirts, pants, and sets. Your jeans and folded clothes are on the shelves across from you. My clothes start after your shelves, then my shelves are at the far end of your hanging clothes. Jennifer washed, dried, and ironed my uniforms, so I'm set for the week. She's absolutely amazing, isn't she? Jennifer loved how large our closet is, and I told her how much we appreciated that she did our unpacking. She said we could always change how she organized our things, but at least we'd have a few days to relax before I start classes."

I smiled. "Sounds logical to me; no reason to mess with perfection. Is there a dresser?"

"No, but there is room for one in the bedroom if we want one. The bed is a queen-sized bed, but the apartment came with only one set of sheets. Jennifer said they were too scratchy for you and was going to buy us new sheets, but Ella found our sheets in storage, so we're using our own."

"I feel really spoiled." I sniffed back a tear.

Larry hugged me. "You're special and deserve every bit of it. Let's finish up the tour."

We left the bedroom and immediately turned, and Larry opened the door to the bathroom. "The bathroom is pretty standard. The switches for the lights and the fan are on the wall on the right, as you go in. There are open shelves for towels and things then a counter that continues to the back wall. The counter has four large cabinets with doors, one sink, and a medicine cabinet with a mirror about midway. The one window is at the end of the counter and has blinds. We have a regular bathtub with a shower. If we continue straight ahead, we have a utility area with a washer and dryer. Jennifer was thrilled when she found it, and actually, so was I. I was fairly quickly burned out by hauling my clothes to the laundry room from my apartment then back up the stairs."

"Ancient history." I snickered.

He chuckled. "Exactly. You and Palace Guard want to explore while I carry in our things?"

"Yes."

After he left, I asked, "What do you think?"

Palace Guard patted my back then made minor corrections in my direction as I checked out each room. When Larry came in through the front door with the warm light of the late afternoon sun behind him, I squealed, "You're a blob, honey! I can see you!"

I rushed to Larry to hug him, but he took two steps and grabbed me up while tears rolled down my cheek, and I sobbed, "I didn't think I'd ever see you again."

Larry hugged me and hummed his version of a fairy tune, and my tears slowed as I sniffled then smiled. *He's trying his best.*

I leaned against him and listened to the vibrations in his chest until he ended his song. "Thank you, honey. That was wonderful."

"It was awful," he said.

"Yes, but it was wonderful that you wanted to comfort me, and I feel better."

"Good. Pick out a chair while I put Jennifer's lasagna into the oven, then we can fight because you picked my favorite chair."

After he walked away, I attempted to sound insulted when I asked, "Is that anyway to talk to your favorite wife?"

"You mean the one who takes my favorite chair or the other one?" he asked as he closed the squeaky oven door.

"Give me a minute, I'm thinking. Are you sure you want me to pick the wife for you?" I giggled, and he laughed as he strode to me and held me until we collapsed together in laughter on the sofa.

We shifted from laughing to kissing, and Larry moaned. "Sweetheart, I love you."

I sighed. "I love you too, Mr. Sexy Pants."

"Ooo. My sexy wife, naked Maggie, used to call me that," he said.

"I'm jealous of that sexy wife; is she your favorite? We will have a very serious discussion about her while I sit in my favorite chair this evening."

Larry laughed. "I call for a truce. It's not fair when you cheat and win."

"I don't cheat." I smirked as I flipped my hair. "Didn't you say the campus library was a short walk? I'd love to get out and stretch my legs."

"A walk sounds good after our long drive. I'll grab your sweatshirt for you; it's starting to cool off."

On our way back from the library, Larry said, "The rest of my class must be arriving tomorrow because only a few apartments are occupied. When I checked in at the office, my packet included a notice for a meet and greet planned tomorrow evening for my class. I didn't sign up because I didn't think it would be something you'd want to do."

"If it's just your class, you should go; if spouses are included, I'd like to go with you, and you won't have to hover because Palace Guard and I can step outside if I need fresh air or if the noise gets to me."

"If you're ready to leave, would you tell me?" he asked. "Never mind; I know you wouldn't. I wouldn't want you to be uncomfortable; Palace Guard, would you let me know if she needs to leave?"

"Ganging up on me," I grumbled.

"Good, then we all agree." Larry chuckled.

"Paul Vargas told me not to worry about the crowd of people at the art show because they were all assassins. I'll be just fine."

Larry groaned. "I'd forgotten about that. I don't understand why that is so relaxing for you, but whatever works."

"I'll ask Jennifer which set she suggests I wear to a party of assassins. I'm suddenly hungry; let's check the lasagna."

After we returned, Larry peeked into the oven. "Wouldn't hurt to give it a little more time. We don't have a porch to sit on, but how about standing around in the backyard with a beer?"

"That sounds great. It's been ages since you were off duty."

Larry put his arm around me while we stood outside with our beers, and I listened to the neighborhood sounds. "The sounds are different," I said. "I hear birds, people, and the speeding traffic from the road that goes past the training center but no dogs barking."

"I understand what you're saying. It's a small town, but we're closer to more activity and shopping than we were outside of Columbus. Let's eat."

After we ate, and Larry put away the leftovers, we relaxed on the sofa, and I leaned against Larry.

I woke when Larry said, "Sweetie, let's go to bed for the rest of your nap."

"It was a power nap," I said as Larry opened the back door to go outside with Lucy.

When he returned, I added, "I'm energized, Mr. Sexy Pants."

"You walk too slow," he said, and I giggled when he swooped me up into his arms and carried me to the bedroom.

* * *

The sound of sizzling bacon woke me. When I climbed out of bed, the cold, bare floor startled me. I'd forgotten I wasn't at Jennifer's house. After I found my bathrobe, I threw it on and hurried to the kitchen and the aroma of coffee and bacon.

"Where are your slippers? Aren't your feet cold? I'll pour you some coffee," Larry said.

"Coffee sounds great. I don't know where my slippers are." I sat at the table and wrapped my hands around the cup that was in front of me.

"I'll be right back."

After he set my slippers next to my chair, he asked, "What would you like to do today? The town library is about fifteen minutes away.

We could walk there and see what is along the way or visit the dog park to see what it's like."

"Let's do both. We should play tourist this weekend too because after school starts, you'll be too busy."

We visited the busy dog park then picked up sandwiches at a bake shop and deli. After we ate lunch, I texted Jennifer, and she called me.

"A meet and greet sounds like fun, and it will give you a chance to get acquainted with others who are new to the area too. It's casual, right? Tell Larry you should wear your green blouse and matching eye patch with your jeans; he'll know which one that is. How do you like your apartment? What about Lucy?"

"There's a dog park not far from us. Lucy wasn't impressed; most of the dogs tore around the park and chased each other or barked. Larry said she stayed out of the way while she relaxed on the grass, then when she was ready to leave, she stood with her nose at the gate."

"She is an old girl and a homebody, but don't tell her I said that." Jennifer chuckled. "What about you?"

"The apartment is great, and there are a lot of stores within walking distance. Larry is required to have a vehicle because some of their training is off campus. That has no impact on me at all. I'll set up my computer, so I'll have plenty to keep me occupied. Larry expects to put in extra study hours at the library, but he'll be close and could run home in less than a minute if I have a problem, so he can relax and do his research."

After we hung up, I said, "Jennifer said my green shirt and jeans, except she said blouse."

"I know exactly which one she means, and I love that shirt on you," Larry said. "Oh no. I forgot to sign up for tonight. I'll be right back."

When he returned a few minutes later, he said, "I signed up, but I didn't notice yesterday that we're supposed to bring something like hors d'oeuvres or a dessert."

"We could take Chef Daryl's shrimp dip. It's super easy, tastes great, and looks fancy. I'll give you a shopping list if you don't mind running to the grocery store."

"That sounds great. How long will it take to make?"

"Chef Daryl's recipe book said five minutes; it'll probably take you and me twenty."

Larry wrote down the shopping list as I recited the ingredients. "Get the cracked wheat crackers we like to go with the dip, and we'll be good to go."

Larry gave me a quick kiss on the cheek then left.

When he returned, he said, "I talked to the seafood guy at the grocery store, and he helped me pick out the small pink shrimp. He told me Gulf pink shrimp are an excellent choice for a dip because they are sweet and sustainable. What do I do now?"

I assigned the chopping and zesting to Larry while I mixed the cream cheese and mayonnaise together. After he was finished, he added the rest of the ingredients to the creamy mixture.

"Is that it?" he asked.

"We have to taste it, then it can go into the refrigerator until we're ready to leave."

"Mmm. This is great. Good choice, sweetie." He opened cupboard doors. "Do you think it's okay to put the dip in a regular bowl? I don't see anything fancy."

"A regular bowl is perfect. I'm wearing out; I think I need to lie down for a power nap."

"Sounds good to me. After I load the dishwasher, I'd like to read."

I kicked off my boots then laid down on the sofa and closed my eye to rest while I listened to Larry load the dishwasher.

I woke when Larry asked, "Did you plan to take a shower?"

I nodded then stretched. "I'd like to try to find everything myself."

"Okay. Just call out if you need us."

After I stepped out of the shower, Larry came into the bathroom. "I laid out your clothes on the bed. Let me know if you need any help."

"I'll need the tangles brushed out of my hair, and if you mention fishing line, you're fired."

Larry chuckled. "Yes, ma'am."

I dressed then carried my hairbrush to the dining room where Larry waited for me. I sat on my chair at the dining table and relaxed as he gently brushed my hair.

"Done," he said. "Your hair has natural curl, and it's very soft. Very pretty." He brushed away my hair from my face with his fingers.

"You have full immunity from any potential firing. After I put on my eye patch, I'll be ready."

As we walked together to the office building, I grabbed Larry's arm. "I won't know if people are smiling at me. What do I do?"

"Just remember they're all assassins, honey, and this is your opportunity to listen and collect data," Larry said.

I smiled, and he said, "See? It's working already; I'll have to ask Paul how he came up with such a genius idea."

When we reached the door, I stopped. "Remember you're not supposed to hover."

"Palace Guard will hover for me. We've got this."

I released my death grip on Larry's arm, and we continued inside. I steeled myself for the onslaught of noise but heard only soft murmurs and occasional chuckles from the meeting room.

"Are you doing okay?" Larry whispered as we entered the room.

"Other than being embarrassed about overreacting, I'm fine." I giggled, and he put his arm around my waist.

"We're at a table with name tags with first and last names and agency. Where do you want yours?"

I put my hand above my right breast, and he patted the nametag onto the spot that I'd indicated then patted my left breast.

"I'm an equal opportunity groper," he whispered, and I giggled.

I pretended to peer at my nametag. "What's my agency?"

"GBI Wifey, except they spelled it wrong, and it says GBI Spouse, Columbus, Georgia. Your name is Maggie Ewing with Kevin in parentheses, so you won't get stuck with the wrong husband. My nametag has Maggie in parentheses, so I won't forget I'm here with the boss. You're all set," he said.

I giggled. "I love my nametag. You're released because it's Palace Guard's turn to hover."

"I think I see a couple of guys with GBI on their nametags. I'll be close."

"I'll wander a bit, so I won't block the entrance and the table."

"You could sit at one of the round tables. You might be comfortable there."

After Larry left, Palace Guard guided me to a chair, and I sat down and listened to the quiet chatter. The chair next to me scraped on the floor, and a small blob sat next to me.

A woman said in a soft Georgia coastal drawl, "Hi, Maggie Ewing. I'm Mary Leigh, and you're the Gray Lady, aren't you? It really tickled me when I first heard about the Gray Lady who was the Gray Man's counterpart. Did dyeing your hair gray really help you to blend in? That was genius, as far as I'm concerned. How are you feeling? How's your right eye doing? That was quite an abrupt explosion of words, wasn't it? I told myself I wouldn't be nervous. Guess I blew it."

I smiled. "I'm casually freaking out like every other one-eyed introvert in the room. I see a little light and shadowy blobs; you look lovely tonight."

"Thank you." Mary Leigh giggled. "I knew the Gray Lady would understand me. I'm an occupational therapist, and we live near Savannah. I've been a Gray Lady fan, just like every other OT in Georgia, since you almost died in the library explosion. When the news got around that Kevin Ewing was going to be here the same time as my Ron, my email exploded with messages from occupational and physical therapists and nurses who wanted me to tell you hello from them. If our conversation really drags, I'll read you the list."

I snickered. "What are other people talking about? Maybe we can pretend we're social too."

"They're all talking about the murder at the bed and breakfast. Did you hear about that? The latest is that a ghost has claimed another victim. We'll have to find a local to tell us the details about the Ghost of Wicked Hollow. The story has evidently been around for at least twenty years, but I think the husband did it."

"Why do you think it's the husband?"

"I don't have any special insights, but the circumstantial evidence definitely points to him more than a ghostly legend, and I overheard two elderly women talking about the murder in the produce department of the grocery store today; one of them said her cousin's hair stylist told her cousin that the husband's friends started the ghost rumor to shift the blame."

"An elderly woman's cousin's hair stylist is certainly an indisputable witness; we've got an open and shut case." I held up my hand, and Mary Leigh then Palace Guard smacked it.

"Look at us," Mary Leigh said, "being all social and high-fiving. Are you up to tackling the buffet, or are you brave enough to trust my judgment as I artfully stack yummy morsels onto our plates? They have a coffee urn, some kind of red punch in one of those large plastic dispensers, and ice water in another dispenser."

"I don't think I can maneuver a buffet; coffee or water sound like safer choices than a suspicious red punch."

"I'm not a fan of a drink that's so lacking in flavor that it's referred to by color either," Mary Leigh said.

While Mary Leigh cruised the buffet, I breathed in the blended aromas of floral and woody soaps, coffee, and food as I listened to the hum of conversations and laughter.

"A witness claimed the husband was in Atlanta when the wife was shot," a woman said.

"I know. That witness is my brother," another woman whispered.

Mary Leigh returned and set plates on our table.

I motioned for her to come closer to me. "Do you see two women talking with no one else around? They'd be behind me at the two o'clock position," I whispered.

"You mean at the far corner?" she whispered, and I nodded.

She asked in a normal tone, "Of course, what else would you like?"

I felt her breath close to my face, and I whispered, "One of the women claimed her brother saw the husband in Atlanta when the wife was shot."

"I'll have to ask. Your plate is in front of you; I'll see you later."

"Thank you; it was nice to meet you."

"You too," she replied as she strolled away from me and toward the two women.

"Hi, I'm Mary Leigh; I'm from Atlanta."

One of the women asked, "Really? Why does your name badge say Savannah?"

The other woman tittered. "You are such a card, Sally."

I started to rise from my chair, but Palace Guard placed his hand on my shoulder.

"Spoilsport," I mumbled; when his hand on my shoulder shook, I knew he was laughing. "Proud of yourself, aren't you?"

Palace Guard patted my shoulder, and I focused on listening.

Mary Leigh giggled. "I didn't even pay attention to that. My Ron was in the GBI Savannah regional office until last week."

"Maybe you know my brother. He's an important lawyer in Atlanta. Here's his card if you need a good lawyer," Sally said.

"Oh my goodness, he is famous; lawyer to the stars, am I right?" Mary Leigh asked. "Is the husband of the murdered woman one of his clients? You know, the woman that everyone says was the latest victim of the Ghost of Wicked Hollow."

"Well, I shouldn't say anything." Sally paused before she whispered, "Yes, he is."

"Congratulations; I know you're proud of him. It was nice meeting you," Mary Leigh said as she walked away from the two women.

"Nice enough girl, I suppose, but don't you wonder who her people are, and did you see what she was wearing?" the second woman asked.

Sally laughed. "She'd certainly never fit in with our small community of exclusive cabins in the mountains of Georgia."

I felt for my knife in my boot, but Palace Guard kept me from pulling it out by holding down my arm.

"Seriously?" I asked.

"Seriously what?" Mary Leigh asked.

I exhaled. "Lawyer to the stars? Did you recognize his name? You were really slick. I need to know, what are you wearing?"

She laughed. "I've never heard of him, but it seemed like she thought everyone would know his name, so I decided he was at least famous to his sister. As far as what I'm wearing, I'm seven months' pregnant, Maggie. I'm wearing an oversized T-shirt stretched across my huge baby bump while I wait for Mom to send me my maternity shirts; I only have the one I wore when we traveled, and it's in the washer. My pregnancy brain forgot to pack the rest of them, so Ron and I went into town and bought me three huge T-shirts. My shirt of choice tonight says, 'Bacon is for winners.'"

I laughed. "Love your T-shirt. So do we believe that the husband's lawyer started the rumor, and what do we think of the rumor?"

"Food first. I put the crackers on one plate for you and a dip in a bowl; I brought you a spoon in case that would be easier to eat your dip as a chaser. Only one dip looked interesting to me, so that's what you got."

"You're really thoughtful, thank you." I picked up a cracker and took a bite before I tried the dip.

"Mmm," Mary Leigh sighed. "This shrimp dip is wonderful. Try it, or better yet, don't, and I'll eat it for you."

I giggled. "Larry and I made the shrimp dip; a Cajun chef shared his recipe with us."

"Wow. You are definitely invited to all my parties," Mary Leigh mumbled through a mouthful of dip and cracker, "if I ever have one."

She crunched another bite of cracker and dip. "I'll get more dip in a minute. I loaded that last cracker with all the dip I had. I'm certain the rumor about the husband is not true, especially since we've discovered the source, but isn't the lawyer interfering with an investigation involving a client?"

"He could claim he never said it."

"True. I'll be right back."

"Are you doing okay, sweetie?" Larry asked.

"I'm great; I have a friend, and Palace Guard's a bully," I said.

"Oh, really? Why is he pointing at your boot? Is your knife there? What were you going to do?"

"Hi, you must be Gray Lady's husband," Mary Leigh said. "The shrimp dip is heavenly. I tried to bring the entire bowl with me, but some interfering man in the line behind me grumbled like I was embarrassing his personal sense of propriety."

"Of course, I did," a man said. "I'm Ron, Gray Lady. It's nice to meet you."

I smiled. "You too." *I like these people.*

A woman bustled to our table. "Come join the group at the front of the room, y'all. We've got a few ice breakers to get everyone acquainted."

I shuddered, and Larry put his arm around my shoulder. "Thanks, but we'll watch from here."

"And listen," I added, and Mary Leigh choked on her water and coughed.

"Excuse me; it went down the wrong pipe." Mary Leigh cleared her throat. "We'll sit here and keep these nice folks company; we're happy to be the cheering section."

"Oh my goodness, of course. Y'all are perfect where you are."

After the woman hurried away, Ron said, "Very slick social avoidance, honey. More dip?"

"Yes, and for the Gray Lady too because I ate most of hers when she wasn't looking," Mary Leigh said.

Larry snorted, and I giggled. "You're hilarious, Mary Leigh."

When Ron returned, he said, "Here's the bowl of shrimp dip, the basket of pita crackers, and our platter of what's left of our bacon, cucumber, and cream cheese rollups."

"What a feast," I said. "I'd like dip and rollups."

"Sounds good, sweetie; I'll smear dip on my rollups too."

While we ate and chatted, the shouts, loud laughter, and shrieks from the icebreaker crowd became so overpowering that I put my hands over my ears, and Larry put his arm around my waist and helped me rise to my feet.

"It's getting too loud," he said.

After we were outside, he said, "Here's your jo, sweetheart. Palace Guard will stay with you while I go inside and get our bowl. Ron and Mary Leigh are leaving too. We'll get together with them another time at our apartment or theirs, but I'm calling tonight to an end."

I exhaled. "Thank you."

CHAPTER FIVE

After we went into the apartment, I said, "Hello, Lucy; Hi, Spike."

Lucy's tail thumped on the sofa.

"I think we woke her up; she hasn't moved from her spot on the sofa." Larry kissed my cheek. "Thank you for going with me; next time we go to a party, we'll know that when icebreakers are announced, it's our cue to leave. The noise hurt my ears; I can just imagine how painful it was for you."

"Did you have enough time to talk to people? I hope you didn't rush any conversations to get back to me."

"I didn't feel rushed at all; I talked to everyone in my class, so I'm less nervous about Monday."

"Good; that was our goal, right? I enjoyed getting to know Mary Leigh and Ron," I said.

"I did too; Ron was glad that Mary Leigh had someone to talk to because he said she's not comfortable with mingling in large groups. I told him you were the same."

"That might have been a minor understatement," I said.

Larry chuckled. "Maybe, but I still appreciate that you went with me."

After I sat on the sofa next to Lucy, Larry said, "We still have the other half of the lasagna we could warm up, and I forgot about Jennifer's peach pie last night. What's your pleasure?"

"I'm too full for supper, but I always have room for pie."

After Larry put the pie in the oven to warm, he said, "Some of the guys are talking about going to the local range tomorrow morning. I thought I might go too, but I didn't commit because I didn't know how you'd feel about being alone."

"I'll be fine. I have Lucy and the men and my computer. I'll catch up on my emails to Jennifer, Ella, Heather, Kate, and everybody else."

"Sounds very social. What are you really going to do?"

"What are you talking about? They would be happy to hear from me."

"Of course, they would. You want ice cream on your pie?"

"Yes, please."

"Come to the table, and I'll put your dessert at your place."

After I took a bite, I asked, "Am I in trouble?"

"It depends. What are you really going to do?"

"Did you know I can hear when you smile? I'm going to research unsolved deaths along a line from fifty miles northeast of here to almost fifty miles straight south of here. It's a very arbitrary line, but I'll expand as I go along."

"Internet search, right? Doesn't sound like you could get into too much trouble if you're inside the apartment on your computer."

He scraped his bowl for the last bit of pie and ice cream. "What do you think about the B&B shooting? A witness saw the husband in Atlanta at the time of the murder; is this another one of the unsolved deaths?"

"If I were the investigator, I'd be asking who is the witness?"

"Good point." Larry cleared our dishes. "Should we celebrate our new apartment with a beer?"

I made myself comfortable on the sofa and smiled when Lucy jumped down and Larry joined me.

He put his arm around me, and we toasted each other and the apartment with a clink.

"Every time we clink our bottles, I remember the first time we had a beer together when we sat outside on the patio at your fancy apartment and wrote notes."

I sipped my beer and giggled. "It was the only place with no microphones. We aren't bugged here, are we?"

He snorted. "I wondered how long it would be before you asked me. There's absolutely no reason why anyone would bug us, but I checked anyway and didn't find any."

Before I finished my beer, I yawned.

"I'll bet you're exhausted. Ready to call it a night?" Larry asked.

* * *

When I woke the next morning, it was still dark, and when I reached next to me, Larry wasn't there, but the pillow and the depression in the bed were warm. I grabbed my jo and opened the bedroom door. I blinked my eye at the surprising brightness of the light that streamed in from the great room windows. I smiled at the sizzle and aroma of sausage and the sound of the last few gurgles from the coffeepot.

"Good morning, sweetie. The curtains do a good job, don't they? You've got time to dress before breakfast is ready, or do you want your coffee first?" He hugged me, and I turned up my face for a good morning kiss.

After a quick smooch, I said, "Be right back."

I dressed in jeans and the first shirt I grabbed. I attempted to make the bed then patted it. "Good enough." I giggled as I hurried to the table.

"I put your coffee on the table. What's funny?"

"I attempted to make the bed and decided it looked good enough to me."

Larry chuckled. "Pretty sharp before you've even had any coffee."

I held my cup with two hands. "It's colder in the mountains of Tennessee than it was in Georgia."

As Larry set my plate in front of me, his phone rang.

"Thirty minutes? Sounds good."

After he hung up, he said, "I'll pick up Ron in thirty minutes. Mary Leigh will call you; she plans to ask you to go to the town library with her."

"Before you leave, would you help me find my Texas Tech ballcap, a sweatshirt, and my warm coat?"

"Sure will, and I'll brush your hair. I think I can do a ponytail too, if you like."

"That would be great." I dragged my last small piece of toast across my plate to pick up every morsel of egg yolk and sausage that I might have missed then popped it into my mouth.

I sat at the table while Larry brushed my hair; Lucy placed her face on my knee, and I rubbed her ear.

"Low or high ponytail?" Larry asked.

"Let's go with low."

"You're wearing an olive-green T-shirt, so I texted Jennifer, and she suggested your navy sweatshirt. I never would have thought of that, but she's the expert." He finished brushing my hair then pulled it back into a ponytail before he handed me my cap. "See how it feels."

I pulled it on. "Perfect."

Larry kissed me good-bye; not long after he left, my phone rang.

"You want to go to the library?" Mary Leigh asked.

"Ready when you are."

"Great. I'm at your front door."

I giggled as I strode to the front door then opened it. "Can I hang up, or do I wait for you to knock? What's the social protocol for going to the library?"

Mary Leigh laughed. "You'll need a coat too; it's cold. Can Lucy go with us?"

"She'd love it. Come on, Lucy. Let's go."

Lucy skidded as she scrambled to the door.

"Just a second, and she can wear her vest at the library."

"I'll open the backseat door for her. I can't bend over far enough to help."

I picked up Lucy's vest that Julie made for her, and Spike helped guide Lucy as Palace Guard and I put it on her.

"You and Lucy are slick," Mary Leigh said. "It was like you had an extra pair of hands helping because the vest just slipped right on."

"Lucy likes her vest; a friend of mine made it for her."

"She's carrying her leash in her mouth. Lucy's the smartest dog I've ever seen," Mary Leigh said.

After Mary Leigh parked, she said, "We need to get you a handicap hangtag, so we can park closer. No one is parked in any of the marked handicapped parking slots. Do you have a doctor here?"

"I have an eye doctor appointment on Monday. Larry wants to see if he can get some time off to take me, but it's his first day, so I think I could take a taxi."

"He doesn't need to take any time off, especially on his first day, and you certainly don't need to go alone because maybe I can take you, or at least go with you. The students have to have their vehicles available during the day for any field assignments, but I'll check with Ron because he told me the first day is all orientation, and he was planning to walk to class. Maybe the librarian can help us research what you'll need for a handicap sticker or designation. I've noticed you call Kevin Larry. Is that a nickname?"

"It is. No one introduced us, and I somehow thought his name was Larry."

"There's much more to that story; you'll have to tell me later or whenever you feel like it. There are no steps going into the library; that's a bonus."

"I'm actually pretty good with steps; just not fast."

"If you do fall, I'll get us help. I'm a great screamer. No, that's not a good plan; I'd hurt your ears. Don't fall."

"Probably the best plan."

Palace Guard guided me on the way to the front entrance, and Lucy walked alongside me.

Mary Leigh opened the door, and I breathed in the familiar, sweet, musky fragrance of old books.

I whispered, "Hello, old friends; I missed you."

Pages rustled in reply, and I bit my lip to keep from crying.

"Will you be okay?" Mary Leigh asked. "Should we have waited outside for you to adjust first?"

I smiled. "I'm fine. I'll go to the desk and talk to the librarian."

"I'll go with you," she said. "I want a library card, if they'll give me one."

When we approached the desk, a woman with a soft, slightly wavering voice that reminded me of Mrs. Smythe said, "You're new; you must be here with your husbands for the law enforcement course that begins on Monday, and who is this pretty girl?"

"This is Lucy," I said.

"Welcome, Lucy. We have a short-term resident library card, if you ladies are interested."

"That's exciting," Mary Leigh said. "Both of us are interested. Is something wrong?"

"Young lady, you're Maggie Sloan, the Gray Lady. I'm Betty, and Olivia was a dear friend of mine. I'd like to shake your hand."

I held out my hand, and she shook it with one bony hand then patted it with the other. "We were all so relieved that you survived that terrible explosion and were devastated when you lost your eye. Your attitude is inspiring, even for an old bird like me. All of my librarian friends agree that we want to be just like you when we grow up." Betty cackled, then when someone at a nearby table shushed her, steel came into her voice. "You can sit in the quiet room to read or work or leave if you can't be nice in front of guests."

I listened, but no one nearby moved or breathed. *I wonder if they're all paralyzed in fear.*

"We'll get those library cards for you," Ms. Betty said in her soft, deceptively shaky voice.

While Mary Leigh filled out her form, and Ms. Betty filled out mine, she said, "I believe you married Kevin Ewing. Are you Maggie Ewing or still Sloan?"

"Maggie Ewing."

"Ah, staying under the radar for a while until you fully recover. Smart move."

After Ms. Betty reviewed and approved Mary Leigh's form and read my form to me, Mary Leigh and I signed where Ms. Betty indicated.

She gave me what felt like an oversized business card. "These are your temporary cards; you'll get your permanent cards in the mail at your apartments next week. What else can I do for you?"

"I'm going to browse the science fiction section to see if you have any space opera series I haven't read yet." Mary Leigh's blob disappeared.

"If you have a break anytime soon, Ms. Betty, I have some questions," I said.

"I'm available for a meeting any time. We have a remarkably intelligent volunteer who does a fine job of filling in at the desk when we're helping a reader. I'll find Wayne then be right back."

When Ms. Betty returned, she said, "Gray Lady, this is Wayne. He's been a volunteer in the regional libraries for years. He started part time on weekends until he retired early from his teaching career in Nashville, and now he's a fulltime volunteer in our circle of libraries."

"I'm very pleased to meet you, Gray Lady. I hope I'm not embarrassing you, but your bravery was a fine example for the young women that I taught, and I thank you for the difference you've made."

I swallowed hard, and Ms. Betty said, "Thanks for your kind words, Wayne. Our Gray Lady's overcome."

Ms. Betty walked around the desk then tapped my arm. "Do you want to take my arm, and we'll go to my office; you are welcome too, Lucy."

After we were inside her office, I squinted as I tried to scan along the walls for boxes of papers like Olivia had. *There is something along one wall under the windows, but I can't see what it is.*

"Sit in this soft chair, Gray Lady. My chair is across from you. This is my version of a conference table. So, what can I do for you?"

After I sat, Lucy flopped down next to me. *I wonder if Palace Guard or Spike went with Mary Leigh to watch over her.* "I have two questions. The first is how do I get a handicap parking permit or tag?"

"The form is simple. You fill it out, then your doctor signs it, but I have a question for you. How much improvement do the doctors expect for your right eye? Do you have a doctor in Tennessee?"

"They're not making any promises, but I'm hopeful that I'll regain if not full sight, correctable sight. My Georgia doctor is continuing to direct my care; I see the local doctor on Monday who will report his findings to her."

"I'd wait until I returned to Georgia, if I were you, but an option is to ask the doctor on Monday for his opinion; he may suggest a temporary permit while you're here."

"That makes sense."

"I helped Walter fill out a form a couple of years ago. It was easy." She rose then pulled out a sheet of paper from a file cabinet. "This is incomplete, and there's nothing on it that isn't online. Take a picture, then you and your husband can review it together; having a copy of the form will be useful to discuss your options."

I pulled out my phone and held it parallel to a position where I thought it might take a picture of the form, but Palace Guard signaled for me to stop.

"Do I have this pointed right?"

"I'm sorry; I wasn't thinking," Betty said. "Shall I do it for you?"

I smiled. "I forgot I probably couldn't see well enough to aim the camera in the right direction until I tried."

Betty snapped the photo. "Done; here's your phone."

I reached out for my phone, and she asked, "What's your second question?"

"Can you tell me about the Ghost of Wicked Hollow?"

Betty chuckled. "This is an intriguing question and much more in line for Gray Lady. The folklore is that the Ghost of Wicked Hollow was a young man who had been happily married for six years. He and his wife did not have any children, and the wife blamed herself. He wanted babies because she wanted babies, but there were no babies year after year, and his once-joyful wife fell deeper and deeper into depression. He came home from his grueling job as a mechanic at the textile mill late one night, and she wasn't in their cozy cabin in the woods near their peaceful lake."

She rose from her chair and opened the blinds on her office window. "I wanted to check to see if it was foggy. Whenever I think of the Ghost of Wicked Hollow, I become anxious about fog."

She exhaled and returned to her chair. "He searched for two days, but all he found on the second day was their small fishing boat when it floated to shore. He jumped into the small boat and searched along the bank all through the night and into the next morning then finally trudged into town and reported her missing. Three weeks later, divers found her body at the bottom of the lake. She had tied the anchor from their boat to her legs then jumped into the deepest part of the lake."

"How tragic," I said.

"It is, but even more tragedy followed. The husband couldn't shake his crushing guilt for not noticing how depressed she was. He left their cabin with their dog inside and hiked through the woods in jeans and his short-sleeved T-shirt in thirty-degree weather until he stood on a train trestle in a heavy fog over a deep crevice; he straddled the tracks with his arms crossed while he shivered and waited for the next train. The engineer didn't see him until it was too late to react, and the engine slammed into him at full speed. There wasn't even enough of his body recovered to bury him. It's said that his ghost wanders the hills as he searches for childless couples who are happily married. He kills the wife before she becomes depressed to save her husband from the guilt that he suffered because he didn't see how deeply his wife had sunk into depression."

"Wow. That is really twisted."

"Yes, it is. There's a custom that has developed in the hills. The men refer to their wives as the old lady, the ball and chain, and other negative terms, so that the ghost will not think they are happily married. Women speak critically of their husbands and complain in public about how their men are lazy, never home, or always drinking. If you listen, couples who have children aren't afraid to speak fondly of their spouses."

"So, have all the deaths been of childless women who have at least a public reputation of a happy marriage?"

"That's the legend. The locals all know the tale, so for the last ten years, the unsolved murders and supposedly accidental deaths of young married women have been those who are childless, happily married, and not local."

"Whoa. So, according to the legend, Mary Leigh is fine, but I'm a target."

"From a theoretical standpoint, yes."

"Like you said, intriguing," I said. "Where is Wicked Hollow? Is it close?"

"Wicked Hollow is an otherworldly place where the ghost takes his victims before he murders them and stages an accident or more frequently, a suicide two or three days later. You're looking into this, aren't you, Gray Lady? How can I help?"

"There are so many interesting ways to slice this. Could it be possible we have a serial killer who started or revived the legend to cover his tracks? Do we know when the first death happened?"

"I'm not sure anyone has asked that. I have an old friend who might know, but she has dementia with good and bad days. I'll give her a call to see if today is a good day."

I rose from my chair to leave her office. "I'll check on Mary Leigh."

"Don't leave. If my old friend is up to it, I'll talk to her with my speakerphone turned on, so you can hear what she says and feed me any questions. She won't hear you because she's very hard of hearing. If she knows who I am, it's a good day for her."

I listened while Ms. Betty tapped the keys on her cell.

"Hey, honey, it's Betty."

"Your voice sounds nice. Do you have any friends? My friends are hungry. Good-bye."

Ms. Betty sighed. "Her good days are getting farther and farther apart. I might know someone else, but I have her number at home. I'll call her tomorrow. Call me Monday or drop by, and I'll let you know if I had any luck."

"Thanks for your help. I have some ideas that I can research to keep me busy."

"I'll walk with you to find Mary Leigh. We have an excellent selection of space opera science fiction. She may need help getting up from the floor."

When we rounded the stack with science fiction books, Betty said, "Mary Leigh's right there on the floor with her books; just like we said. Oh dear, I'll leave you here if you don't mind. One of our patrons is having trouble maneuvering her walker."

After Betty left, Mary Leigh said, "I was so excited about the books, I sat on the floor to look through one before I remembered it's been two months since I could get up without help."

"You're a hardcore reader, Mary Leigh." I held out my hand to help Mary Leigh up, but Wayne said, "I'll help."

Mary Leigh said, "Thanks, Mr. Wayne."

While Mary Leigh grunted as she rose to her feet, Palace Guard gave me a push, and I stepped toward her. When I put out my hand, I brushed past Wayne's right side and felt the imprint of a pistol, and he quickly stepped away.

Mary Leigh grabbed my hand and pulled me toward her, and I said, "Thanks, Mary Leigh. I took a misstep and would have fallen if you hadn't caught me."

She came close to me and slipped her arm through mine. "You must be tired. I found some books that I may not have read, but we can come back next week after I finish unpacking and can check my books."

I nodded, and we walked together to her car.

After she started the engine, she asked, "How did you know?"

"Know what?"

"While Wayne helped me up, I had a strong sense that I had to get you away from him, then you pushed him away."

"I didn't know I pushed him away. I was reaching for you and must have bumped him."

She clicked her seatbelt then pulled out of the parking spot and headed toward the training center. "Mmm. Interesting. He definitely jerked away from you; that's why I thought you'd pushed him."

"My antimagnetic personality?" I giggled.

Mary Leigh giggled too. "Whatever it is, you're definitely electrifying."

When she stopped, she said, "Car in front of us ran the red light. My Ron would be chasing them down."

I nodded.

"Do you have a concealed permit?" she asked.

"Of course, what made you think of that?"

"The sign on the door said no guns, knives, or brass knuckles, but it was in graphics not words."

"That is interesting; I guess my sword hidden inside jo is fine then." I smirked.

"Wouldn't that be cool?" she said. "Why did you name your cane Joe? Never mind; you're going to tell me Dave was already taken, right?"

I laughed. "You're right."

After she parked, she said, "Tell me the real reason later, if you want to; meanwhile, I like our version. I've parked in front of your apartment. Are you okay from here?" Mary Leigh asked.

"I'll be fine. I'm planning to take a nap."

"Good idea; I'll do the same."

I opened my car door, and Palace Guard helped me out. As her car pulled away from our apartment, I waved toward the sound then unlocked the door, and Lucy bounded inside and dashed to her water bowl, and a wide shadow followed her while a tall shadow stood next to me.

"Palace Guard, I can see shadowy you next to me, and shadowy Spike, you're next to Lucy. Yay!"

I held up my hand, and two shadows smacked it.

"I'll celebrate with some hot tea."

When I thought I'd reached the stove, I discovered Palace Guard had diverted me to the refrigerator. "Okay, sweet tea, but I'd be perfectly fine making tea with your guidance."

After I poured my glass of sweet tea, I powered up my computer and pulled out the list of names that Mother gave to Jennifer. I scanned in the list then started my search for each name. After I finished, I repeated listening to what I'd found.

"Of the list of twelve women who were found dead in the past five years, either by suspected suicide or murder, only four of them are not from around here. That blows the theory of how to be safe from the Ghost of Wicked Hollow."

I glanced at the Palace Guard shadow that was more formed and widened my eyes. "I saw you shrug."

He smiled, and I returned his smile. I scanned the great room for Spike, but I couldn't see him or Lucy.

"Did Lucy and Spike go outside?"

Palace Guard nodded.

"This is wonderful. I saw you nod."

I heard Larry's truck pull into the spot in front of our apartment. I opened the door as he came inside. I inhaled his aroma of gunpowder and coffee, and when he kissed me, I tasted coffee, sugar, and cinnamon.

"Ready for some lunch? What would you like?" he asked as he headed toward the kitchen.

"Sandwiches for lunch and leftover casserole for supper," I said.

While Larry put together his sandwich and my half sandwich, he said, "Some of the guys were talking about the B&B murder, and after one of the locals told us the husband had an alibi, I asked who the witness was, but nobody knew. The guys and I talked later, and one of the guys will make sure the investigator hasn't dismissed the husband as a person of interest yet. Anyway, the locals told us about the Wicked Hollow Ghost and how the locals protect their wives from the ghost by making sure their marriage doesn't appear to be happy, at least in public. Have you heard anything like that?"

CHAPTER SIX

"I heard the husband's lawyer was his witness, and I heard about the locals' theory. Mother gave Jennifer the names of twelve women who were murdered by the Wicked Hollow Ghost in the past five years. I looked each one up, and only four of the twelve were from somewhere else."

"You're not helping my complaint that you're smarter than I am," Larry said as he cut my half sandwich into two smaller halves. I smiled at the pride in his voice.

He continued, "What do you think about hot apple cider with your lunch? One of the locals told us about the Saturday farmers' market, and Ron, two other guys, and I bought some apple cider. The old man told us not to tell anybody where we got it from because he sold us what he called, 'the good stuff.' We all laughed, but you and I are supposed to check it out before Ron will pour any for Mary Leigh."

Larry opened a bottle and sniffed. "Whew, sure smells like good old-fashioned hard cider to me." He opened a cupboard then said, "I've poured a small amount into a glass. See what you think."

He handed me the glass, and I sniffed the liquid and sneezed before I took a tiny sip then sputtered and coughed. "Took my breath away. This would be great heated up and stirred with a cinnamon stick after supper in front of a fire, except we don't have a fireplace."

I handed the glass to Larry, and he took a sip then coughed. "We should tell Ron this isn't appropriate for Mary Leigh. I'm substituting our hard cider with hot tea for you and regular apple cider for me. While I'm waiting for your tea to steep, I'll text Ron."

After he sent the text to Ron, he laughed when his phone buzzed a reply text. "You'll love this, sweetie, Ron said he opened the bottle, and Mary Leigh asked him why he brought home moonshine."

"She certainly has a keen odor detector," I said. "I'll have to ask her if she has a similar sensitivity problem as I do with hearing."

I glanced at Larry then peered at him before I blinked my eye to focus on him.

"Your tea's ready; let's eat. Why are you staring at me?" Larry sat next to me and reached my hand. "Are you okay?"

"I was admiring my blurry hunk of a husband. Did you just blush?"

Larry put his hand on his cheek. "Sure is warm in here. I'm a blurry hunk? Not a blob?"

I gazed at him and smiled. "You've always been a hunk; I've missed seeing you."

He knelt next to my chair as he hugged me then stroked my hair and kissed my eye. "I always knew your eye would heal."

"I still have a way to go, but blurry is probably correctable, so I finally have hope."

I bit into my sandwich while he sat.

"Blurry is an incredible improvement," he said.

I finished one of the halves of my half sandwich. "Mary Leigh will take me to the doctor on Monday, so you can attend your classes. Palace Guard will be with me, and I'll text you from the doctor's office. This is just a routine checkup for our Georgia doctor. Your classes need to be our priority, especially since we know I'm getting better."

Larry ran his finger around the lip of his cup then sighed. "I don't know; you've always been my priority."

"Good because it's important to me that we're here for you to take this course only one time, so you have to study like crazy and do your best. You wouldn't be happy with anything less."

"You're right about that, but I'd feel guilty because I was ignoring you."

I snorted. "You've never been able to ignore me before."

He laughed. "You win. I'll go to class and complain about how you're so much smarter than I am."

I tried to roll my eye and sighed. "I haven't quite got down the one-eye roll yet." I stuck out my tongue at him. "That will have to do for now."

"Ouch." Larry laughed harder, and I giggled.

After we ate, Larry cleared our dishes. "What are your plans for this afternoon?"

"Probably a nap. The library trip was a little exhausting." I sat on the sofa and pulled the afghan over my legs.

"Sounds sensible." Larry joined me on the sofa. "What are you really going to do?"

What a suspicious man. "After my nap? Maybe some more computer research. Why?"

"I thought I'd go to the library on campus and check it out. I understand we need to be ready to hit the ground running on Monday; we've been warned there will be no coddling or introductory anything."

"Sounds rough, but you've always attacked your challenges head on."

"You've trained me well, sweetie. Ron and most of the other guys in my class plan to go too. We thought we might start organizing study groups."

"I need a relaxed afternoon, so take all the time you need."

Larry rose. "I'll heat up the kettle before I leave. It should stay hot enough for a while for you, at least."

After the kettle whistled, Larry turned off the burner and threw on his jacket then kissed me. "Text me if you need me."

I leaned back on the sofa, put up my feet, and closed my eye. "See you later."

After he left, I waited a few minutes then rushed to the table and turned on my computer and opened the email from Kate that included her notes about Dean's wife and links to public documents about her murder.

I saved copies of the public records then read Kate's notes and the documents I'd saved. *Sounds exactly like the other Ghost of Wicked Hollow murders, except she was shot in a public place rather than being reported missing then found later. Did the ghost go outside his usual pattern?*

I reviewed the names that Mother gave me before I called Paul.

"Hey there, Maggie. I thought we were going to talk on Monday."

"Larry's gone to the library for a while, so I thought I could catch you up on a few things. Are you busy?"

"Ella and I are the only ones in the office today. I'm in Glenn's office and was actually doing some research on the murders in Tennessee."

I told Paul about the list from Mother, my findings, and the local tale about the Ghost of Wicked Hollow.

"Good work. I have a list of seventeen more women in the past fifteen years who were found dead in similar circumstances as the ones on the list your Mother had; I asked Sarge for a copy. I didn't find anything about any ghost, but I was checking public records."

"Could the Ghost of Wicked Hollow be an old legend that the killer resurrected to hide his crimes?"

"Makes sense to me. I'll check to see how long the legend has been around. I have some friends who are deep into southern history and legends, and they would know. What else?"

I told him about Dean's wife. "Now I wonder if there are other murders that are outside the local lore of the bodies being found two or three days later. I'm not sure we've uncovered the killer's pattern yet."

"I'll look into that murder a little deeper to be sure we don't have a domestic like the B&B. I also need to read up on serial killers; this isn't quite as clear cut as I thought. What else?" Paul asked.

"The locals claim all the murdered women have been happily married and childless. Is there any way you can check your list to see how true that is?"

"A little harder, but at least it's more concrete and another data point to check. You don't mind if I ask Julie for help with that, do you?"

"Not at all. Am I asking for too much?"

"Not at all." Paul echoed my words then chuckled. "Notice I didn't ask, what else?"

I smiled after we hung up. *Paul loves attacking a puzzle as much as I do.* I furrowed my brow. *It doesn't make sense to duplicate what Paul is doing.*

I padded to the stove, dropped a teabag into my cup, and added hot water under the supervision of the hovering Palace Guard. After my tea steeped, I carried it to my computer and picked up my phone, and Palace Guard stepped close to me and leaned over my shoulder as I pulled up the photo of Wayne's partial application for the handicap permit.

"Mary Leigh had a strange feeling about Wayne, and you pushed me to step between them. It's odd that Wayne retired so young then a few years ago applied for a handicap permit for his car. There weren't any cars parked in the library's handicapped spots when we were there earlier. Odd."

I sent the photo of his application to my computer then opened my text-to-speech app to listen; I frowned then replayed it a second time. "According to his application, he retired eighteen years ago from a private school outside of Nashville, but according to his birthdate, he was thirty-three when he retired. Odd. I keep saying that, don't I? Of course, he could have received an inheritance that allowed him to retire. I'll see if I can find him on an old census record for Nashville."

After a half hour of searching census records, I stretched then turned off my computer. "This is too hard. Maybe I'll be able to read next week. Let's go outside and practice with my knife."

When Palace Guard and I headed to the back door, I smiled as Lucy clicked across the floor from the kitchen to the sofa. After we were outside, I walked the perimeter of the fence with my right hand on the fence then returned to the back stoop. "I wanted to get a good feel for where it is. I'm ready."

Palace Guard tapped my arm to move away from the house. I counted my steps; he tapped me to turn left then we stopped. *We're not quite halfway to the back fence and didn't make a full ninety-degree turn.*

A small rock fell to my right, and in one smooth movement, I removed my knife from its holster then flung it at the rock. Palace Guard tapped my arm and we moved until he indicated a stop. I bent low and felt the grass until I found the small, round pebble.

"Here's the rock. Where's my knife?"

I squinted to see Palace Guard, and he grinned while he shrugged.

"You're no help," I grumbled.

I slowly looked around but couldn't see anything on the ground except for the blurry brown grass. I got down on my hands and knees to search for my knife with no luck. When I rose, I asked, "Are you standing where my rock was?"

Palace Guard nodded then pointed.

"I see the direction you're pointing, but I don't see the knife," I growled. He tapped my arm, and I walked in the direction he led me.

When we stopped, I searched with my foot and found my knife that was buried to its hilt in the soft dirt.

"How far is this from the rock?" I asked, and Palace Guard guided me back to the spot where the rock had fallen.

"Wow, I've gotten really rusty. Let's do it again."

Palace Guard lobbed the rock, and I threw my knife; Palace Guard insisted that I find the rock and the knife with no help. I finally found them, then we repeated the process again and again: toss, fling, and search. When I finally found my knife next to the rock three times in a row, Palace Guard patted my back, tapped my arm, and led me back to the house.

Lucy woke when I flopped down on the sofa next to her. I closed my eye and Palace Guard tapped my shoulder then guided me to the refrigerator. "Thanks, I was parched and didn't know it." I poured a large glass of iced tea and drained the glass before I returned to the sofa.

I kicked off my boots, leaned back, and closed my eye. I smiled when the afghan floated over me. I heard the slight click at the door when Larry returned, but I was too tired to stir. When I heard the creak of the oven door, I yawned then sat up.

"Hi, honey; I've been home for a while." Larry chuckled. "How was your nap?"

"I didn't think I was that tired. How was the library? What time is it?"

"It's five o'clock. Cold or hot tea?"

"Cold."

Larry joined me on the sofa and handed me my glass of sweet tea. "We spent almost all afternoon there; I'm glad I went because there are a lot of resources that I might have assumed weren't available and might never have found in my rush to start on my research. I got home maybe a half hour ago. How long did you and Palace Guard work out?"

I frowned, and he chuckled. "Your boots have brown grass all over them. How did you do?"

I drank half of my cold tea then handed my glass back to Larry. "I was as rusty as the grass. I missed the rock with my knife then couldn't find either one. I don't know how long it was until I finally found the rock with the knife practically on top of it. Palace Guard tossed the rock a few more times, and I threw my knife right next to it. I would have kept going, but Palace Guard made me come inside."

"Good job, Palace Guard." Larry and Palace Guard high-fived, and I snorted.

"What else did you do?"

"You mean after Palace Guard tortured me by refusing to help me find the rock target and my knife then made me come inside when I actually figured it out? Nothing."

"I've made arrangements for us to go to the range tomorrow morning before they open to the public. We'll have an hour and a half to practice your shooting skills, and if you want to clean rental guns after that, you can."

"You are the best husband in the world." I threw my arms around his neck and kissed him. When I released him, he laughed. "I certainly feel like the most appreciated husband, that's for sure."

"I think I could make a salad," I said.

"I did that while you were napping, sweetie. Sorry."

"You are not."

"Maybe not because I was glad that you were napping, but I'm sorry I didn't give you a chance to show off your knife skills."

"Okay, I'll pretend like that was a wonderful apology because you arranged for us to go to the range."

He hugged me and buried his face in my neck. "I'm going to get as much mileage out of that as I can."

I giggled. "That tickles. Did you shave this morning?"

"Nope; all us guys decided last night we're not shaving until we pass the course. It's a tradition."

"Really? I can't wait to see your beard."

He kissed me before he rose to his feet. "I knew you'd like it."

I smiled as I followed him to the kitchen. *I'll bet it will be red.* "I'll set the table."

While we were eating, Larry said, "Your sight is really improving, and that's wonderful, but do me a favor: keep using your jo. I think it will be to your advantage to have it at your side, especially when I'm in class or at the library. People tend to focus on your cane and your eyepatch, making you the ultimate Camo Lady."

"Can we go for a walk after supper? I've missed our runs." I took another bite of the lasagna.

"Great idea; I've missed them too."

"I'd like to explore the campus."

"That would be good for me too. I should have thought of that earlier. I've got a map but walking past the buildings, especially where my classes will be, in person will give me a better feel for how long it would take me on foot. We can have dessert after we get back."

Lucy, Spike, and Palace Guard joined us on our walk.

I pulled my coat tighter around my neck. "I'm always surprised how much chillier it is right before the sun goes down. I'm glad I wore my heavy coat."

"Let me know if we need to turn back."

"It feels great to walk without being afraid that I'll bump into someone."

When we turned back to go to the apartment, Lucy and Spike ran ahead of us.

"Lucy's ready to be back inside where it's warm," Larry said.

I slipped my arm through his. "I don't have enough light to see where I'm walking."

He put his arm around me. "I'm sorry, sweetie."

"Don't be sorry; I like to have your arm around me. Isn't this romantic?"

He stopped and kissed me. "Let's hurry back to dessert."

As we headed back to our apartment, I asked, "Have you heard of an instructor named Dean? He's tall with premature gray at his temples and looks very distinguished."

"Are you thinking of Dean Sanchez? The guys say his classes are hard, but he's one of the best."

"Are most of the instructors fulltime faculty, or do they work for other agencies?"

"I'm not sure; does it matter?"

"I was just curious; I can see advantages either way."

"Tell me why you were asking about Dean Sanchez while we eat dessert."

I snuggled closer to him as we hurried back to the apartment.

When we rounded the corner, Larry chuckled. "Spike and Lucy are playing with a stick. He tossed it to her, and she jumped and missed then picked it up and trotted it back to him. Can you imagine what it would look like to a neighbor?"

I giggled. "I never thought about that before. Do we tell Spike to play in the backyard with Lucy?"

"No, that's where they usually play. We were just too slow getting back this time."

When we went inside, Lucy trotted to her water bowl and took a long slurping drink.

"I'll turn on the oven to warm our pie; why don't you relax on the sofa?" Larry headed to the kitchen, and I took off my coat and tell-tale boots and curled up on the sofa with the afghan on my legs.

When Larry carried our bowls of warm peach pie with the melting ice cream on top, he handed me my bowl then sat close to me. After we finished our dessert, he said, "I'll rinse our bowls, then you can tell me why you were asking about Dean Sanchez."

I frowned. *Why is he angry?*

"I don't think I'm supposed to say anything, but I know you won't tell anybody. You won't, will you?"

"I'm waiting," Larry growled.

Definitely angry.

"Kate told me she met him on a case she's working in Virginia. She's known him for three months, and from the way she talked, she has a crush on him. I won't be surprised if Kate pops by regularly."

"Kate? Kate has a crush?" Larry's voice conveyed his surprise. "That's not what I expected for you to say at all. Have you met him?"

"No, but I suspect I will eventually after Kate comes to visit."

"Will Kate be here overnight? We have only one bedroom. Where will she sleep?" Larry asked.

"On the floor."

Larry gasped. "What?"

"Don't feel sorry for her. She taught me camping by giving me a tent and a sleeping bag, then she sat on the back porch of Glenn's cabin and read a book for three hours while I struggled to pitch the tent. I put my sleeping bag on the ground and spent the night trying to sleep on sticks and rocks. If you'd feel better, we could put rocks and sticks on the floor for her. I know I'd feel better."

Larry guffawed. "I don't think I'll ever understand the bond between you and Kate, but I'm getting an idea why Glenn always said he was glad he had only one daughter, and why Jennifer frequently tells you to call a truce. Would you like some hot apple cider?"

"I'd cough with every sip. How do you think half apple cider and half hot tea would taste?"

"Let's try it. If we don't like it, we'll dump it and have beer."

While our tea brewed, Larry heated the apple cider then mixed it into our cups. "Here you go, sweetie." Larry handed me my cup and waited for me to taste it.

"Aren't you having any?" I asked.

Larry lifted his cup. "Here's to you."

"Sometimes you remind me of my cousin." I sipped the apple cider and tea. "Mmm."

"That bad? I'll get the beer." He took my cup from me.

"How did you know?" I asked as he opened two beers.

"You're seeing better which means you're getting back to your sassy self, so that was my hint to be on my toes. After you told me I reminded you of your cousin, I was ready for the ambush that would be your version of rocks and sticks on the floor."

I giggled. "My husband understands me."

As we sipped our beer, I asked, "Were you worried about Dean Sanchez?"

Larry snorted. "Of course not. Why would I be worried about Dean Sanchez?"

"We're even."

"Wait, how are we even?"

"If I told you, we wouldn't be even anymore." I held up my bottle; when Larry leaned closer and clinked it with his, I kissed him. After he returned my kiss with increasing passion, I matched his passion with an even longer kiss. When we broke apart for air, we laughed and finished our beer.

"You tricked me when you held up your bottle and ambushed me with that kiss," Larry said. "Am I losing?"

"How could you possibly be losing?" I asked.

He carried our bottles to the kitchen then returned to the sofa. I held out my hands, and he helped me up.

Larry took me into his arms and whispered, "Let's discuss this further in the bedroom. I'll help you undress."

* * *

After a restless night of listening to the loud footsteps over my head, a harsh voice and a slamming door woke me. A sliver of light peeked between the curtains, and Larry's arm across my back held me in place. When I wiggled to sneak out of bed, he chuckled. "I was waiting for you to wake up, but I think I dozed off for a second; I'll get the coffee going."

"It's my turn to make coffee," I said.

"Why don't you get dressed, then I'll hover while you make biscuits and gravy."

"I can only make sausage gravy but not before we have coffee," I grumbled and stepped out of bed. When my bare feet hit the cold floor, I shivered and jerked them back up. "Ooo. Cold."

"We have sausage patties and a package of sausage for gravy, courtesy of Jennifer; your slippers are by your side of the bed, your sweatshirt's on your dining room chair, and I'll get the coffee going." He quickly dressed while I squinted to see if I could see enough to leer at him properly.

"I saw your cute bottom," I said. *I wish I could see his cute bottom.* I sighed.

He was blurry, but I was certain he sashayed out of the bedroom, and I laughed.

I found my slippers and hurried to the closet for a long-sleeved T-shirt. After I put on the first one I found, I finished dressing then carried my matching eyepatch that Jennifer had put on the hanger with my shirt to the bathroom and brushed my hair.

When I went into the great room with my hairbrush in hand, Lucy slid off the sofa in slow motion then nudged my hand, and I rubbed her ear. "Good morning, pretty girl."

Larry said, "Coffee will be ready in a few minutes. What do I need to pull out for you to make biscuits?"

"Flour, butter, unsalted if we have it, and baking powder. I don't suppose we have buttermilk, so I'll need milk and vinegar; I'd like to make gravy too. Do we have any chicken broth?"

"We have everything you need. Jennifer shopped for what she called 'staples' while she and Ella were here. Coffee's ready."

While he filled two cups with coffee, he asked, "Did you brush your hair?"

"Sort of, but I'll need a ponytail after we have some coffee."

Lucy padded to the back door, then I heard the door open and close.

"Spike took Lucy outside," Larry said. "I couldn't get her close to the back door earlier. I think she was waiting to tell you hello."

While I mixed then formed the dough into a rectangle, I asked, "When do we leave for the range?"

"We'll leave here a little after eight thirty; we have plenty of time." I folded the dough to create the flakey layers before Larry cut out round biscuits with a drinking glass then popped the biscuits into the oven.

"How do you want your eggs?" I asked.

Larry refilled our cups. "However you cook them."

I sipped my coffee. "Scrambled goes good with gravy."

"You have me convinced you can do anything. Do you want me to crack the eggs for you?"

"I'd appreciate it," I peered at Larry and smiled. *I'm sure he's smiling.*

He put his arms around my waist and gazed at my face. "You saw my smile?"

"I still see you through a foggy blur; you'll have to let go of me, so we can start the gravy."

Larry chuckled as he released me. "It would be romantic to say I'll never let you go, but then I'd have to list all the exceptions and that definitely includes gravy to go with our biscuits."

CHAPTER SEVEN

"Would you wrap half of the sausage and put it back in the refrigerator then brown the other half for me? I'm not sure you'd be happy watching me stick my face close enough to be sure there's no pink left."

"You got that right." While he broke up the sausage in the pan, he said, "It's actually impressive that you asked me to brown the sausage instead of cooking it yourself and scaring me."

Palace Guard peered over Larry's shoulder at the browning meat.

When I headed to the bedroom to make our bed, Larry whispered, "Tell me when it's browned all the way."

I managed to stifle my snicker and kept walking.

When I returned to the great room, Larry said, "It's all browned, but I was surprised because there's not much grease at all."

"Can you spoon out a little of the grease and put it into a pan for me to scramble eggs? It'll give our eggs a little extra sausage flavor."

"Okay, done. What's next?"

"Put the sausage into a bowl, then we'll check the biscuits and make gravy." I opened the oven and peered inside. "What do you think? Are they golden?"

"Not really."

"Let's give them a little more time; check them in two minutes, and I'll get busy on the gravy."

As I stirred the butter and flour mixture, I felt it become a thick paste then sloshed in some chicken broth and stirred.

Larry said, "Two minutes; time for me to check the biscuits."

I stood back while he opened the oven and pulled out the cast iron skillet, then I added more chicken broth until I was satisfied with its creamy feel as I stirred with my wooden spoon.

"Add the sausage for me and a generous sprinkle of black pepper." I stirred the sausage and gravy mixture then said, "Would you add the eggs to the pan with the sausage grease, and I'll scramble them."

I added a little more chicken broth and stirred the gravy while I scrambled the eggs. "Gravy and eggs are ready; could you plate our eggs?"

"Got it. I poured the gravy into a bowl and put scrambled eggs on our plates. One biscuit for you?" Larry asked.

"Yes, please." I set our plates on the table, and Larry dropped one hot biscuit on my plate and two on his.

Larry inhaled. "Ahhh. This smells great."

I split my biscuit with my fork before I spooned gravy over my biscuit and egg with the gravy ladle. "I don't need the ladle," Larry said.

I squinted as Larry split his biscuits then poured gravy from the bowl over his biscuits and eggs.

"I'm very much into efficiency," he said, and I smiled.

After we ate, Larry asked, "What do I do with the biscuits? There's no gravy left."

"Wrap them individually, and we can put them in the freezer; we can make gravy whenever you want it."

I carried our dishes to the sink, then Larry loaded the dishwasher. "I'll fix your ponytail as soon as I get this going."

"What color shirt did I pick out?" I asked while he brushed out my tangles.

"Hot pink."

"I did not." I squinted and raised my right arm close to my face. "It's a little foggy, but is it some kind of tan color?"

"Something like that. It looks a little greenish to me, but you'll have to admit, hot pink would be a great disguise. Nobody would recognize you as the Gray Lady."

"Including you." I giggled. "I'll tell Spike and Lucy we're going; it will give me a chance to check the weather."

When I stepped outside, I was surprised at how warm it was. "Larry and I are going to the range. We might be a while."

Lucy yipped, and I smiled.

"What's the verdict?" Larry asked.

"It's foggy and warm; unseasonably warm. I'll wear my sweatshirt, but I'll take my coat along in case the weather changes."

On our way to the range, I said, "If we were in Georgia, I'd be worried by the sudden warm weather. Do we have a front or anything headed our way?"

"Not yet, but it's worth keeping an eye on it. Are you worried about a storm?"

"I like to read the weather, and the weather today feels unstable."

"The fog is thinning enough that I can see the car ahead of me on the road."

When we pulled into the range, I heard the pop of a pistol, and I cringed.

"Are you okay?" Larry asked.

"I'll be fine. When Kate and I went to the range on Wednesday, I had the earplugs she gave me and hearing protection earmuffs, but I still had a headache after I shot six rounds. I have my earplugs and thought since my eyes were better, I wouldn't be so sensitive to the crack of gunshots."

"How did you shoot?"

"According to Kate, great. I had a wonderful time cleaning Skip's dirtiest pistol that someone abandoned in a locker, so I was happy we went."

"Wait here."

Larry climbed out of his truck and closed his door. Palace Guard patted me on my shoulder.

"Thanks for coming. Was Larry mad?"

Palace Guard patted my shoulder again, and I said, "Thanks. I was just wondering."

When Larry returned to the truck, he said, "The owner is training his grandson to shoot and be safe. Their goal is for the boy to be ready for the next turkey season. I told the owner we had a conflict and won't be here today after all, and he seemed really grateful for the extra time. Is that okay?"

I exhaled. "That's perfect. I've always enjoyed going to the range, but I guess for now, it's not for me."

"I'm glad you know you didn't lose your skills. There are some hiking trails not too far away. Does that sound good?"

"It does, except the weather has me on edge."

"There's a park nearby with a walking trail. How about that?"

I exhaled. "Fresh air would be good for me. Let's do that."

After Larry parked, he helped me out of the truck then took my hand before we walked the foggy path around a large pond.

"The fog is thicker around the pond." I clutched Larry's arm, and he slowed our pace. I listened to the fish splash as they jumped for the flying insects that skimmed the water. "I'm not sure I'm comfortable living in a two-story apartment building, and the weather has me spooked. I seem to be more on edge in unfamiliar places since my sight became so limited."

"You had a restless night; was there noise from upstairs that kept you from sleeping?"

I sighed. "Someone paced all night. I wanted to go upstairs, knock on their door, and ask if they'd like to borrow a book."

"I thought it was something like that; someone with the jitters, do you think?"

"I suppose; hopefully they'll settle down by Monday."

"Maybe, but I want you to be comfortable and happy, sweetie. What do you want to do?"

I exhaled. "Maybe I need a week or two to adjust."

Larry put his arms around me, and he pulled me close. "I've never known you to need any time to adjust. We have our allowances, so money's not an issue. What would make you comfortable?"

I smiled. "I've never heard you admit that both of us have allowances, but you're right that money is not an issue. I never lived in an apartment with someone above me. Now I wonder if Taylor and I disturbed the people downstairs with all our traipsing back and forth from our apartments to Mr. Morgan's."

"Maybe, but I'll bet they were more disturbed when we cordoned off the parking lot after the bomb scare or by all the shooting when Mr. Morgan was shot near the apartment." He hugged me. "Good old days, right?"

"Yep, back in the day. Tell me again why you shifted from being my new boyfriend, which is what Kate said, to being my cousin?"

"You could have broken up with a boyfriend, but you couldn't have dumped your cousin."

"You are so smart."

"Of course, and it worked too, didn't it? We're still related." He chuckled, and I giggled as we continued around the pond.

"Fog's not as thick now that we're walking away from the pond." I grabbed his arm and whispered. "Someone is walking toward us."

Larry spoke in a soft voice. "I don't see anyone."

I felt his muscles tense and released my hold; after we stopped, I prepared to throw my knife.

Palace Guard patted my back, and Larry said, "A woman and a girl are on the path. The fog hid them. Can you see them now?"

"No, I can see blurry you and blurry Palace Guard, but I don't see…now, I do; they're shadowy blobs. How could that be?"

"I don't know; do you suppose you know us so well that your mind interprets our blobs?"

I exhaled. "Sounds reasonable to me. Palace Guard told me they were okay, but I was already in panic mode."

"I need to fix that. You need a little time for your eyes to heal, but there has to be a way to help you feel safe in the meantime."

After we were in the truck, Larry said, "I think you're hypersensitive from not sleeping. Why don't you try wearing your earplugs that Kate gave you to bed tonight?"

"I'll have to think about it; my hearing is all I have to warn me of danger."

Palace Guard poked my shoulder, and Larry said, "Not true, and you're lucky Spike didn't hear that."

"I apologize, Palace Guard."

Palace Guard lightly tapped the back of my head. "You're right. Spike would have smacked me upside the head, as he always told us kids he would do when we got out of line. Not me; the other kids." I giggled, and Larry chuckled.

After we were home, Larry said, "Relax on the sofa, and I'll bring you a drink. What would you like? Sweet or hot tea? Mimosa? Please don't say mimosa because I have no idea what it is, but it sounds fancy."

"Fancy hot tea sounds perfect," I said.

"I saw a fancy drink at a hotel restaurant when I went to a training course in Atlanta. It had a pearl onion at the bottom of the glass. We don't have any pearl onions, but we've got garlic cloves. I could drop one of them into your cup."

"Eww." I wrinkled my nose. "I think I'll go with the usual plain hot tea."

"Whatever you wish, my dear."

Larry sounded smug. *He's proud of himself.*

While I sipped my tea, Larry sat next to me, and I snuggled close. He told me who the guys said were good instructors and how to avoid getting on the wrong side of other instructors. I listened to the excitement in his voice and relaxed. *This is where we should be.*

Larry's phone buzzed a text, and I smiled when he tried to reach it without disturbing me. *He is such a sweetheart.*

I sat up, so he could check his phone. "Ron wants to know if I'm free to go for a long run before lunch."

"Go right ahead; I might get in a little computer time."

Palace Guard tapped me on the shoulder.

"Palace Guard would like to go too, if you don't mind, but remember he runs fast."

"That would be great; you could take the lead, Palace Guard, and give us a workout."

He's forgotten how fast Palace Guard is.

"I'll have Spike and Lucy, so don't feel like you have to cut your run short on my account."

After Larry and Palace Guard left, Spike stood in front of me with his arms crossed.

"Don't tell me you would have told Larry that Palace Guard will run them ragged. You wouldn't even have mentioned that Palace Guard runs fast, would you?"

Spike exaggerated his shrug by throwing his hands up, and I laughed.

When Lucy whined to go out the front door, I said, "I know you love to run, but they'll be running much too fast for you and me. Let's go to the backyard; you can run with Spike, and I'll run behind you. It will be good practice for me."

Lucy trotted around the perimeter twice with Spike walking next to her. I followed them and was grateful when Spike headed to the back door after our second lap; Lucy loped alongside him.

I bent over as I tried to catch my breath. "Good run, Lucy and Spike. I'm ready to go inside too."

Spike danced with his hands in the air, so I did too, and Lucy pranced and yipped. After I opened the door, Lucy dashed to her water, Spike closed and locked the door, and I moaned as I collapsed on the sofa. "We should probably do that again, but not today. I am out of shape."

After I cooled down, I turned on my computer, put on my headset, and searched for Wayne Dillard in Tennessee. Lucy had fallen asleep on the cool kitchen floor, and Spike sat next to me with his elbows on the table as he propped his chin on his hands.

"He lived in a town over fifty miles from Nashville. That's why I couldn't find him on the census, but why does he have the Nashville post office box number as his address?"

Spike shrugged.

I listened as I searched the census records for Wayne Dillard's hometown. "Found him. He lived with his parents."

I searched for his parents and found their obituaries. "Father died when Wayne was twenty-two. That may have been about the time he graduated. If his father had been ill, that might have been why he stayed with his parents."

Spike shook his head. "I know you don't approve, but he might have been the caregiver for his father. His mother died right before he retired, so both of them might have been ill."

Spike shook his head more vigorously. "I'll check to see what his father did; maybe he left his family a lot of money or a profitable business that Mrs. Dillard sold."

After more research, I said, "Mr. Dillard owned a large textile mill; it must have been extremely profitable when he died. If Mrs. Dillard invested wisely, she would have had quite a nest egg for her and for Wayne, so he could have retired at thirty-three."

Spike crossed his arms. "Okay, Mr. Suspicious, I'll research cause of death for Mrs. Dillard and Mr. Dillard while I'm at it."

After I exhausted my limited resources, I said, "I can't find anything; I'll hand it off to Paul."

I sent him a text: "Call when convenient."

My phone rang immediately.

"Was that code, Maggie?"

"Not at all. I wanted you to know it wasn't urgent."

Paul exhaled. "I sure wish this was a video call where you could blink twice if you needed help."

I smiled. "I blinked once; what does that mean?"

"It means a one-eyed married woman just winked at me, so now I know everything you say will not be true." He chuckled, and I giggled.

"So, whatcha got for me, Married Lady?" Paul asked.

"I need the cause of death of a husband and wife."

After I gave him all the information I had, he asked, "Priority?"

"Filler work because I don't know whether it's important yet."

"On it." Paul hung up.

I sighed as I set my phone on the table. "Have you ever noticed everyone hangs up on me?"

Spike sat on the kitchen floor next to the sleeping Lucy.

"Was that your version of hanging up on me, Spike?" I smiled at my puny growl.

Larry stumbled into the apartment, and Palace Guard followed him.

"How was your run, honey?" I asked.

"Palace Guard kicked our butts, and Ron thinks I'm nuts. You knew he could run rings around us, didn't you?"

"Who do you think taught me to run so fast?"

Larry collapsed on the floor and lay on his back. "I forgot; and I also forgot that you can outrun me. When I yelled, 'Palace Guard, slow down,' Ron asked me if I was okay."

I giggled. "What did you say?"

"I remembered you warned me that Palace Guard runs fast, but I wasn't paying attention, so I pretended my selective hearing tuned Ron out too."

"Can I get you some sweet tea?" I asked.

He sat up. "I'll get myself some in a minute and make us sandwiches. What have you been doing?"

"Lucy wanted to go with you, so the three of us went for our run in the backyard. Two laps around the yard, and we were done. We'll work on that."

As Larry rose to pour a glass of tea, he said, "Ron and I agreed we're going to run early every morning before breakfast, except not so far or so fast. Palace Guard and I agreed that he'd run behind us, and we'd let Ron set the pace."

When I heard the rush of a sudden gust of wind, I hurried to the back door and opened it. The wind slammed the door into me, and I lost my balance. Larry caught me before I fell.

"Wow, that came up fast. You okay?" he asked.

I shivered when a second blast of cold wind hit me. "The temperature's really dropped. We definitely have a front rolling in."

Larry held me as he closed the door. "I'll brew you some hot tea."

"What if the power goes off?" I sat at the dining table.

"We couldn't cook because the stove's electric, and we wouldn't have any heat. Jennifer told me she put some candles in a drawer in case we wanted a romantic candlelight dinner. I'll find them, and I could boil some hot water then put it into a thermos, so we can brew some tea."

"We have biscuits and cheese, so we could eat sandwiches, and we could even boil some eggs for egg salad," I said.

"Here's your hot tea. I'll make our sandwiches; talking about scrounging for food makes me hungry."

He opened the refrigerator. "This is not a bad drill for us; we need a propane camp stove and a kerosene lantern."

Larry opened a cabinet door. "We have crackers, canned chicken, and canned tuna. We'll be fine without electricity for at least a couple of days."

"No, we won't. What about coffee?" I asked.

"Good point. We'll need a coffee pot that we can heat on our camp stove; our glass pot wouldn't work."

"I'll make a list." After I recorded our list on my phone, I said, "We need a cabin like the Coyles' cabin."

Larry set a plate in front of me. "Here's your sandwich. A cabin would very definitely be a good use of our allowances, wouldn't it?"

Rain slammed against the back of our apartment, and I shuddered while I ate.

"Let's sit on the sofa and look for a cabin until we lose the internet. While you get set up, I'll boil the water for our thermos."

I turned on my laptop. "What are our must-haves for a cabin?"

"Fireplace, dishwasher, gas stove, gas water heater, and no nearby neighbors," Larry said.

"Porch," I added. "What about bedrooms? One or two?"

"Two would be nice, but is it a must-have?" Larry asked.

"A big question is where do we start looking?"

"Why don't we see what's around the Coyles' cabin?" Larry asked.

I searched for cabins; Larry looked at the photos, and I listened to the descriptions.

After we expanded the location of our search a little farther north, we trimmed our possible cabins to six.

"What's that?" I asked as I removed my headset. "Did the wind stop?"

When Larry opened the front door, I heard the soft rain. "Wind has died down, and it's raining. Want to go shopping for our emergency supplies? We can start at the hardware store."

Lucy wagged her tail, and it thumped against a dining room chair.

"Lucy's ready," I said. "I'll send you our list, so you can read it."

"It's turned a little cooler; you'll want your sweatshirt," Larry said. "I'll put Lucy's new vest on her."

After we were all in the truck, Larry said, "I heard there is a camping store in town, so we have options if we don't find what we want."

When we went into the hardware store, Lucy carried her leash and stayed close to me.

Larry grabbed a shopping cart, then when he joined us, he whispered, "You and Lucy are collecting a whole new set of admirers. You are the gorgeous woman with an eyepatch and the brilliant service dog that carries her own leash."

I tried to watch people as they came into the store, but the fast-moving blobs blurred into each other.

"I'll start at the top of our list; first is the camping stove," Larry said. "Let's check near the outdoor grills."

Larry pushed the cart, and we followed him. The grills were near the entrance, so we didn't have far to go. Lucy, Spike, and I waited next to a large barbeque grill while Larry and Palace Guard searched the nearby aisles.

"They have two, but they aren't exactly what I want. Let's go to the outdoors store."

Lucy trotted to the checkout line. "I have a treat for you in the truck, Lucy," Larry said.

When Lucy remained in line, the cashier said, "Here you are, pretty girl. Can you sit?"

Lucy tore past the customers in line and dropped into a sit for the cashier, and the customers laughed. "Good girl," the cashier said.

On the way to the truck, I giggled. "Lucy, you are shameless, but you pulled it off like the rock star you are."

After we were in the truck, Larry started the engine. "A guy looking at grills told me the camping and hunting store was open today. I'll look up the address, then we can go there."

When we walked into the camping store, I inhaled the familiar aroma of my favorite gun oil. "Can I clean your gun after we go home?" I whispered.

"I always clean my gun after I shoot," Larry said. "I just didn't get to it yet."

"Thank you, then I'll clean it after we're home."

While we stood in front of the camp stoves, Larry said, "Weight isn't a factor for us because we won't be hiking with our stove. I think this one is the one we want."

Larry put it into our shopping cart. "The propane for portable stoves is here too. I'll grab two cylinders. Next is a kerosene lantern. We're in the camping section; they're probably right around the corner."

After we moved to the next aisle, he said, "We can get two lanterns. We'll get a large one that we can put on the dining table; it will light up the great room. A smaller one would be good for those times when we're relaxing on the sofa and don't need a bright light."

Larry stopped in every aisle as we wandered through the camping section. "I'm getting distracted. I picked up a few more candles and a pair of candle holders. Coffeepot is next, then I think we're done."

We backtracked.

"Ready. We have a coffeepot and a couple of pans that we can set aside for our camp stove and not worry if the pot we want is in the dishwasher," Larry said. "We need our cabin, so we can get everything else we're positively certain we can't do without."

As we headed toward the checkout counter, I breathed in a sweet, vanilla fragrance and stopped. "Mmm. Smells good. What is it?"

"Candles; they do smell nice, don't they? Do you want to pick out a couple for the apartment?"

I frowned. "Glass jars?"

"Yes, but I can hold the candle jar and take off the lid, so you can decide which one you want." He held a jar under my nose.

"Vanilla? Nice; let's get that one and see what we think."

After Larry put the candle in our cart, I said, "This store is a bad influence; I didn't know vanilla candles were on my must-have list."

"I'm going to take a quick look at their camping chairs for our backyard. Can you manage the cart? I'll meet you at the checkout counter."

"Go ahead; I'll push, and Palace Guard will guide me."

"Lucy and Spike are with me," Larry said.

As we headed to the checkout counter, I heard slow, quiet footsteps behind me and frowned. *Most people stand while they search for their item or hurry to another aisle, and people who walk slowly don't try to be quiet.*

CHAPTER EIGHT

Palace Guard grabbed my arm, and we made a sharp turn and hurried down an aisle until he guided me to a kiosk. When we stopped, I felt the items. *Sunglasses?* I tried on one pair after another until Palace Guard patted my shoulder. I added the pair of sunglasses that I wore to the cart, then we continued to the checkout counter.

When Larry joined us, he said, "I hadn't thought about sunglasses for you, but it makes sense. Your idea?"

I shook my head.

When we reached the apartment, Larry carried in our shopping bags then returned to the truck for our new backyard camping chairs. While he loaded the new pans and coffeepot into the dishwasher, I dropped onto the sofa, then he joined me.

"Want your afghan? The storm affected me more than I would have expected. While we were on our way home, I kept thinking I needed to do our laundry before we lost power."

"I'm just happy to be home; I'm ready to clean your gun."

"If you're sure, I'll bring you my gun and cleaning supplies."

"Do we have an old towel we could put on the dining table? I'd rather work there."

"I'll light your candle and get you all set up, then I'll start a load of laundry."

After I sat at the dining table, Larry said, "I lit the candle, and everything is laid out. Can I help you find what you need?"

"Nope, if it's in my reach, I'll find it. The candle smells nice, thank you."

"You sure are easy to please. All I have to get you is a candle, a gun to clean, and a cabin." Larry chuckled, and I smiled.

I hummed while I took the gun apart, cleaned all the pieces, and put it back together. "That was fun. Do you have any more?"

Larry whistled. "I can't believe how fast you are. I watched, and your fingers flew. I've never seen anyone clean a gun as thoroughly as you do, either. Kate said you were amazing; I should have known she wouldn't have exaggerated."

While Larry put away his gun and cleaning supplies, I washed my hands then stretched out on the sofa. Larry tucked the afghan around me then kissed me lightly. "See if you can nap a bit and catch up on your sleep."

I yawned then rolled to my side and listened while Larry put clothes into the washing machine.

When I woke, Larry asked, "Ready for supper?"

"Did I sleep that long?" The afghan was wrapped around me like a cocoon, and I struggled to untangle myself.

"Hold on, honey." Larry chuckled. "You're making it worse."

I sighed in disgust and quit flailing at the afghan. "I was about to pull my knife on it, but I couldn't get my arms free," I grumbled.

"Hold still, I've almost got it."

When my arms were free, Larry hugged me. "You aren't going to slice the afghan, are you?"

"Is that why you're hugging me, so I can't?"

"You know me as well as I know you." He lifted me off the sofa and hugged me tighter. "Did you hear anything before you and Palace Guard went to look at sunglasses?"

"Why?"

"Oh, nothing." He released me and headed to the kitchen.

I snorted. "Right. I'll go first. I heard someone behind me that was walking slowly and quietly, then Palace Guard grabbed me, and we hurried down the aisle to the sunglasses. Now, you."

"Fair enough. I asked Palace Guard what gave him the idea for you to get sunglasses, and he crouched and crept toward you like he was going to grab you. When I asked him if someone was stalking you, he nodded. He described the man as tall as I am, muscular like Spike, and older than me."

I shuddered then kicked the sofa before I yelled at Palace Guard. "Why didn't you tell me? Who was it?"

I watched Palace Guard as he mimed pulling a hoodie over his head then wrapping a scarf around his face.

"Do you remember seeing a man with a hoodie and a scarf, Larry?" I asked.

"No, he could have left immediately when you made your abrupt turn."

I peered at Palace Guard. "You followed him, didn't you? I kept trying on sunglasses until you told me I had the right ones, but I didn't know you weren't there the entire time because I was focused on sunglasses. Did you see his vehicle?"

Palace Guard motioned that the man hurried away on foot; he didn't try to follow him.

Larry said. "Makes sense to me, Palace Guard; you wanted to get back to Maggie."

I exhaled. "I appreciate it, Palace Guard. He might have had an accomplice. So, where does that leave us?"

"As far as I'm concerned, packing up and moving to our cabin," Larry growled.

"Just as soon as you finish your certifications, but we'll have to find our cabin and buy it before we can move."

Larry shook his head. "I'm glad you had Palace Guard with you. If he'd thrown a small item at the man, you'd have nailed the guy, and the two of you would have run away."

"And you'd be listening to me moan about how sore I was from running so fast," I added. "What's for supper?"

"Cheesy chicken and rice casserole, courtesy of Jennifer. Wash your hands, and we can eat. I even made a salad."

After I sat at the table, I asked, "How did you know it was cheesy chicken and rice?"

He chuckled. "It's labeled, and I have a master list of the casseroles; Jennifer instructed me to mark off the ones we eat, so we'll know what we have left. Beer or sweet tea?"

"Sweet tea with supper; beer with dessert."

"We've got summer sausage made from venison courtesy of Paul for an appetizer if we want to try out our new camping chairs and relax in our backyard sometime with a beer before supper."

"I'd like that."

While we ate, I asked, "What are we going to do after we've eaten all of Jennifer's casseroles?"

"I've been thinking about that. If we plan our meals for Sunday through Friday, we can make casseroles or soup, but plan on leftovers for Monday, Wednesday, and Friday."

"I like it; cook one day, leftovers the next. What about Saturday?"

"Go to a restaurant or order pizza."

"We could pick out a recipe from Chef Daryl's cookbook on Saturdays."

"Even better; I'll be your sous chef."

After supper, we relaxed; Larry read, and I searched for more information about Wayne Dillard and his parents. When I discovered his mother had earned a degree in Fine Arts from the University of Tennessee, I searched deeper to see if she pursued a career in the fine arts field after graduation. I smiled when my search led me to her photographs in a Nashville travel magazine; she had retained her maiden name as her professional name after she was married: Noreen Weber.

"I should have thought of that," I mumbled then glanced at Larry. *Still reading; good. He would not be impressed that I'm stalking my potential stalker.*

Larry's phone buzzed a text, and he smiled as he read it. "I'm not the only one that's nervous about tomorrow. Ron's set up a group of five of us on his text message."

While he tapped in his reply, his phone buzzed again. "My phone might be busy for a while." He went out back, and Lucy and Spike followed him.

"Was I ever like that?" I asked.

Palace Guard raised his eyebrows.

"You're right; I'd forgotten you weren't with me when I started college; I don't think I was. Is it because Larry's more social than I am?"

Palace Guard nodded.

"That whole social thing is fascinating to me."

I picked up my headset and continued my research on Mrs. Dillard.

When Larry, Lucy, and Spike came inside, Larry said, "I'm so sorry, honey. I didn't mean to be outside so long, but I feel better knowing everybody else has a case of the nerves too. Ron told Mary Leigh it looked like the baby was really getting big then spent the rest of the afternoon apologizing for implying that she was fat. He verified we don't need our vehicles tomorrow, so Mary Leigh can take you to the doctor's office, and he and I are walking to class. Are you okay?"

"I might not be; a taste of that summer sausage might help."

Larry chuckled. "Good idea. Beer too?"

"That would be fun. We'll celebrate the rampant class jitters y'all have."

"Meet me at the sofa," he said, "It got too buggy outside, so we called it a night; otherwise, we'd probably still be talking."

While we munched on the summer sausage and crackers and sipped our beer, Larry said, "I owe you an explanation; it's been bothering me. When you mentioned Dean Sanchez, I overreacted.

When I calmed down, I told you the guys said he was a good instructor, but that's not all." He cleared his throat. "He was kind of a jerk before his wife died; he was stringing along a couple of young women your age. After she died, he took advantage of sympathetic older women who gave him large sums of money; he depleted their bank accounts then dumped them."

I cocked my head as I peered at him. "You were worried that I'd give him money?"

"No, I was shocked when you asked about him right after I heard what a snake he is, and I went into instant protective mode but not in a good way."

I exhaled. "I'm so glad you aren't perfect; I couldn't take the pressure. Do we tell Kate?"

"If she comes here to see him, yes." Larry hugged me. "You're amazing, you know that?"

"Am I your favorite wife?" I side-glanced him; he pulled me close and gazed at my face. "You know it."

He kissed me, and when he started to lean back, I pulled him even closer and wrapped my leg over his leg while I kissed him; he moaned then slid his hand up my shirt.

When I finally released him, he whispered, "I love you, favorite wife."

* * *

After Larry fell asleep, I listened to his quiet breathing and to the pacing upstairs that sounded more like stomping.

I tried to cover my ears with my pillow, but the footsteps sounded even louder. I threw off the covers then froze. Did I wake Larry? I sighed in relief as his breathing remained slow and even then tiptoed with my jo to the great room.

I walked to the front door then tried to peer out the dining room window. *It's either blurry or foggy out there.*

I counted my steps to the back door, and Spike joined me. He pointed at Lucy and put his index finger over his lips, and I frowned. He cocked his head and held up two fingers and crooked them for bunny ears; when his hand bunnies hopped around, I snickered.

"It's only bunnies hopping around upstairs, right? I can listen to the bunnies and go to sleep," I whispered, and Spike grinned and nodded.

"You always were a smart man, thank you."

I returned to bed and relaxed as I listened to the bunnies play upstairs.

* * *

When I woke the next morning, it was dark, and Larry was deep in sleep. I untangled from him and slipped into the closet for my clothes. *Being mostly blind is a huge advantage when it comes to getting dressed in the dark.* I smiled as I selected my clothes and quickly dressed.

I quietly closed the bedroom door then tiptoed to the kitchen without bumping into anything. *The nightlight is enough for me to see my way. Thank you, Ella.* I jumped when Palace Guard appeared next to me.

"What time is it?" I whispered. He held up four fingers. "Good. I'll have time to make coffee before Larry wakes."

After I started the coffee, I mixed the dough for cinnamon rolls by hand then covered the bowl for the dough to rise. At four thirty, I smiled at the quiet scraping sound when Larry opened the bedroom closet door. *I finally have coffee ready for him for a change.*

"What are you doing up so early?" He sauntered into the great room.

"I wanted to have coffee ready for you before your run and get cinnamon rolls prepped, so you can cut them after your run."

"I don't think Ron will make it this morning. I expected a text from him by now."

"Palace Guard and I can run with you, at least part way; Palace Guard can run me back then catch up with you."

"Are you sure about running in the dark?" he asked as he poured our coffee.

I laughed.

Larry chuckled. "Why don't I drink my coffee before I say anything else that I have to apologize for the rest of the day?"

"Good plan; give me one second to drink a bit of coffee and another second to change, then we can go."

After I put on my running shorts and shirt, I grabbed my jo and crammed on my Texas Tech ballcap. "Ready."

"You're running with your knife?" he asked. "Not a bad idea."

It was chillier than I expected outside, and I shivered. *Maybe I'll warm up with the run.*

Larry and Palace Guard ran one block with me before Palace Guard and I turned back. After I was inside, Palace Guard sped away from the apartment to catch up with Larry, and I snickered. *I'll bet Larry's trying to run full speed, so Palace Guard can't catch up with him.*

I took a warm shower and dressed; while I brushed my hair, Lucy padded into the bathroom. "I'll put on my sweatshirt and my warm coat and pour myself some more coffee, then we can go out."

I picked up the coffeepot, and Spike crowded me. "Fine; just tap my shoulder gently when I should stop."

When Spike smacked my shoulder hard enough to knock me down, I had braced for it and set down the coffeepot, then the three of us went out back. I sipped my coffee and listened to the murmur of the voices from the surrounding apartments and the mournful call of an owl while Lucy wandered the yard, and Spike strolled alongside her. I caught a faint whiff of burning wood and smiled. *Our cabin has to have a wood-burning fireplace.*

Lucy trotted to the door and turned to stare at me.

"It's cold out here, isn't it? I'm ready to go back inside too; even though I have two layers, I'm freezing."

After we went inside, I dished up her food and checked her water. "It's full enough until Larry gets back, then he can fill your water bowl before he goes to class, Lucy." *Wonder if I should make him a sandwich or if he'll come home for lunch.*

I rolled the dough into a rectangle and slathered the top with my butter, sugar, and cinnamon mixture then rolled it into a log. While I waited for Larry, I decided to preheat the oven.

"Bad plan. I can't see the dials. Can you turn on the oven for me, Spike?"

Spike waved his thumbs in a random pattern in front of my face. "I get it; you're all thumbs," I grumbled. "Can you show me which dial is for the oven?"

He pointed, and I turned it halfway in the only direction that it would go. I touched each burner, and none of them felt warm. "Even if I didn't turn it high enough, it will have a start toward a preheat." I held up my hand, and Spike smacked it.

I touched the burners one more time. "No burners are on; that's good. We'll know in a few minutes whether the oven is getting warm; otherwise, I turned on the time, and I'll definitely jump when it buzzes. If it was gas instead of electric, we'd have heard the gas ignite when it hit the pilot light. Our cabin needs a gas stove, but Larry already put that on our list."

I put my thumb inside my cup and poured coffee until my thumb was wet then opened the oven. "Yay, the oven is warming. Thanks, Spike."

I set my coffee on the table next to my computer and resumed my search for Wayne's mother, the photographer.

When Larry and Palace Guard returned, I smiled as I inhaled Larry's aroma of vinegary sweat.

"What a workout," Larry said; I heard his pride in his performance. "Thanks, Palace Guard."

"Before you take your shower, honey, cut the cinnamon rolls for me and check the setting for the oven temperature."

Larry strode to the kitchen. "Oven's set at three-fifty."

"Three-fifty is perfect."

"Dough's cut. I'll shower."

I giggled. "Thank you, honey."

"Ha, ha." Larry pulled his shirt over his head as he hurried to the bathroom.

Palace Guard held up his hand, and I smacked it.

When Larry came out of the bedroom wearing his forensics T-shirt and khakis and with his curly hair slicked down, I squealed, "What did you do with my husband?"

Larry laughed as hugged me. "Down the drain, honey."

I inhaled. "I love you when you're sweaty, but I really love the sexy smell of your soap."

He kissed me. "I love your sexy cinnamon sugar smell. When will the cinnamon rolls be ready? Do you want an egg this morning?"

I hugged him with my head against his chest. "Egg sounds good. Are you coming home for lunch, or do you need a sandwich?"

"I don't know. Some of the guys said at the meet and greet that lunch is provided. We get our schedules today, so I really don't want to carry a sandwich around."

"The cinnamon rolls smell like they're ready to come out of the oven. What time's your first class?"

"Not for another hour, but I'd like to get with the guys before class starts."

"We can have cinnamon rolls and coffee, then you can meet with the guys."

"Shall I scramble an egg for you?"

"Not today; maybe tomorrow. Anything I can do for you? I feel like I'm sending you off to your first day of school. Sit at the tiger table."

"What?" Larry laughed. "I'll remember that."

After Larry wolfed down his cinnamon roll and tossed down his coffee, he kissed my cheek. "You'll explain the tiger table to me later, right? I love you, sweetie."

"I love you too. Knock them dead. That's break a leg for cops, you know."

Larry chuckled as he left, and Palace Guard stared at me.

"What? He thought it was funny and wasn't nervous when he left; that was my goal."

I loaded the dishwasher, added the detergent, and after I closed it, I asked, "Where do I push to start it?"

Palace Guard pointed to a spot on the dishwasher's panel, and the dishwasher hummed after I pushed on the spot.

"Thanks." I turned on my computer. "Back to Noreen Weber, photographer."

After an hour, I stretched. "I found Noreen Weber's online blog. She doesn't write much in her blog, but there are a ton of photographs of the area; she does mention a portfolio that she maintained of her pictures that aren't included in her blog. I wonder where that is; let's go to the library on campus and ask."

I put on my ballcap, zipped up my heaviest sweatshirt and put on my coat, and grabbed my jo then waited at the door for Palace Guard. "Are you ready?"

He trudged to the door. "Oh don't be so grumpy. Larry would be happy that I'm getting out for some fresh air."

Palace Guard rolled his eyes and shook his head, but when I headed for the library, he tapped my arm to help me stay in the middle of the sidewalk. After we went inside, Palace Guard pointed to the women's room, and I went inside. I washed and dried my hands, so it wouldn't look like I was lurking then stood out of the way like I was waiting for a friend.

Palace Guard appeared next to me, and as we exited, I whispered, "You were checking for my stalker, weren't you? Did you get a good enough look at him to identify him if you saw him?"

He shrugged then shook his head as he guided me to the main desk. I listened to the rustling of papers and waited until a woman mumbled, "Is there something I can help you with?"

She must have glanced up because she added in a clear voice, "Oh, I'm sorry; I didn't notice you were visually impaired. What can I do for you today?"

I smiled. "I'm interested in the nature photography of local and regional authors. Have you heard of Noreen Weber?"

"Oh my, yes. She was one of my personal favorites. What would you like to know?"

"I've listened to her blog, and she referenced a portfolio of all her photographs that aren't included on her website. Have you heard of her portfolio?"

"I have; it's actually in our campus library in Nashville. Shall I order it for you? It will be here by Wednesday or no later than Thursday."

"That would be great. Do you have any audio books on photography? I'd like to understand it better."

"We should, but we don't. I can think of three that you might like; I'll order them too. Is there a specific area of photography you're interested in?"

"What about surveillance photography?"

"You're the Gray Lady, aren't you? I should have recognized you because we all knew you were going to be here with your husband, and Olivia Chandler Edwards was a dear friend of mine; she spoke very highly of you." She sighed. "Sometimes, I get too overwhelmed by all the administrative trivia. Was that the same for you? I'm Lily. Could I shake your hand?"

I smiled and held out my hand, and we shook. "It's funny that you've become interested in Noreen Weber's work. She developed a keen interest in surveillance photography and was one of the foremost lecturers for the forensic photography classes until her untimely death. She was an absolute artist with a camera in her hand. She definitely saw things no one else did."

"I didn't know that. Are there any of her lecture notes or slides that are available?"

"We have all of her presentation slides and notes. Do you have text to speech software? I can send you a link to her presentations and notes, and you can check them out. I'll set you up with your library card with us, if you can give me a few minutes. Shall I make it for Gray Lady or Maggie Ewing?"

I giggled. "Better make it Maggie Ewing."

"Good idea; stay incognito. Would you like to sit in one of our reader chairs? I'll show you where—"

"I think I'll wander a bit. I enjoy the sounds of a library."

"Isn't that the truth," she snorted. "People don't realize how much librarians hear. I keep saying I should write a book, but I'm a reader not a writer. I won't be long."

Palace Guard and I wandered toward the back of the library.

"If there's a body there with a knife in its neck, I'm warning you, I'll freak," I whispered, and Palace Guard patted my back.

While I stood toward the back of an aisle, I breathed in the beautiful aroma of all the books.

A woman in the next stack whispered, "Did you hear about the Ghost of Wicked Hollow? He's claimed another victim."

"Not another one." The woman's voice was shrill, and her friend shushed her.

"Yes; one of the wives of a young man from the new class went for a walk and disappeared. She was supposed to meet a friend, but when the friend showed up twenty minutes late, she assumed the girl had gone without her and returned home. The husband reported her missing not long after dark."

"That's horrible," the second woman lowered her voice. "I'll bet that has everyone on edge."

"As it should; the school should have warned them about the ghost."

I waited, but their conversation turned to how to repel a ghost, so I headed to the main desk with Palace Guard's help.

"There you are," Lily said. "I've got you all set up. I'll give you your card, and you can scan it in when you get back to your apartment. Is there anything else?"

I held out my hand for my card. "I keep hearing rumors about the Ghost of Wicked Hollow. Do you have anything I could read about that? Does anyone know where Wicked Hollow is?"

"These legends just don't die, do they? We have a memoir written ten or so years ago by a woman from Nashville, according to her bio. You can check it out and listen to it. I'll write down the name for you, and to answer your question, Wicked Hollow isn't on the map, but according to the locals, it's just one hill over."

I cocked my head and squinted to see her blob. "One hill over from where? Like wherever you are, it's one hill over?"

"Exactly."

I giggled. "I don't know why I find that so funny, but it's very convenient for the ghost, isn't it?"

She chuckled. "Let me know what else I can do. Are you okay going back to your apartment by yourself?"

"I'm fine; thanks for everything."

As Palace Guard and I returned to the apartment, I said, "That was a profitable trip, wasn't it?"

Palace Guard guided me as I unlocked the door. Before I took off my coat, Lucy whined, and we all went outside to the backyard.

I sat in my camp chair with my hands pulled up into my coat sleeves and listened to the traffic on the highway that went past the campus and a mockingbird that flitted from tree to tree.

"What time is it, Palace Guard?"

He held up ten fingers then one.

"Eleven? I'll text Mary Leigh."

I pulled out my phone and sent the text: "Are we still on for two?"

My phone rang. "Hi, Maggie. I should have checked with you earlier, but would you like to go to lunch before your appointment? I could pick you up at noon. I found a nice sandwich shop that my husband would hate. It's only five minutes away."

"That sounds really good; I'll be ready. How are you doing?"

She giggled. "I'm fine; I was pampered all day yesterday after the klutz I married mentioned my girth. I wish you could have seen his face the second he realized he'd made a huge mistake that was as big as my belly." She burst into laughter, and I joined her.

"I'm so glad you're here," she added. "It's so nice to have someone to talk to that I don't have to worry about saying the wrong thing."

After we hung up, I said, "I'm going inside. It's too cold out here for me, and I'd like to download the memoir."

I hung my coat on the back of my chair but kept on my sweatshirt when I sat at my computer; the hairs on the back of my neck and my arms rose as I listened to the memoir. I was deep into the story when I realized I needed to check the time.

I stopped the audio and asked, "Is it close to noon?"

Palace Guard nodded.

CHAPTER NINE

I shut down my computer. "The memoir was published twenty years ago and is the author's retelling of stories her grandmother told her about the ghost when she was a child. The legend is old, but it isn't the same as the current legend we've heard."

I shuddered. "I know that logically the old legend most likely isn't true, but it's really creepy. In the old legend from the memoir, the girls were lured to the ghost's shack in Wicked Hollow, and he put them under a spell before he killed them by scaring them to death. I didn't know ghosts did spells, but I guess there aren't rules for what ghosts can and cannot do, and even legends are allowed literary license. I've never been into tales about ghosts, but the author's storytelling style is very compelling. I wonder if she wrote anything else. I'll have to check after I finish this."

I rose from my chair and felt my hair. "I'm not sure I've brushed my hair today."

When I pulled my brush through my hair, I said, "Ouch. I didn't. Maybe I should get my hair cut, so it won't be so painful to brush."

I pulled my hair back into a ponytail and peered at the blob in the mirror. *Why can't I see myself?*

I shrugged and put on my eye patch, and my phone buzzed a text from Mary Leigh: "I'm here."

I put on my ballcap, my coat, and my new sunglasses and hurried outside with Palace Guard and my jo.

"I am freezing," Mary Leigh said on our way. "Is your coat warm enough? I need a coat that will close and fasten in front, but when I told Ron I couldn't see spending money for a coat I'll wear just a few more months, he told me we could always have more babies, so I would get my money's worth out of a larger size coat. When I told him it was a serious infraction to mention more babies to a pregnant woman, he told me he'd bring home supper tonight. It's not all bad having a klutzy husband. Want to help me find a coat after lunch?"

I snickered. "I'm not much of a shopper except in a pawn shop or the hardware store, but I wouldn't mind seeing if I could find a warmer coat and some gloves."

"Gloves is a brilliant idea," Mary Leigh said. "I need gloves too."

When we went into the sandwich shop, I smiled at the soft classical music playing in the background and the pervading aroma of vanilla.

"Tell me about the décor," I whispered.

"The tables have white tablecloths with eyelet trim, and the cushions on the seats are pale pink and yellow florals. The front windows have white lace curtains, the wooden floors are gleaming with polish, and the painted white, faux brick fireplace has pots of geraniums on the hearth."

"Sounds like Larry and Ron would collapse from sweetness shock if they came inside."

"Pretty much." Mary Leigh giggled. "Reservations are required. Can you believe it? I asked to be seated at a table where we wouldn't be too close to others, so we could whisper about the other people, except I told them that you were hypersensitive about noise. I understand most of their lunch business is between one and three; isn't that weird?"

"Good afternoon, ladies; please follow me to your table. I have a braille menu, Mrs. Ewing."

"How kind," I said, and Palace Guard poked me.

After she seated us and handed us our menus, the woman said, "Your server will be here in a second with your sweet teas. Take all the time you need to decide; I recommend the lightly battered and fried river trout."

After the woman hurried away, Mary Leigh said, "What are you having?"

I rubbed the menu with my fingertips. "Oh, there's just so much to choose from; I'll just have what you're having."

Mary Leigh snickered. "I'm thinking about the thin-sliced ham half-sandwich with the small side salad of greens, avocado, pecans, and blue cheese."

"That sounds good, but I'm not sure I could manage a salad in public; I'm still working on eating without making a mess."

"A Cuban half-sandwich with a small side of sweet plantains might work for you," Mary Leigh said.

"That's perfect."

As our server set our sweet tea on the table, she asked, "Have y'all decided?"

"I'd like the Cuban half-sandwich with a small side of sweet plantains," I said.

"Excellent choice, Mrs. Ewing. It was our original owner's signature sandwich. And you, Mrs. Lassiter?"

"I'll have the ham half-sandwich with the small side salad of mixed greens."

"Yes, ma'am. Bleu cheese dressing?"

"Yes, please."

"I won't be long."

After she left our table, a group of women came into the shop.

"Four women, and they're all wearing dresses and light coats. They must be freezing," Mary Leigh said in a soft voice. "One of them is Sally, from the meet and greet. We'll have entertainment with our lunch."

After they were seated, another group of women came in.

"Another group of four. The second group of women are wearing dresses and sensible, warm coats. The two groups have been seated close to the front near the front windows. Sally's group is on the same side of the room as we are."

"How do they carry their guns?" I asked.

Mary Leigh snorted. "I'm so glad I wasn't drinking my tea at that particular second. Okay, let me figure this out."

"Do they have large purses?"

"Two of the women in the newest group have backpacks, and the other two have large handbags. One woman from Sally's group put a phone she had carried in her hand on the table. The other three women, including Sally, from Sally's group set small clutch purses on the table."

"Were any of the women from the new group at the meet and greet? We might like them, even if they do wear dresses," I said.

"I'm not sure; I think they might be. I'll be right back."

I stared at Mary Leigh's blob as she headed toward the front then looked at Palace Guard; he shrugged.

"Everyone needs a friend like Mary Leigh," I muttered, and he nodded.

"I'm Mary Leigh; I don't mean to interrupt," Mary Leigh said, "but I had to come say, 'hey' because y'all look so familiar."

"Hey, Mary Leigh. I remember you from the meet and greet. Ron's wife, am I right?" a woman with a young voice asked.

"Right, and you're John's wife?"

"Yes, I am."

"I'm Bud's wife," another woman said. "Is that Kevin's wife with you?"

"It is; we'll have to all get together again sometime," Mary Leigh said.

"I'd love that. I'll check to see if we can hold a weekly get together at the meeting room at the office," Bud's wife said. "I'm a planner."

"That sounds great. Just let us know what we can bring. Nice to see you again," Mary Leigh said.

After Mary Leigh returned, she said, "You nailed it. The women with the backpacks were at the meet and greet and are John's wife and Bud's wife. The other two smiled politely; they weren't there. Sally's table was being very quiet; did you notice?"

"Sure did; I'm sure they were listening as intently as I was. Were you surprised that someone actually responded to your get together idea?"

"Not really; all of us are new to town and live within walking distance of each other. I expected a party organizer to jump at the chance to put her talents to work."

Sally stage-whispered to her friends, "She is really a social climber, isn't she? She's definitely not in our league."

The women chuckled, and I rose from the table so quickly that my chair clattered.

Mary Leigh said, "If Sally said something, consider the source. Let's eat."

I muttered, "She's a jerk," as our server picked up my chair.

"Anything I can do to help, Mrs. Ewing?"

"Thank you, but I'm fine; I lost my balance for a minute."

While we were eating, two more groups of women came into the shop.

"A group of four is at a table on the same side as we are; a group of three is opposite them. Is it getting too loud for you?"

"So far so good. I'm listening to Sally."

"Full report after lunch?"

I nodded.

Sally continued. "I mean, I was with her on Saturday. It could have been me. I've never been so frightened in all my life."

"Did you hear how she disappeared?" a woman asked.

"I heard her husband left early yesterday morning to pick up a few things at her parents' house for her, and when he came back late last night, she was gone. He wasn't in class this morning; nobody knows if he's going to stay with the program," another woman said.

"My husband is so helpless. He'd starve if I wasn't home to order out for us," Sally said.

"You don't cook?" a woman asked.

"Never learned and don't care to." Sally's cackle set me on edge.

"Maybe she had a boyfriend and left her husband," another woman said. "What? It happens."

"Oh no, she told me everything; she didn't have a boyfriend," Sally said.

"If I had a boyfriend, I wouldn't tell you," a woman said, and I smiled at all the laughter.

"There's no sense in making a snarky remark at the expense of someone else," Sally said.

"Right, you wouldn't do that, would you, Sally?"

"Thank you, I most certainly would not."

"Did you save room for dessert?" Our server asked. "We bake our pies here every morning. We have tart cherry today."

"Pie?" Mary Leigh asked, and I nodded.

"You talked us into it; two slices of pie, please," Mary Leigh said.

"Right; warm pie topped with our homemade ice cream." Our server cleared our dishes before she left the table.

"Did you want ice cream?" I whispered.

"No, I was just being polite."

"So was I." I snickered, and Mary Leigh joined me.

"There really should be a dress code," Sally said quite clearly over the other chatter in the room. "There are some real hicks around here. Have you noticed?"

When I heard the laughter, I frowned. "Are they really that mean?"

Palace Guard nodded.

Mary Leigh asked, "Who?"

"Sally and her friends are very judgmental," I said.

Bud's wife interrupted one of her friends who was talking about buying flowers for her yard. "You know the old saying, be nice or leave."

A chair scraped, and the front door slammed.

The friend who had been interrupted said, "I was about to say the same thing. Sour attitudes like that spoil the digestion, don't they? Thank you."

"That was interesting; Sally just left in a huff," Mary Leigh said. "You heard it all, didn't you? I'll pump you for details later."

"Well, everybody leave money on the table for your bill, and let's go," one of Sally's friends said.

"The rest of Sally's table just got up, plopped a few dollars on the table, and left. What a bunch of cheapskates," Mary Leigh said.

"When Bud's wife tells us there's a party, we're going," I said. "She's a force. I can't do much cooking by myself, but I've got some awesome recipes that we can do together."

"My cooking repertoire is pretty limited. I'd love to learn some new recipes. That shrimp dip of yours was scrumptious."

When I heard the server approach, I said, "I'll take the ticket."

"No, wait, I invited you—"

I interrupted Mary Leigh. "You can get it next time. I wouldn't have come here if you hadn't invited me, and I enjoyed it. Thank you."

After the server left, the woman who greeted us at the door bustled to our table and leaned next to me to whisper, "I'm Cassandra, the owner. May I add a twenty percent tip to your bill for our server, Mrs. Ewing?"

"Please do, and if any of the other tables were a little light with their tip, please add the additional to mine."

"That is so generous, but are you sure? One table of customers left without leaving any tip at all."

"That's too bad, and I'm positive about the tip. I have a little extra mad money, and I can't think of anything else that could make me madder."

Cassandra chuckled. "Mrs. Ewing, I heard the Gray Lady studied with Chef Daryl and was an awesome cook before she was injured; it's a pleasure to see you back in circulation, even if you aren't cooking. Your lunch is on the house; I'll let you pick up the tips for you and Mrs. Lassiter and the other table if you'll come back sometime before we open, so we can visit, and of course, Mrs. Lassiter is also welcome to come with you."

"Thank you, Cassandra; I'd love to hear more about your café and talk to your chef."

Mary Leigh and I rushed through the cold to her car; after we were inside, she said, "I know the perfect place to look for coats, and it's not far from here. I didn't know how talented the Gray Lady is. You can cook?"

I snickered. "After I graduated from college and was on my own, I could burn a grilled cheese with the best of them. My best friend taught me to cook when I worked with her in a diner. Her rule was that our customers should not know who was cooking in the kitchen on any particular day, and I learned that a recipe was just a step-by-step formula to a final product. Tell me what you want to learn to cook, and I'll find us a good recipe."

"Bud's wife will probably plan a morning coffee group. What could I learn to make?"

"Cinnamon rolls. That was the first thing after coffee that my best friend taught me."

"I could never make cinnamon rolls," Mary Leigh said.

"You might be surprised," I said.

"I don't know; I'm kind of a hard case. Tell me what Sally said."

I told Mary Leigh about Sally's friend who disappeared and examples of how self-centered Sally was.

"Do you think it was the Ghost of Wicked Hollow or the copycat?"

"I really don't have enough data to know what to think."

Mary Leigh chuckled. "You're right; we haven't found the right recipe."

"I have another surprise for you," I said. "Cassandra invited us back to the café before opening hours to visit. That would be an excellent way for you to pick up some cooking tips. Cooking fast for a crowd of hungry customers may not be in your future, but the shortcuts you'll see aren't taught in any cookbook."

Mary Leigh sniffled. "I was so worried about being lonely and bored while Ron was in his classes. My mom wanted me to stay with her where I'd be around friends, but you've opened up my world, Maggie, and you thought you weren't social."

"If you call hanging out in a café kitchen before the crowds arrive as social, that's me." I giggled.

Mary Leigh made one last turn then slowed and parked her car. "We're about twenty minutes early, but my doctor's office here told me to be fifteen minutes early to fill out paperwork. Ready to go in?"

"Not really, but I probably have to because Larry will ask me about my appointment."

Mary Leigh went in with me. After I checked in, we sat together near a window.

"I brought one of the books that I checked out at the library, so don't worry about the time."

A woman approached us. "Mrs. Ewing, if you come with me, we'll update your records with us. Are you okay with your cane, or do you want to take my elbow?"

"It might be better if I take your elbow. I'd worry I might trip someone with my cane."

"It would serve them right for not giving you space," she said.

After I verified the information my doctor had sent to them, a tech led me to an exam room and tested my vision.

After she finished, she said, "The doctor won't be long."

When the doctor came into the exam room, he said, "How are you doing?"

"I see some light and vague forms of people; I call them blobs. I see people I know very well, like my husband, more clearly."

"Good description. How does your vision compare with your sight before your surgery?"

"It's not at the same level, but I was happy when I could finally see light."

"When was that?" the doctor asked.

"Last Wednesday; the first time I saw a blob was on Thursday then yesterday I saw my husband's blurry face well enough to guess that he smiled."

"Can you see my face?" The shadowy blob moved close to me.

I strained to see eyes, a nose, or a mouth. *Nothing.* "No, I can't."

The blob moved away. "It's too soon to write off any more improvement, so don't be discouraged until I tell you to be discouraged."

I smiled. "That's encouraging."

He chuckled. "Good. Are you having any pain from either surgery? Any phantom pain?"

"No; my doctor told me pain on the left side is normal, but I've been fine."

"I'm going to examine your eye, but first I'll administer some drops. You may not even see the blobs until tomorrow; your husband has my cell phone number. Have him text me if you don't see his blob in the morning."

After the examination, he said, "Do you see any light?"

"Yes, thank goodness. I was afraid I'd be in the suffocating dark again."

"It makes sense that dark could be described as suffocating after regaining then losing partial sight. I'll see you again next Monday."

The nurse said, "I'm here; shall I help you with your coat?"

"Thanks." I rose from the chair.

"Right arm first," she said.

I smiled. "Not your first rodeo."

She giggled. "No ma'am."

After we put on my coat, she patted my arm. "I'll walk you out if you want to take my arm."

I found her forearm and held on. Palace Guard patted my back, and I sighed in relief. *I knew he was there, but it was nice to hear from him.*

"We'll schedule your appointment on Monday for two again, if that's okay," the nurse said as we went into the waiting room.

"That's perfect. Thank you."

Mary Leigh said, "That was fast."

After Mary Leigh started the car engine, she backed out of the parking spot. "How was it? Are you too worn out for shopping?"

"I liked the doctor. I think he and my surgeon had higher hopes for my rate of recovery because I caught a sense of disappointment. I think he suspected I knew what he was thinking because he told me he'd let me know when I should be discouraged."

"What a great doctor." Mary Leigh chuckled. "I'll go with you again next week. Maybe I can finish my book."

My phone rang. "Hi, Gray Lady. It's Betty. I talked to my friend about the Ghost of Wicked Hollow, and she said the first death she knows about was nineteen years ago, but she added that the original story and the tale going around now aren't the same. She said she might have a book about the old folktale, but she'll have to look for it. I'll let you know when I hear from her."

"Thanks." After we hung up, I said, "Ms. Betty is doing some research for me. She called with an update."

Mary Leigh slowed then stopped. "We're here. Ready to shop?"

"Not really, but I want warm clothes."

When we walked into the store, I smelled leather and chicken feed. "Where are we?" I whispered.

"We're at a farm store," she giggled. "I figured the best coats for us would be here."

"You are smart."

Palace Guard guided me to the rack of women's coats and tapped a coat for me to try on.

"That looks good on you." Mary Leigh was at the far end of the rack. "It's brown and looks like it would be heavy duty. You picked it out by how it felt, didn't you? I'm down to two and can't decide."

Palace Guard guided me to her then tapped my left arm. I touched the one on my left and felt the material and the thickness of the jacket. "This one; it feels like it would be soft and warm."

"I thought that one too," she said. "It's warm, sturdy, and a beautiful royal blue."

"What color is the other coat?" I asked.

"Kelly green. Let's look at gloves."

"Seriously, Palace Guard? You picked her coat because of the color?" I whispered as I listened to Mary Leigh walk away.

Palace Guard shrugged.

"You have no shame, you know that?"

He grinned then tapped my arm to follow Mary Leigh.

"Try on these," she said when I joined her.

"I love these gloves; they're so warm. Thank you."

"I have the same gloves; yours are dark brown, and mine are dark blue, so we'll be able to tell them apart."

When I laughed, she giggled. "Don't you dare tell my klutzy husband that I forgot you can't see."

While we stood in line at the checkout counter, Palace Guard tapped our 'be ready' signal on my left arm then tapped for me to turn away from Mary Leigh. I turned away and stared at what I hoped was a candy rack across the aisle. When the candy rack moved, I heard the quiet whisper of shoes with foam rubber soles as someone sneaked away from us toward the front door. When the person opened the door, I turned my head toward the blast of cold air, and Palace Guard patted my back.

We asked the cashier to remove the tags for us after we bought our gloves and coats, so we could put them on before we left.

When we went outside, I was tense until Palace Guard patted my left arm. *All clear.*

"This coat is soft and warm. Ron better be jealous because I have a new cuddle buddy," Mary Leigh said, and I smiled.

It didn't take us long to get from the farm store to campus. Mary Leigh stopped her car. "Here's your place. I'll talk to you later. Are you okay from here?"

"I'm fine."

After I opened the car door and climbed out with my purchases, Palace Guard poked me. "Thanks again for driving me to my appointment and for taking me to the farm store. I actually had fun."

When we went inside the apartment, Lucy rose from her afternoon nap and nosed the back door; Spike took her outside.

I held out my left hand. "Was the stalker following Mary Leigh or me?" I held out my right hand, and Palace Guard tapped my right hand.

"Following me, thanks. I'm glad he wasn't following Mary Leigh. Is it the same guy as the one at the camp store?"

Palace Guard tapped yes.

I hung up my new and lighter-weight coats but left on my sweatshirt. While I headed toward my computer, my phone rang.

"Is now a good time to talk?" Paul asked.

"I just got back from going to lunch with a new friend. Lunch was delicious, and I have more gossip. It's a perfect time to talk. What do you have?"

"I'll start with the women being murdered, which includes suspicious suicides, over the past fifteen years. The only news I have is that there is absolutely no overall pattern. If I worked for me, I'd fire me." Paul chuckled.

"That's funny. I think Larry would like it if I were fired too. We'd just have to break it to the bad guys."

Paul snorted. "I can give you a long list of what has no pattern. The married women were happy, unhappy, or not known. The murders include unmarried women, which, if we give any credence at all to the ghost theory, is a complete surprise. There are only two common factors: every victim was between twenty-one and twenty-five; and they all were living within fifty miles of the training center when they were murdered. The investigators haven't uncovered a common cause of death; many were smothered, some were shot in a public place in front of witnesses, others were knifed, clubbed, or strangled. The killer may be using the Ghost of Wicked Hollow as a way to mock the investigators, but's that's my gut speaking. I found a two-year gap of no murders, and five years before that, there were a few sporadic murders with the same pattern of age, but no other pattern, around Nashville. I found those by mistake when I was poking around on the deaths of the Dillards. I have a friend looking deeper into those deaths. I believe Nashville was the early years of our killer, and his biggest mistakes would have happened when he first began."

"That was a good find."

"Yeah, but moving on to the Dillards, that wasn't a filler. The cause of death for both of them was generic; dementia for him and depression for her. Julie's taking a little trip to Nashville to visit our friends there."

"Oh no, I didn't mean to make her take a special trip like that."

"Don't worry about it; she should have been the detective in our family. She's ecstatic, and my friend is a heavy-handed klutz like I am. He asked if she could come visit him and his wife because he needs Julie's finesse. He told me Julie could sweet talk the warts off a toad. I told him not to tell Julie that, or she'd turn around and come home, and he'd be stuck."

I snickered. "I think I might understand his level of diplomacy. I learned more about Mrs. Dillard that you can pass on to Julie. She was a talented photographer and was an expert in surveillance photography. She was an instructor here at one time. The campus library ordered her lecture notes and presentation slides for me to review. She used her maiden name, Noreen Weber, as her professional name. I don't know how this fits with anything, but Julie might find it useful."

"I've heard of Noreen Weber," Paul said. "I have a copy of some of her lectures. I never knew her lecture notes were available. I think you'll enjoy studying them. It's right down your spy alley."

I smiled. "The library had a copy of an old memoir that includes the legend of the Ghost of Wicked Hollow. The old legend doesn't have much in common with the newer version. We had another disappearance here last night, according to unreliable gossip I overheard at lunch at a local café."

"We have quite a lot of nothing, don't we? What else do you have for me?"

I told him about Dean Sanchez and his reputation. "Could you check him?"

"No can do. Kate's orders, and you don't know this, but she expected you to want to investigate him when she mentioned his name."

"If you can't, you can't."

"Glad you understand. Again, here's something else you don't know: Glenn's looking into said person's past. He'll get with you later this week to make sure everything's going okay with you, and, at my suggestion, he wants to be sure you aren't mistreating Larry."

"Again," I giggled. "You forgot to add that part."

"Right, again. What else?"

CHAPTER TEN

"Wayne Dillard. My new friend and I went to the library, and Wayne Dillard was helping Mary Leigh up from the floor where she'd been sitting. Palace Guard pushed me between Mr. Dillard and her, and I felt an imprint of a pistol in his pocket. She grabbed my arm and pulled me toward her then later told me she had a strong feeling she had to get me away from him. Vague, I know. I plan to ask Ms. Betty about carrying a concealed weapon inside the library; I'll be interested to hear what she has to say. I haven't been carrying my gun, but I will from now on."

"Kate said your shooting skills hadn't deteriorated at all. That's great."

"I can't stand the sound of gunshots, though. I had a raging headache after Kate and I left the range, but it did give me the confidence boost that I needed."

"I'll see if I can uncover the creepy side of Wayne Dillard. Sounds like Palace Guard doesn't trust him either. What else?"

"That's it."

"No, it isn't. You're talking to me, Maggie. I was a master at lying for years. You're not even in my league, girl."

"I could use something, but I don't know what: maybe a Heather gadget. I have a stalker; he's very bold but obviously unsure how limited my sight is. I've heard him, but of course, I can't see him. If I turn in his direction or even act like I saw him, he leaves quickly, almost at a run. I have the sense that he's tall and muscular, but that's it."

"Dammit, Maggie. You don't need a gadget. You need an old man like me guarding...wait, Palace Guard. He's sticking with you and told you what the man looked like, didn't he?"

"Yes."

"That's a relief; I guess I don't have to see how long it takes before I get a speeding ticket between here and Tennessee, after all. You keep your knife and carry piece close too, don't you?"

"Yes."

"You need a way to take a picture of him. There are cameras in pens and tiny nanny cams, so I'm sure I can find a camera in a pommel or a way to make one. We could put it on top of your jo."

"That sounds perfect. Is there such a thing?"

"If there isn't, there will be before the end of the week," Paul said. "What does Larry say?"

"Well—"

Paul interrupted me. "Of course, you haven't told him because he would blow a gasket, and for good reason. If I ask Heather for help, she'll know it's for you and that you haven't said anything to Larry; she won't either. I almost forgot to ask you about your doctor's appointment. Jennifer and Ella will ask me as soon as I hang up," Paul said.

"My eye is improving, but not quite fast enough for me. I have a follow up appointment next Monday."

"Slower than we hoped, but Jennifer and Ella will be happy to hear your eye is continuing to heal."

After we hung up, I turned on my laptop and carried it to the sofa to listen to more of Noreen Dillard's lecture notes. I felt a chill, so I set down the laptop and pulled up the afghan. *I'm supposed to let Della know when I'm settled.*

I picked up my phone. "Send a text to Della, 'I'm settled.'"

"Message sent."

I wrapped the afghan around my feet and leaned back.

The sound of a key in the front door lock woke me. When I sat up, I was disoriented and meant to lean against the back of the sofa, but instead, I rolled off onto the floor. I laughed as I tried to get up before Larry came in the door.

"Sweetie, why are you laughing, and how did you end up on the floor?" Larry strode to me and lifted me up into his arms. "Are you okay?"

"I'm okay." I inhaled his unique Larry aroma to regain my composure. "I had dozed off, and when I woke, I thought I was at our old house, and rolled off the sofa. I blame the earth's axis."

Larry chuckled. "You're fine; only my sweetie would shift the blame to an entire planet. Why don't you rest a minute to give your head a chance to clear while I pop a casserole into the oven. How was your appointment? What did the doctor say?"

While Larry preheated the oven, I carried my laptop to the table and plugged it in. "I think the doctor expected more improvement than what I have so far, but he told me not to be discouraged. He put in a couple different drops, and I'm back to blobs again. I have another appointment next Monday."

"Were you disappointed?" Larry asked.

"A little, but I'm not sure when I'll have time to mope. Mary Leigh and I had a full day. We visited the campus library this morning, and I learned that a photographer from Nashville was an expert in surveillance photography and taught classes here. The library had some of her lecture notes; I've listened to most of them. They were easy for me to follow even though most of the information was over my head. I'm positive I missed ninety percent of the depth of what she said. Does that make sense? I thought you might like to read her notes. Her name was Noreen Weber."

"Noreen Weber? She's a legend around here. I bought the camera and equipment for the photography class based on her preferences. I'd love to read her notes. I'm not sure anyone knew they were available."

"I don't know why not; they were in the library."

He opened the oven door for the casserole then closed it. "Spoken like a true librarian."

"The oven door squeaked. Did you put in the casserole?"

"Sure did, but I didn't hear the squeak. It will be a while before the casserole is ready; would you like to go for a short walk? It's not quite as cold as it was earlier."

"I'd like that. Mary Leigh and I went to a small café for lunch, then after my doctor appointment, we went shopping, and both of us bought ourselves much warmer coats and gloves."

"You went shopping for clothes? Mary Leigh is a miracle worker."

"She's actually brilliant too because we got our coats and gloves at the farm store."

"I should have guessed. I'll get your coat for you."

"I hung it up when I got home, and my gloves are in the pockets."

When we stepped outside, the shock of cold air almost took my breath away. I opened my mouth in a wide O then forcefully exhaled as we strolled down the sidewalk. "At least it isn't cold enough that I can see my breath."

Larry laughed. "That was hilarious, sweetie. I thought you were trying to steel yourself for the walk. Tell me about the tiger table."

"I was so excited to start first grade because I was certain I'd finally learn calculus."

"That's my girl," Larry said.

"I knew you'd understand. When I walked into the classroom, I almost heaved."

"Color overload?"

"Yes, and worse. There were no desks; instead, the room had small tables that seated four and were painted with bright, garish, primary colors; each table had a different cartoony animal painted in the middle. The teacher told us to find our nametags and match the animal on our nametag with the animal on the table. My saving grace that kept me from dropping out of school at age six was she had assigned me to the tiger table and not to one of the others that went beyond cutesy."

Larry chuckled. "You have always been the Gray Lady; you were just a tiny version of yourself in first grade. So, did you learn calculus that year after all?"

"Yes, I sneaked in a calculus book to study while the others read the preschool children's picture books."

"You did not."

"Maybe not, but I should have. What were you like in the first grade?"

"I always wanted to be a cop, just like Dad. I read every crime book that I could get my hands on, but the elementary school library's supply of books on murder, fraud, and cold case investigations was woefully lacking. Dad had books that he let me read after I did my homework."

"I'm not a bit surprised. Your dad is a wise man."

"I was like you: I loved to read, and I loved math. Dad taught me how to multiply and divide, and I'd race through our simple math pages in class then daydream about long division math problems and solve them in my head. I got sent to the office at least three times a week for not paying attention."

"What about the guys?" I asked.

Larry stopped. "How did you know? Two kids in my class had dads who were in law enforcement. The guys and I stuck together all through elementary school."

I nodded. "You always find your guys."

As we continued our stroll around the campus, I asked, "Do we have the fixings for hot chocolate?"

"We might, but if we don't, it's a quick trip to the grocery store to get some. Let's head back; I'm getting cold, so I'm sure you are too, and our casserole is probably hot enough to come out of the oven."

On the way back, Larry said, "We have homework; Ron and I and a few other guys plan to meet at the library after we eat. Will you be okay? All the married guys in class wanted to eat dinner with their families first; the single guys went to the library right after class then will probably eat together somewhere in town later."

"That's fine; we expected you to have to put in extra time at the library. I appreciate that we have a little time together in the evening, though."

"So do I."

After we went inside, I said, "Feels good in here."

"Sure does. I've turned on the burner under the tea kettle and removed the casserole from the oven. While it cools, I'll pull together salads for us: a small one for you, and a regular salad for me."

"Your huge salad, you mean." I put two forks and the salad dressing on the table.

After we ate, I cleared our dishes while Larry covered the casserole and loaded the dishwasher.

"I'll run to the grocery store; I checked Jennifer's recipe, and we need milk for our hot chocolate; is whipped cream okay with you?" Larry asked.

"That's perfect. I'll get my coat."

"Why don't you stay here where it's warm? It's such a short trip, the truck won't have enough time to warm up."

"I'd like to ride along, but I can't argue about staying where it's warm."

Larry gave me a quick kiss as he left, then Spike coaxed Lucy out back for a brief break. When Lucy dashed back inside, she leapt onto the sofa next to me, and I hugged her. "You're cold, girl. No wonder you came back inside so quickly."

After she leaned against me and fell asleep, my phone buzzed a text, and I pushed to move her off me. "I need to check my phone, Lucy; it might be Larry with an urgent hot chocolate question."

She shifted her weight enough that I could get up and pick up my phone I'd left on the table next to my laptop.

Spike crowded me as he leaned over my shoulder, and Palace Guard tapped my arm to let me know he was standing next to me; the three of us listened to the text from Kate: "Will be there Tuesday. I'll cook."

"This is not good. How can I subtly ask her why she's coming?"

I stared at my phone. "Send my reply: 'Cool. You coming to see Dean?'"

Palace Guard elbowed me, and I shrugged. "It's kind of subtle."

"Kate replied: 'No.'"

"Whoa. I didn't expect that. Shall I ask her why not, or would that be pushing my luck?"

Spike's blob jumped around, and I sighed. "Your wacky dance. Got it."

"Hi, honey; I'm home." Larry strode to the kitchen. "I got milk, whipped cream in a can, ice cream, root beer, in case the weather warms up, or we decide we need root beer floats, and a surprise. I'll get busy on our hot chocolate."

While he made our drinks, I said, "I got a text from Kate. My phone's on the table."

"I poured our hot chocolate, but it might be safer if we sit at the table. I read the texts; I'm surprised you didn't ask her why not."

I sat with my hands wrapped around my mug for the warmth. "I thought about it, but Spike did his wacky dance."

"He's right; thanks, Spike."

I listened to the sound of a long spray as Larry spritzed a tower of whipped cream on my hot chocolate.

"I found some crushed candy canes on sale for seventy-five cents and couldn't pass them up," Larry said. "I added crushed candy cane on top of your whipped cream. I'll give you a spoon."

I used my spoon to eat the crunchy whipped cream down to my cup's rim then stirred the rest into the chocolate to cool it. "You've taken hot chocolate to a whole new level. I loved the peppermint crunch whipped cream."

"It is good, isn't it? I can't take full credit for it, though. A ten-year-old boy and his mom were getting milk the same time I was; when he saw the ice cream and the can of whipped cream in my cart, he told me the broken candy canes were on sale."

I found a sliver of peppermint in the bottom of my cup. *That explains the peppermint hot chocolate. Yum.*

"What's that for, Spike?" Larry asked. "Why would Spike pat me on the back, sweetie?"

"Because you're smart enough to listen to an expert," I said. "Speaking of expert, would you like to read Noreen Weber's notes? We can copy them to a flash drive tomorrow."

"That would be great," Larry said.

He kissed me then smacked his lips. "Yum. You have a chocolate mustache."

I blotted away my mustache, and he kissed me again. "You're yummy even with no mustache. You don't have to wait up for me if you get tired. We'll probably stay until the library closes at ten."

After Larry left, I called Kate.

"What's up?" I asked. "Larry's gone to the library, so I've got all evening to talk."

"I'm glad to hear your doctor appointment went well. Thanks for letting me know." She hung up.

"Kate will call me back; she can't talk right now."

I turned on my laptop to search for more works by the author of the memoir but didn't find anything. When I switched to searching her name on the internet, all that came up was the memoir.

I leaned back in my chair and sighed. "She used a pen name for the memoir. Ms. Lily may know whether the author wrote anything else under another name, but the campus library will be busy tonight; we'll go tomorrow."

My phone rang, and Kate said, "I need for you to stop."

"Stop what?"

"Paul's looking into Dean Sanchez, and I know you're behind it. Tell Paul to stop; he'd be suspicious if I told him to back off."

"Why? Would Paul find something?"

"Doesn't matter. He has to stop. I'll be there tomorrow, and we can go for a long walk."

Kate hung up.

"Did you hear? Kate wants me to tell Paul to forget investigating Dean Sanchez, but he isn't."

Palace Guard patted my back, and I picked up my phone.

"Send a text to Paul. 'Kate called me. Can we talk?'"

My phone responded, "Message sent."

Less than a minute later, Paul called me.

"Did she set your hair on fire?" Paul asked.

I snickered. "Pretty close to it. She wanted me to tell you to stop investigating Dean Sanchez, and she'd be here tomorrow to talk to me."

"What did you tell her?"

"You say that like you think she gave me a chance to talk. I asked her if you would find something, and she told me it didn't matter, and we'd go for a long walk, then she hung up."

"I'll let Glenn know Kate's on the warpath. I'll think of a way to let Ella and Jennifer know I'm focused on the Dillards and nothing else right now. Do you have anything else?"

"Of course, but it's minor and gives me something to do while you're busy with the Dillards."

Paul chuckled as he hung up.

I returned to my computer and searched for the copyright of the memoir, and Palace Guard stood next to me.

After spending the rest of the evening on the computer, I yawned. "I can't find where the memoir was ever registered with the copyright office, but I could have missed it because I didn't use the right search word. Text to speech is fine for reading straight text, but for an organic search, it's painfully tedious. The book was published before social media was widespread, so that removes the potential for an author to reveal her identity accidentally. I'll bet a weekly local newspaper published an article about a local woman who wrote a book."

I slammed my laptop closed. "I need my eye, so I can read."

I tried to stomp to the sofa, but Palace Guard stopped me.

"I left my jo at the table," I whined.

Palace Guard guided me back to the dining table, and I grabbed my jo.

"What time is it?" I growled.

Palace Guard tapped my arm ten times.

"I need to shake it off. Larry doesn't need to come home to a grumpy wife, and you're very patient for putting up with me."

Before I reached the sofa, Larry had unlocked the door and was inside.

"Hi, honey, I'm home; are you exhausted?" Larry strode across the room and hugged me. "I'm a little wired."

"I'm fine. How did your studying go?"

"It was great. Can you stay up for a bit? Care for a glass of wine?"

"I think I'd crash if I had a glass of wine."

We sat on the sofa together, and Larry put his arm around me. "Ron and I and a couple of the other married guys got organized, and I have all the notes from the library that I'll need this week for my classes on my computer. I can study at home the rest of the week, then our small group can get together early on Saturday for a study session. What do you think?"

"Whatever works best for you is fine with me," I said. "I'd love to have you around in the evenings; you can study, and I'll listen to books. I'll see if Mary Leigh would like to get together on Saturday while you're at your session, so there wouldn't be any need for you to feel like you had to cut it short."

Larry kissed me. "I told Ron that's what you'd say."

I snuggled against him as he told me about the articles he found to supplement the class material. While Larry talked, I relaxed and closed my eyes.

"Ready to wake up and go to bed, honey?" he asked.

I mumbled, "I didn't know I was asleep."

"You dropped off right in the middle of my fascinating summary of our calculus class." He chuckled.

After he and Spike took Lucy outside for a quick break, we walked together to the bedroom. "I didn't know you were back in first grade."

"Yep, sitting proud at the tiger table."

* * *

I woke to the sound of the shower and shivered when I climbed out of bed. I grabbed my jo and hurried to dress. While I was putting on my socks, Larry came into the bedroom.

"I thought I heard you. Good morning, sweetie, coffee's ready." He kissed me. "Want me to bring your cup to you?"

"No, I'll come to the kitchen; it's warmer."

"How does oatmeal sound?" Larry asked.

"Perfect for this polar weather."

While Larry cooked the oatmeal, he asked, "What are your plans for today?"

"Mary Leigh and I will probably get together sometime; we don't have any special plans, though. Kate's going to be here, but I don't know what time. I'd like to go to the campus library this morning to see if the author of the memoir I read wrote anything else. I really like her style of writing."

After breakfast, Larry said, "Have a great day, sweetie. Text me if you need me." He gave me a quick kiss then left.

I put on my warm coat, then Lucy and the men and I went outside to the backyard. A crow called out, and other crows answered. As more crows gathered and joined in, their cries sounded more and more frantic.

"Is there a predator like a hawk in the neighborhood?" I asked.

Palace Guard patted my back. When the crows continued their calls as they flew away, I asked, "Are they chasing it?"

I glanced at Palace Guard, and he nodded then reached for my back to pat yes.

"The thought of a predator really spooked me. I'd like to tell Larry, so he could tell me it's okay, but he might think he needs to leave his class," I said. "Do you think it would be okay if I text Larry to tell him I can see you more clearly? It's not an emergency, so he won't rush home."

Spike punched my arm gently, at least for Spike, and I smiled.

I went inside and peered at my phone. *Not quite ready to send a regular text.*

"Send a text to Larry: 'Saw Palace Guard nod.'"

Larry replied immediately. "Great news. Thanks."

"I feel better; let's go to the library."

When we left, Lucy and Spike were on the sofa; Lucy snored softly, and Spike nodded off.

As Palace Guard guided me to the library, I said, "I'll be interested to see if there's any change in the blobs."

He held up a thumb, and I smiled.

When we went inside, I saw two blobs strolling through the aisles. *Tourists in the library?*

I stood at the desk, watched the blobs hurry to the exit, and listened as the door opened then closed.

"The parents of a high school girl that is interested in a forensic science career just left," Lily said. "I'm not sure why they decided to stop at the campus library on their way home to Kentucky from a Florida vacation because all they did was take a power walk through the stacks, but I understand books much better than I understand people."

I turned and peered at her blob and sighed. *I hoped I'd see Lily.* "Maybe they wanted to be sure there weren't any unsavory people around."

Lily snorted. "They should have been here yesterday and last night. I swear our law enforcement officer students get younger every year, and every single one of those youngsters was packing heat. That's how us thugs talk, you know." Lily chuckled. "Thanks,

Gray Lady, for letting me get that out of my system. So, what are you up to?"

"I read the memoir; it's really well-written. Has the author written anything else?"

"That was a pen name. Hold on, I might have a record from the publisher. I'll be right back."

I listened to the silence that only a library has and sighed at the memories of my first job where I met the tall, new recruit, Officer Ewing, but didn't remember him when I saw him as an undercover officer and dubbed him Larry. I missed the creaking of my cart as I went from stack to stack and reshelved the returned and misplaced books in their proper place before anyone else came into the library.

I bit my lip. *I miss Olivia who died in the library explosion, and I miss Parker Coyle who was my first boyfriend. He would have approved of Larry and been a great friend to both of us.*

Lily returned. "You have card catalogs in your blood, don't you, Maggie. Do you miss it?"

"I have good memories and bad memories."

"I'm sorry, sweet girl. Sometime after your eye heals, we'll rock on my front porch, drink moonshine, eat sugar cookies, and swap stories."

I giggled. "Deal. Thanks for that. I'm having a little trouble...adjusting."

"You'll do it; I did. So, back to our author. I don't have anything from my records, but I have friends, and I love a puzzle. Can you give me one day?"

"You've got it. I'll see you tomorrow."

Before Palace Guard and I walked through the parking lot, he guided me to turn away from the apartment then stop, and I cocked my head and peered at a blob that appeared to be doubled. When one blob ducked behind a car, the other blob disappeared. I placed my left hand alongside my leg in readiness to snatch up then throw my knife. When a car pulled into the parking lot, Palace Guard signaled that I could continue, and we walked home.

We went into the apartment, and I said, "I very briefly saw a double blob before it hid behind a car. You aren't double. Should I be worried about my eye seeing double blobs? Was it the same guy we've seen before?"

Palace Guard shook his head and pointed at me.

"What? There's a second stalker following me?"

Palace Guard sighed and stared at me then pointed at me again.

"I don't get it. I need my camera pommel, so Larry could see him."

My phone rang.

"What are you your plans for today?" Mary Leigh asked.

"A friend of ours is coming to see us; she said she'd cook supper, but I don't have any idea when she'll be here. What are you thinking?"

"I heard the faculty is talking about hosting a get together for the class at a local park this Saturday. This certainly is a social lot, isn't it?"

"It must be some team building theory or something. Larry's great at networking. Is it going to be potluck or something?"

"Yes. I don't mind the socializing in small doses, but I'm hyperventilating over the potluck. According to the gossip, they'll assign the items to bring: hors d'oeuvres, salad, vegetable, or dessert, but I don't know when, so I'm stressing."

"We'll go with our team approach; my recipe and directions, and your hands."

"I got myself in such a state of panic, I wasn't thinking. Are you going to have to stay home and wait for your friend, or would you like to go somewhere for lunch? I heard of a great diner that specializes in grilled cheese sandwiches."

I snickered. "Sounds pretty specialized to me. I really don't expect her before late this afternoon."

"I'll pick you up around eleven thirty."

"Wait a minute; how are you going to do that? Ron needs the car for school."

Mary Leigh giggled. "I knew I wouldn't be able to slip that past you. One of my aunts showed up to clean our apartment and offered me the use of her car to get me out of the way. She and I are really close, so she knows the rules about the car for Ron. She told me she can't clean when I'm around because I talk too much, but really, she's the one who talks all the time. She asked me if I had a friend I'd like to take to lunch, so I called you."

After we hung up, I turned on my computer; while I listened to the memoir again, Palace Guard stood next to me and read the screen.

He poked my arm, and I stopped the narration as he pointed to the screen, then I listened to the previous thirty seconds.

CHAPTER ELEVEN

"The author mentioned her friend, Noreen, twice, and I missed it both times. According to the author, Noreen had been friends with the mothers of many of the girls who had disappeared during the time the memoir was written. The author's story wasn't just about the long-ago Ghost of Wicked Hollow legend her grandmother told her because she included the disappearances and murders in Nashville from twenty years ago. If she hadn't mentioned Noreen, I don't think I would have caught it. The author blended the old and the new seamlessly, but now that I've listened a second time, I can hear the style change in the last half of the new part, so that it has a more current feel."

I closed my laptop and stretched. "Let's go out back. I need the fresh air to think, and maybe Lucy and I can run again."

Lucy trotted and I jogged around the yard once, then I jogged around it two more times.

I was out of breath and at the point of collapse when we went back inside. I braced myself as I leaned on the sink then held a glass under the faucet. After the water overflowed, I turned off the faucet and spilled out part of the water into the sink. I gulped down my glass of water. "I need to call Paul."

When Paul picked up, I said, "I have more for Nashville. Can you check for disappearances, murders, and suspicious deaths from thirty years then forward to twenty years ago?"

"Sounds like you've narrowed in on something. What?" Paul asked.

"I listened to the memoir a second time, and Palace Guard read along and noticed a reference to someone named Noreen who was friends with many of the Nashville victims' mothers. If it's Noreen Dillard, she died about twenty years ago, and the book was published about twenty years ago. The author made the transition so smoothly from the legend to essentially a current event at the time the book was written that I'd missed the reference twice."

"I can throw another twist at you, hang onto your socks. Do you know where Dean Sanchez was twenty years ago?" Paul asked.

"No, but don't tell me. You're sounding so smug it must be Nashville."

"You are right, so do we pin this on Dean Sanchez or Wayne Dillard?"

I exhaled. "Or someone completely different."

"I'm listening," Paul said.

"I either have two stalkers, or I've started seeing double when the blobs aren't close. I think I'm seeing double, but Palace Guard said no. I saw double this morning when I left the campus library. If there are two, Palace Guard is the only one who has seen both."

"Are there two? Would he recognize them again?"

I looked at Palace Guard, who stood next to me, and he nodded.

"Yes."

"Are you sure?" Paul asked, and I giggled.

Paul snorted. "Never mind. I forgot for a second that he can see and hear me, but I can't see and hear him. At least I didn't tell you to give him the phone, so I could talk to him."

"Would Dean Sanchez have any association with the missing girls?"

"We'll know pretty quick, won't we? My boss man is a tenacious bloodhound when he's given a scent to follow."

"You be safe, Maggie. Are you sure you wouldn't be safer here for a while? Never mind. There's no way you'd leave Larry alone for more than a day unless you were hospitalized and unconscious, but please don't do that. It's a toss-up which one of you is more protective. Kate's our courier for the pommel camera; she or Larry can install it for you on your jo."

After Paul hung up, I said, "Did you hear that? Kate's bringing the camera. Why couldn't she just say so instead of being so mysterious?"

My phone buzzed then announced, "From Mary Leigh. 'I'm here.'"

I grabbed my coat and jo and checked my knife and holster. "I should probably practice with my knife while I'm wearing gloves."

Palace Guard nodded.

I glanced at Mary Leigh on our way to the diner. *Only one blob.*

She said, "I'm really excited about all the different grilled cheese choices. After lunch, I'd like to find a couple of shirts that are a little more stylish than my T-shirts. Do you mind?"

"Not at all. I'll be happy to have an opportunity to listen to the latest rumors."

"I want to go to a maternity shop near the diner; it should be a regular baby pool of gossip."

"Are there many wives on campus that are pregnant? Isn't there a mother's club or something?" I asked.

"There are six or seven expecting, and there's a small group that I think is planning to meet regularly. Before you ask, I don't fit in. I'm an Asian occupational therapist and seem to be the only one who finished college."

"Reverse snobs?" I asked.

"Something like that. Did you know I'm as short as you are?"

"Seriously? You're not only a college graduate but also short? They must be reeking in jealousy. My best friend in high school was shorter than me. I'll have to tell you about Taylor and me sometime. She became a kindergarten teacher and married a middle-school teacher, then they moved to a big city because he wanted to make a difference."

"They sound like really cool people."

I nodded.

"My best friend in high school towered over me," Mary Leigh said. "Kids in school called us Mutt and Jeff, but nobody knew who was supposed to be Mutt or Jeff because nobody knew what that meant except me. I looked it up in case I needed to start a fight. I didn't." She giggled, and I smiled.

"Where is she now?"

"She and her husband run a ranch in Montana. Can you believe she went from Savannah to Montana? I get chilled to the bone just thinking about it. I told her she always was a softie for a cowboy, and she told me she was surprised I married a cop after being such a thug in high school."

"You two sound more like me and Kate," I said.

After we were seated, Mary Leigh said, "I didn't realize the tables were so crowded together. What do you think about takeout?"

"That's fine. Get me whatever you order. If they have milkshakes, I'll have chocolate."

I stood with her at the end of the line to order until the line extended to the door, and I felt the crush of bodies, even though no one was touching me.

"I'll wait outside," I whispered.

When Palace Guard and I went outside, he pointed to me then turned me to my right, and I saw one blob then another blob as it hurried into the shop next door; I blinked. *Double blob? I'll bet Palace Guard is right. I wonder if they're working together.*

I glanced at Palace Guard. *Only one of him.* "Let's go."

Palace Guard shook his head, so I took off by myself. He caught up with me just in time to keep me from crashing into a lamp post.

As I waltzed into the shop, I inhaled the familiar aroma of a pawnshop: leather, gunpowder, mildew, old books, and machine oil and steel from old tools. I smiled, and Palace Guard patted my back then guided me to the counter. I stared at the blob behind the counter. *Only one.*

"Can I help you, miss?" a woman wheezed before she broke into the wet cough of a smoker.

"Do you have wallets? I'd like to get my husband a new one."

"Sorry, but we don't have any at all. The hardware store down the street has some nice ones, but maybe you should have a friend go with you."

As she resumed coughing and walked away, Palace Guard guided me to the front door then outside.

While he guided me toward the diner, I asked, "Were the guys who have been following me in there? Did you get a good look at them?"

Palace Guard rolled his eyes, held up one finger, and nodded.

"You only saw one of them in there? I'm definitely confused. What is it that I'm missing?"

He shook his head and poked my arm with his index finger.

"I don't get it."

When we reached Mary Leigh's car, I peered at her. Only one Mary Leigh blob. *Do I see double when a blob is farther away?*

As I closed the car door, she asked, "Where did you run off to, and how do you get around so easily? Are you getting some of your sight back?"

I giggled. "I'm glad it looks like I know what I'm doing. I've been trying to practice moving without hesitation with my jo every chance I get. I've picked up a few tricks listening to some videos, and Larry said I look like I have radar, but I thought he was just being nice."

"You're doing great. Where do we want to eat?"

"Why don't we go to my house? I know where everything is, and we can relax and be warm."

"Perfect. Mom keeps telling me to relax now while I can."

After we sat at the table, Mary Leigh unpacked our food, and I unwrapped the sandwich she put in front of me while she opened a small bag of chips.

"I ordered both of us grilled ham and cheese sandwiches. What do you think?" Mary Leigh asked as she shook the chips into two small bowls.

"Thanks." I bit into my sandwich. "Is this gouda? I think I have my new favorite sandwich."

While we ate, Mary Leigh asked, "That's your computer, isn't it? I don't know what I'd do without mine. Just to be snoopy, I looked up our friend, Sally Overman. She has blogged for years but suddenly quit six months ago; I'd love to ask her why. Six months ago is when Ron told me he was accepted to the crime investigator course, and I threw up on his shoes. That was my first hint that I was pregnant. I wonder if Sally's husband learned he was accepted at the same time, but why would that be a reason to quit blogging? I mean, she could have just thrown up on his shoes. I'm pretty sure she snapped the beautiful photos of cotton fields, barns, horses, parks, and streams herself because her descriptions of the surroundings and weather were too real to have been stock photos. Two of her pictures had a single figure in them, usually off in the distance; it looked like the same man in every shot, but I don't see how it could be. It wasn't her husband because it was an older man; at least, that was my impression."

"That's interesting. I've always been fascinated by photography and have read a little about the craft; I don't know very much, other than enough to know how difficult it is." I chuckled.

After we ate, Mary Leigh threw away our trash.

"Thanks for lunch," I said. "Do you blog?"

"Just sporadically."

"Send me a link to your blog, so I don't have to spend all afternoon trying to find you. I'd love to read it."

"Really? It's not very good. One of the women here with a toddler started an online moms' group for the students' wives. The other pregnant wife in the moms' group found it and told me she loved it, but she's the nicest person in the world."

"Even nice people are allowed to say nice things," I said. "If it makes you happy, it will make me happy."

"Okay, but you don't have to read all of it; it's not well-written at all, and it's boring."

"Well, with a recommendation like that, I'll have to read every word." I smiled.

Mary Leigh sighed. "Don't say I didn't warn you. I'll send you the link before I lie down for my nap; otherwise, I'll forget."

After Mary Leigh left, I called Paul. "Can you talk?"

"Yes, sir, I've got that in my office; I'll call you right back. Five minutes."

After he hung up, I said, "Paul had an audience. Shall we take Lucy out back for a bit? I'll try another run."

Palace Guard, Spike, Lucy, and I went to the backyard. Palace Guard ran backwards in front of me. When I got mad and ran faster, he sped up but continued to run facing me. We ran five fast loops, then he veered to the back door, and I followed him.

Lucy went inside, and Spike did his wacky dance in the doorway.

"Cut it out, Spike. I can't see you, anyway."

Spike and Palace Guard laughed so hard that Spike grabbed the door jamb to keep from falling down, and I bent over with my hands on my knees as I gasped for breath and laughed with them until I was laughing and shivering.

My teeth chattered. "Move out of the doorway; I'm freezing."

Spike moved but kept laughing as he swept his hand toward the kitchen in his annoying, 'After you, Princess,' way.

I was breathing heavily when Paul called.

"What's wrong with you? You sound out of breath."

"Palace Guard and I went for a run in the backyard, but he cheated: he ran backwards."

"I'll be polite and pretend like I understand why that would be cheating. You've got something important, or you wouldn't have called."

"A longshot, but Sally Overton, whose husband is in Larry's class, was a blogger but hasn't blogged for six months. Her photos sound like they may be countryside landscapes of the region, but all of them appear to have a man in the background. Could you add that to your list?"

"Sounds strange. I'm on it."

I checked my email and found Mary Leigh's email with the link to her blog.

I chuckled as I listened, and Palace Guard and Spike read over my shoulder.

"This is really funny, but I'm not surprised. I'm glad she told me she planned to take a nap, or I'd be waking her up with a fangirl phone call." I snickered.

Spike pointed to the sofa, and I shook my head.

"Kate could be here anytime. I don't want to be groggy when she shows up. I want to reread the memoir to make sure I understand the differences between the old legend and the more recent events."

I listened carefully, then after an hour, I said, "I've found the transition. The motive of the killer in the legend was tragic because, in his mind, he was saving other young couples from the pain of depression and suicide; the more recent killer's motivation is not focused on a couple, but instead is a fixation on his selected victim. The Ghost murdered his victims at his shack, but the current killer is more opportunistic rather than selective with the murder site. Geographically, the Ghost found his victims in this region; the current murders began in Nashville then moved to this region. I'll be interested in what Julie finds."

Spike made a fierce face as a car pulled up in front of our house. "Kate's here?"

I hurried to the door and unlocked it. After a car door slammed, I took my position to ambush Kate when she opened the door.

When she reached the door, she knocked then shouted, "Truce!"

I opened the door and peered at a blob then frowned. *I thought I'd see Kate.* "That was sneaky."

"Blame Mom; I'm shackled by cookies." She hurried inside and slammed the door. "It's colder here than it is at Mom and Dad's. Hi, Spike. Hello, Palace Guard, wherever you are."

When she flopped onto the sofa, Lucy whined and scrambled to her.

I smiled. "I think Lucy missed you."

Lucy rolled over onto her back for her belly rub then whined a low rumble that sounded like a purr while Kate rubbed her.

"Have you been around Ella and Moe lately?" Kate asked. "Dad said he goes into sugar shock by noon every day. Dad, Paul, and I had a pool betting on when they'd announce their engagement, but Mom found out and said it was disrespectful, so that was the end of that. I'm going to pour myself some sweet tea. You want any?"

"Too cold outside for me."

"I'll make you some hot tea."

After she brought my cup to me, Kate said, "I have the new pommel for you to make your jo fancy. Heather put a little bling on it. She said you'd like that, which I thought was strange. I would have painted it black or gray for you."

"Bling will remind me of Heather; it's perfect."

"Can't argue that. Heather is the best blinging cop I've ever known." Kate laughed at her joke, and I chuckled, so she wouldn't hide my jo from me.

"Heather told me she'd send you an email this evening because there's a little history around that pommel that she thought you'd like. I think it's Heather's version of your reward for busting up the jewelry and embezzlement racket at the senior center."

I smiled in case that was a joke too, but Kate didn't laugh, so it must not have been.

"Sounds like Heather," I said.

When is Kate going to get to the point? Why is she here? Since when is she a nice delivery person? Do I tip her? I am so funny.

I practiced rolling my eye, but Kate didn't say anything, and I sighed.

Kate took my empty cup to the kitchen and asked, "Are you okay? So, what are you doing with yourself?"

"Lucy and I have been walking in the backyard, and Palace Guard and I walk to the campus library. The librarian set me up with some online books. What about you?"

"You know, just work. So, I know I said I'd cook, but what do you think about going out to dinner instead?"

Hate the noise. "We could relax here; I'm sure we could find an interesting restaurant that delivers or has takeout. Larry won't be studying after his classes are over and could pick up our food."

"We'll do that next time. A friend of mine invited us to dinner tonight and made reservations for four."

My mouth felt dry. "Really? Somewhere fancy?"

"Absolutely not. He told me the food was good, and the atmosphere was casual." She giggled.

I tried not to stare at her blob. *Kate giggled? Sounded scary.*

"Your friend, Dean?" I asked. *Good opportunity to meet him.*

"You must be tired because I clearly said Dean. I need to check in at my hotel. I'll text Larry the restaurant address. Our reservation is for six, so I'll see you there."

You clearly said a friend of mine. I'm not tired; you're tired, Kate.

Kate rose and strode to the door. "Bye, Lucy and Palace Guard. See ya, Spike."

She left, and I snorted. "Good-bye, Mother."

Palace Guard shook his head, and the Spike blob jumped around.

I hurried to my computer and turned it on then brought up Heather's email while Palace Guard and Spike leaned close to the screen to read it.

"All I can see is your blob head, Spike," I grumbled. "Not that it matters."

I pressed the listen key. "Call me when Kate leaves."

"That's an interesting history." I called Heather.

"I guess you figured out that Kate doesn't know about the special features of the pommel," she said.

"Kate was weird; I think she's possessed. Tell me about my pommel."

"Are you holding it?"

I grabbed my jo. "Yes."

"The pommel is cherry wood, which is actually a good match for your jo, so that it won't look like an addition. Ask Larry to see what he thinks. On the front of your pommel is a heart outlined by tiny fake emeralds. In the center of the heart is the camera. The emeralds are for your green eye. It was Paul's idea; he is such a romantic." She snort-laughed, and I laughed at her.

"I feel the heart."

"Good. You should have seen Paul's face; he was really grumpy when I told him I'd tell you that."

Now I get why it was so funny. "The pommel's shape is perfect for my hand."

"Good. On the back of the pommel, which would face you, are three inset fake pearls in a line. The top one snaps a picture; the middle one takes a video and includes audio. The bottom one stops the recording. The picture and the video instantly load to a cloud. If there's a connectivity issue, just for your inquiring mind, the pommel saves the data until it can connect."

"Found them; I really like the spacing too; I won't stress over accidentally hitting the wrong one, but they're close enough that's it's not obvious that I'm trying to find a button to push. What about on lower left side? What's that?" I asked.

"It's a pearl. When you carry your pommel in your right hand, it's a reference point for you."

"That's perfect. It leaves my left hand free for my knife."

"That was my idea. That's basically it; do you have any questions? Did I go too fast?"

"This is great. What's the range of the camera?"

"I don't know; you're field-testing it." Heather giggled.

"Don't you think you're having way too much fun with this?" I snickered.

"Probably. The pictures and videos go to my private cloud. Like I said, field testing, so take some pictures at different ranges and videos."

After we hung up, I put on my coat, and we all went to the backyard. I pressed the video button while I aimed my jo at Lucy in the backyard. "I'm sure it was just an oversight on Heather's part, but she forgot to tell me about the GPS tracker on the pommel."

I turned my heart toward me and raised my left hand. "High-five, Palace Guard."

Palace Guard smiled as he smacked my hand, then I waved at the camera before I turned off the video.

"Let's go back inside; I'm freezing."

After we were inside, I said, "I sure wish we had a fireplace or a little gas heater, but I can't say anything to Larry because he'd run out and find a house for me with a fireplace and a gas heater. He definitely loves to fix things."

I dropped down on the sofa and sighed then rested my eye for a few minutes.

I opened my eye and yawned. "I might have dozed off. What time is it?"

Palace Guard held up five fingers.

"I snoozed longer than I thought. Larry will be here soon. Do I have a gray shirt?"

Palace Guard nodded. "Good. I'm going to the informal dinner in disguise."

We went to the bedroom, and Palace Guard pulled out a shirt from my closet and put it on the bed. When he left, he closed the bedroom door. *He's such a gentleman.*

The shirt felt thin and silky.

"Do I have a gray sweater?" I asked as I went into the great room with my jo.

Palace Guard nodded then pointed to my bedroom.

"Oh. You pulled it out for me. I didn't think to check the bed for a sweater. Thanks."

"Feels good." I held up my jo like a microphone. "I need Heather to brush and braid my hair."

I snickered, and Palace Guard grinned.

My phone buzzed. When I picked it up, my phone announced, "Text from Heather: 'Thanks, smarty pants. I won the bet.'"

My phone rang, and Heather was laughing when I answered.

"I was worried for a while because you fell asleep, but I was sure you'd be awake before Larry came home. I bet Paul you'd find the audio buttons before six. I now have Gray Lady bragging rights. What gave them away?"

"It was easy. Nicely placed pearls for me to what? Tell my right hand from my left hand with matching pearls on each side? That didn't make sense because everything you do has a reason. When I pressed on the left pearl, it went in, so I pressed on the right pearl. Left pearl on; right pearl off made sense to me," I said.

"I suspected you found them when you turned it off after you asked for your sweater; I was positive you knew how they worked when you turned it back on and said I needed to braid your hair. Was your sweater on your bed? Never mind; it was."

"How did you know where the sweater was?" I asked. "I didn't have the video on."

"It's what Palace Guard would do. Before you go, this really is a field-test. Turn the audio on as frequently as you can because I'm testing its range."

"Will do, Boss," I said.

Heather snorted. "Not falling for it. Later, Gray Lady. One more thing, I set up a shared cloud for you and me. You'll find it when you check your drives. It's called Gray."

Larry unlocked the front door then quickly closed it. "Hi, honey, I'm home. It got cold out there; I'm glad we're staying in."

He tossed his coat across the room toward the soft chair, but it landed on the floor. "Pretend you didn't see that. What are you all dressed up for?"

"Kate wants us to go to dinner with her and Dean. He made reservations at a restaurant at six. Kate said she'd text you the name and address. Did she send it?"

Larry snorted as he picked up his coat then checked his phone. "Just got it. That's an expensive, popular place, and it would be noisy. Are you sure you want to go?"

"I'm positive it sounds awful, but I hate to let her down."

He said, "I'm not. You don't do well with cold right now; it's bone-chilling outside, and you certainly can't handle an over-crowded, fancy restaurant. Why don't you change into warm clothes? I'm calling Kate."

"I'll change after you call Kate." I moved close to Larry to listen while he called.

When Kate answered, he said, "Kate, going out tonight doesn't work for us. It's turned too cold for Maggie to go out, and she's not quite up to dealing with loud noise yet."

"It's not that noisy, Larry."

"Maybe not for most people, but that's an issue for her right now. We'll plan on something here the next time you're in town. It doesn't make sense for us to go out into the cold because we wouldn't be able to stay through dinner; it's better if we cancel, so you can have a nice dinner this evening."

"I'll bring dinner to you; crack a bottle for me at six thirty." She hung up.

CHAPTER TWELVE

"Now, I'm really worried," I said. "Kate's suddenly all concerned about my well-being? She's coming here because she needs to talk to both of us."

Larry cleared his throat, and I asked, "Could you tell I just rolled my eye at you?"

I raised my chin for my most haughty look. "I'll go change to warmer clothes."

I flipped my hair then strode to the bedroom.

Larry laughed when Palace Guard caught up with me and tapped my arm, so I would go into the bedroom instead of slam into the wall.

After I was in my room, I remembered to turn off the audio. *Need to work on finding the bedroom door for my grand exits and to turn off the audio.*

I changed into the first pair of warm pants and the first long-sleeved T-shirt that I found then pulled out a long-sleeved flannel shirt to wear over my T-shirt. I carefully placed my dressy clothes on the bed or maybe on the floor then hurried to the great room.

"I feel much warmer. Will Kate make fun of my color choices?"

"If she doesn't, we'll know she's desperate for our help. Good strategy, sweetie." Larry chuckled as he kissed me.

"Ha, ha, but that was exactly what I had in mind."

Larry laughed. "Can you tell I just rolled my eyes at you? Do you want hot tea, hot chocolate, or a beer?"

"Hot chocolate sounds good," I said.

"I'll change out of my uniform and make some for both of us."

After he returned to the kitchen, he mixed then heated our hot chocolate.

I asked, "How were your classes today?"

"I got a lot out of them. Ron and I agreed it was helpful to have read everything in advance. I'd never thought of that before when I was taking classes. I'm putting your hot chocolate in your thermal cup, but I'll let it cool a bit before I put on the lid. Wonder what Kate's bringing for our supper. Is she staying here tonight?"

"Wouldn't it be great if she brought tacos? She told me she has a hotel room for tonight, so she won't be staying with us."

"Tacos are for Galveston. You owe me a real honeymoon trip with no killers tagging along."

"I'll ask Jennifer to arrange Galveston if you talk to Kate about the killers," I said.

"You make it sound—"

Larry was interrupted by a knock at the door.

"Truce!" Kate shouted.

"Is that necessary?" Larry asked as he opened the door.

"What do you think?" Kate-blob breezed past him. "Good call on the cold. I thought I had a reservation for tonight, but I don't. I stopped at the camping store and bought a cot and a sleeping bag; you've got company tonight, after all. Here's supper. I'll set my backpack down then grab my cot and sleeping bag."

"Need help?" Larry asked as he handed the large paper sack that smelled suspiciously like burgers to me.

"Wouldn't mind. I also have beer, cheese, dip, and crackers in the car in case we decide to have a party."

"Is this cheeseburgers and fries?" I asked as Kate and Larry came back into the apartment.

"Cheeseburgers, fries, and hot peach cobbler." Kate dropped her sleeping bag near the front door, and Larry carried in the folded cot.

"I'll turn the oven on low to keep the cobbler warm," she said. "I'm hoping y'all haven't forgotten the importance of ice cream when it's cold."

"Of course not. Cold ice cream makes your body warm up, so it can melt the ice cream."

"Do I open beer to go with our burgers?" Larry asked while Kate and I sat at the table.

"Perfect," I said.

"Set that roll of paper towels on the table," Kate said. "I heard these are the juiciest burgers in Tennessee."

Larry cut my burger into half for me, and I took a bite. "They are juicy, aren't they? I'll take a paper towel for my chin."

We clinked our beer bottles then chowed down in silence.

After I ate half my burger and more fries than I really needed, I said, "Really good choice, Kate."

Kate mumbled, "Thanks."

After Larry and Kate finished eating their burgers and finished off the fries, he asked, "Everybody leave room for peach cobbler?"

Kate cleared the table while Larry dished up the cobbler and vanilla ice cream. When he put my bowl in front of me, I dipped my spoon into the soupy ice cream and the sweet crust of cobbler with the embedded peach slices.

"This was a really good find, Kate."

"Mom used to send Ryan and me back with soups, casseroles and desserts when we were students at the training center, which seems like eons ago. Peach cobbler was Ryan's favorite dessert."

Kate sniffed back a sob then brushed away her tears with her sleeve, but I pretended not to notice. "I still miss my wonderful husband; he was a true hero and my best friend."

Kate spooned ice cream over her cobbler then poked at her cobbler with her spoon. "Is Ms. Lily still at the library? She was a remarkable source for information. Ryan and I thought we were hot stuff, but her information recall put us to shame."

"She's still here. She set me up with audio books from the library the first time I walked in."

"I'll bet she knew the Gray Lady, didn't she?" Kate asked.

"I was surprised at first, but she told me she knew Olivia. I'd like to hear what Olivia was like when she was younger."

"I'm sure Ms. Lily would love to talk with you about Olivia. She was always willing to spend extra time with people. She always claimed she was a reader, not a writer, but she was definitely a talented storyteller."

"I'll be sure to ask her, so what happened with Dean and the restaurant, and what did you want to talk to us about?"

Larry snorted, and Kate exhaled in disgust. "Fine. Enough social talk; you actually did quite well."

"I'll clear the table and do the dishes." Larry rose and picked up my bowl.

"Don't run off and leave me alone with this crack interrogator, crime man," Kate said.

I think I actually rolled my eye. I glanced at Larry, and he smiled and nodded.

Palace Guard guided me to the sofa.

"Slick." Kate-blob sat across from me. "How do you do it? Palace Guard guides you, doesn't he?"

"He has a remote control."

"Aghh. Sorry I asked."

"Waiting."

"Care for another beer?" Kate asked.

I worked on a Jennifer glare, but it must have been more of a Spike wacky face because Larry coughed.

"The reason Dean is off limits is because I already have someone investigating him, and I didn't want you to mess it up," she said.

"All you had to do was tell me you had it covered. What exactly are you investigating? Is he a suspect in the Ghost of Wicked Hollow murders?"

"What? No, not murders at all; what do you mean a ghost?"

"If you aren't investigating a murder, then it's spy stuff, isn't it?"

Kate sighed. "It's very mundane. Someone is selling our secrets to a foreign party, and I have someone who is working to rule out Dean. That's all. Can we talk about something else? Tell me about that ghost."

I told her the current tale of the Ghost of Wicked Hollow.

"That's really interesting. Sounds more like a serial killer hiding behind a legend to me," Kate said.

"That's what I thought too."

"No proof other than we're smarter than the entire world, right? Let's kick it around. What do you have?" she asked.

I told her about the creepy vibes from Wayne Dillard and the rumors about Dean Sanchez and the coincidence that each of them was in Nashville and near the training center during the time that murders happened at the two different locations.

"Mostly hearsay and at best, flimsy circumstantial evidence. Makes a good story for one of them to be the killer, but lousy corroboration of any wrongdoing."

"That's exactly what I think," I said.

"For all we know, Dean was assigned to find the murderer," Kate said.

"Right, and Wayne is just a jerk."

Kate snorted. "Much more plausible than the killer theories."

Larry chuckled. "Ready for a beer?"

I yawned. "I don't think I could stay awake long enough to drink a beer."

"I have to get up extra early too, so I can be on the road before daybreak," Kate said. "Mind if I take a shower?"

"Go right ahead, but first, tell me about the reservation."

Kate sighed. "Dean called and said something came up, and he had to cancel dinner. Right after that, Larry called, so I canceled the hotel and ordered takeout. Now?"

"Certainly. Don't blame me, though. The shower gel is from your mom and Ella."

"Oh, man," Kate moaned as she headed to the bathroom with her backpack.

Larry joined me on the sofa and put his arm around me. "So, what do you think?" he whispered.

"I think Kate is an accomplished liar because I can't quite sort out what's true and what's a lie."

"So, what do we do?"

"Not much. Normally, I'd say to keep listening because liars always trip themselves up, but Kate won't give herself away unless she wants to."

"I agree with you. Like you said, accomplished."

I snuggled against him. "I'm really glad you canceled going to that fancy restaurant. You're my hero; thank you."

He hugged me. "It's my job to make you happy, sweetie."

When Kate came out of the bathroom, I inhaled deeply and giggled.

"Don't even say it, Camo Girl," she growled.

"I don't get it," Larry whispered, and I nodded.

"How are your classes going?" Kate asked.

While Larry talked about his classes, and Kate gave him advice, I closed my eyes until Larry whispered, "It's late, sweetie. Let's go to bed. Kate's changing in the bathroom."

* * *

The next morning, I woke while Larry dressed in the dark for class. When I sat up, he said, "Go back to sleep, sweetie. It's early. I'll set up the coffee for you and Kate, so you can have coffee earlier.

"I'm awake. I'll be ready for coffee as soon as I get dressed. Kate's up; I hear her."

"I don't hear anything. Your hearing really is keen, isn't it?"

I grabbed layers of warm clothes for the day and dressed then hurried with my jo to the kitchen. Palace Guard guided me around the cot, or I would have run right into it.

"Coffee's almost ready," Larry said.

"I'm cooking breakfast, diner style," Kate said. "What's your order?"

"One egg medium, sausage, and a cinnamon roll."

"Gotcha," she said.

"Don't you have to leave pretty soon?" I asked.

"Show her, Palace Guard," Kate said.

"We'll show you, sweetie," Larry said. "Let's go to the backyard."

When we went outside, he asked, "What do you see?"

I shivered then blinked my eye to focus. "Nothing; I can't even see the neighbor's bright security light. It's really cold too. What's going on?"

As we hurried back inside, Larry said, "This is the heaviest fog I've ever seen; interstate is closed to traffic except for emergency vehicles."

"I got a call early this morning; I have the day off," Kate said.

"Which my stomach appreciates," Larry said, and I giggled.

"You're going to hang out here today, aren't you?" I asked.

"Yep. You can put me to work cleaning or cooking or both, as long as you keep me company."

"That's awesome, Kate," I said.

"Does this mean I'm fired from my job as the housekeeper and chef?" Larry asked. "Not that I mind."

I giggled. "You're on sabbatical."

While Kate prepared Larry's breakfast, she said, "You have a sandwich and a container of homemade chicken noodle soup in the fridge for your lunch. The soup is courtesy of Mom. We had a microwave in our breakroom when I was here; it might be the same ancient one we had."

"Thanks, Kate," Larry said.

After he kissed me and rushed out the door, Kate cooked our eggs and sausage.

She refilled my cup then joined me at the table.

"He took both containers of soup, so he could share with a friend. Things haven't changed. Someone was always bringing something homemade to share at lunch when I was here. It was a nice break from the standard school food."

She sighed. "I expected fog this morning, but nothing like this. When I woke up, I thought we had a power outage until I realized I had just checked the digital clock on the stove to see what time it was."

Kate cleared our dishes and refilled our coffee. "Tell me more about this Wayne Dillard."

After I told her about Wayne, the coincidences, and the strange sense of alarm that Mary Leigh, Palace Guard, and I had independently of each other, she said, "You've got nothing except radar alerts from a blind, crazy lady, a quirky pregnant woman, and an imaginary man."

"Exactly," I said.

"So, what's next?"

"Paul's looking deeper into Dillard's employment and the Nashville murders for me."

"Looking for a tie in?" Kate asked.

"Not really. Right now, we're just gathering facts. We could miss something if we start trying to force a correlation. If the killer's not Dillard, I don't want to have to loop back around to the Nashville murders."

"I'm glad you see that. What can I do?"

"Paul will be gathering information from public records and gossipy neighbors. Could there have been an earlier investigation into a possible serial killer?"

"That's an idea. I'll check into it then point Paul to the right people if I find anything."

"I have something else. I'd really like to talk to Ms. Betty at the library in town today. If the fog lifts enough to drive on the town streets, could we go?"

"The forecast is for heavy fog through tomorrow, but we'll see how it looks around lunchtime. We should call before we leave; the library might be closed because of the fog."

While Kate was busy on her laptop, I listened to one of my books.

When I found my mind wandering, I turned off my computer and put on my heavy coat.

"Ready to go outside for a break, Lucy?"

Lucy, Spike, and I went out back while Palace Guard stayed inside with Kate.

Lucy and Spike disappeared into the foggy backyard, but I could hear Lucy as she sniffed the ground. I stamped my feet to warm my toes but quit because I was afraid my brittle toes would break in my boots.

"Are we ready to go inside yet?"

Lucy and Spike appeared through the fog then hurried past me.

When Lucy scratched at the back door, I grumbled as I made my way to the stoop and opened the door, "You walked right past me, you know."

I reached for the door and almost fell inside as Kate opened it. "Was Camo Lady too slow for you, Lucy?"

"Guess I was; she was definitely anxious to come inside." I shivered. "It's brutal out there."

"Must be; I'm getting cold just standing next to you. I'll make us hot tea." Kate rummaged through the cupboards. "You have only plain, regular tea. We need to get you some fancy teas."

After I sat at the table with my cup, I asked, "Have you been researching Wayne Dillard?"

"Sure have. I'll probably have a couple of things to send to Paul by this afternoon."

Palace Guard stood next to Kate-blob and shook his head.

Kate didn't know Palace Guard stayed inside because she can't see him.
She's lying, so what was she doing?

My phone rang. "It's my friend, Mary Leigh. I'll call her back."

"No, go ahead and talk to her. I can tune you out while I work," Kate said.

"You've done it often enough," I mumbled as I answered.

"How are you doing? I've been worried about your friend, Kate. Did she leave this morning? Everybody knows Kate Coyle was visiting you because she's a legend here, but in a good way; not like the Ghost of Wicked Hollow." Mary Leigh giggled.

I snickered. "She's still here because of the travel restrictions."

"I called to share the latest from the moms' group, but since Kate's still there, I'll talk to you later."

"She's working on her computer. I'm extremely busy trying not to interrupt her and hiding from the cold, so what's the latest?"

"You are so funny, Gray Lady. The news isn't good; another woman disappeared, but this time it's someone from town."

"Has Sally's friend been found?" I asked.

"Everyone's afraid to ask, but I don't think so. Want to hear the big news?"

"It depends; is it good or bad news?"

"I think it's totally bizarre, so I don't know if it's bad news or good news. Three of the moms are fangirling over the new maintenance guy. According to them, he's a famous movie star who is undercover here to get a feel for what it's like to live in a small town in Tennessee. They told me the movie star's name, but I never heard of him, so I didn't bother to remember. Anyway, they planned to send a daily report to the group by email with the subject line, *Operation Hottie*."

"Don't they know stalking is against the law?"

"Exactly. They're all wives of cops; they should have known that. When I asked, one of the moms said her dad is a defense lawyer and will get them all off with a plea of insanity. The other two women decided to bail."

"Have you seen the new maintenance man?"

"Only briefly; at the time, I didn't know what an item of discussion he would become. I thought he was very distinguished looking in a rough sort of way. His face is weathered, and he has streaks of gray hair. He moves like a cat: really lithe for an older man. I noticed when a couple of students walked past him, he appeared much older and almost arthritic, but I guess actors have to be good at diving into their role."

"I might have super hearing, but you certainly have a powerful talent for observation," I said.

Mary Leigh giggled. "Thanks. Ron once told me I had the observational gift of a nosy neighbor but claimed it was a compliment after I got mad; he washed, dried, and folded the laundry for two days after that. He's not what you call a quick learner.

Mom gave me a slow cooker and a Mediterranean chicken and vegetables recipe. Ron will be surprised; it sounds fancy, and Mom said it smells amazing while it's cooking, but it's real simple. I'll dump everything into the cooker then take my nap."

"Let me know how it turns out. I'd like to surprise Larry sometime as soon as I can see more than blobs. I've been wondering, did you ever ask Sally about her blog?"

Mary Leigh tittered. "She's on my radar. I was meeting with one of her friends this morning, but we had to postpone. I may not know Sally, but I definitely understand her personality; she'll accidentally pop in because she's so nosey. I plan to wear my bacon shirt since it's her favorite."

I laughed. "Good choice. That reminds me: I read your blog, and speaking of fangirling, you are hilarious. I'm following you, so I'll be notified when you post."

"Doesn't count; you're nice too."

"Ha! I've been called a lot of names, but I've never been accused of being nice."

Mary Leigh snorted. "Only because everybody else is afraid to tell you."

I giggled. "There's something missing in your logic, but I can't quite put my finger on it."

After I hung up, Kate said, "I need to make a few phone calls. I may be a while, so I'm going to the campus office breakroom, so you won't have to tiptoe around me." She picked up her computer on her way out the door.

I shivered from the blast of cold air.

"Did you hear Mary Leigh while we talked? Kate's right. All we have is gossip, except we do know someone has been following me."

Palace Guard held up two fingers.

I nodded. "The double blob was actually two, and I've been asking you who was following me when I should have been asking better questions."

Palace Guard raised his eyebrows.

"Okay, I should have thought of that sooner; I blame the eye surgeon. Let's start with the first guy. Do we know him?"

Palace Guard shook his head.

"Dang, that rules out Dillard."

Palace Guard raised one finger.

"I stand corrected, it rules out Dillard for the first guy. Was the second guy following me or the first guy? Do we know the second guy?"

Palace Guard held up one finger on one hand and two fingers on the other hand then moved the two fingers to the one finger and nodded.

"The second guy was following the first, at least when I saw two blobs, and we know the second guy. Was it Dillard?"

Palace Guard shook his head and pointed at me.

"Right, it's that guy: the one that you point at me, and I'm going around in circles."

Palace Guard grinned.

I made my way to the sofa to sit. "Kate told me to call Della after I was settled. That's not right now because I feel really unsettled, and my feet are cold." I put up my feet and threw the afghan over them.

"Camo Lady, you ready for lunch?"

I yawned. "I didn't realize I'd dozed off."

"You were beyond dozing," Kate said. "You never used to snore; are you getting soft?"

I growled as I sat up, "You're lucky we're under a truce. I don't snore."

Kate cackled. "Come to the table. I made soft tacos for our lunch."

"You made tacos?" I hurried to the table.

"I found all the fixings. The tortillas are a little rustic; it's been a while since I made homemade tortillas."

I picked up my taco and took a bite. "Mmm. Rustic, sturdy tacos are my new favorite."

"Sturdy is a good word too," Kate mumbled with a full mouth.

Before she took another bite, she said, "I made an enchilada casserole for tonight; it's in the refrigerator. The highways opened for traffic, so I'm leaving after we eat lunch. Is it okay if I leave my cot? I'll break it down, then you can tell me where you want it; several possibilities come to mind: under the bed or in a corner of your closet. I like the idea of having my sleeping bag along, so I'll roll it up and store it in my trunk."

I nodded. "Will you be sending Paul what you found on Dillard before you leave?"

"What?" She took a big gulp of sweet tea. "Oh, Dillard; I'll get it to him sometime tonight or tomorrow. Are you going to eat all your taco, or do you want me to wrap it up for you?"

"I'll finish it."

She rose from the table and whisked away my plate. "I'll give you a paper towel for your taco. Finish your lunch, and I'll do the dishes then fold up the cot. Where do you want it?"

"In a corner near the dining table is fine. Larry and I can decide when he gets home."

Palace Guard and Spike stared at Kate.

"What are you looking at, Spike? I've already missed almost a full day's work as it is." Kate turned to load the dishwasher.

After she wiped down the stove and the kitchen counter, Kate rubbed Lucy's face then grabbed her backpack and sleeping bag and waved as she left.

I powered up my computer and checked highway travel in Tennessee and listened.

"Well, according to the local news, highway travel is still restricted to emergency vehicles and the state police. I guess if anyone stops Kate, she can pull out her FBI badge. I suppose it must not be as bad as it was early this morning."

Spike frowned.

"I don't believe me either, and I certainly don't understand Kate."

My phone rang, and I shivered with excitement. *Finally, Paul.*

"I've got a little on Dillard," he said. "For starters, you were right about him. He had a juvenile record, and while I couldn't get any details, Julie came through and found some folks in his old neighborhood who remembered him. He was first sent to juvie for attempted kidnapping when he was in high school. He stalked a classmate who wasn't interested in him. After he punched her, he pushed her into his car. He ran into a fence, and the girl jumped out. There were different versions of why he lost control and ran into the fence, but the basic story was the same."

I sighed. "It doesn't give us much to go on, though, does it. Is there anything traceable?"

"For what it's worth, Julie said the most plausible explanation of the events that she heard was that the girl's best friend jumped into her boyfriend's car, and they followed Dillard. The boyfriend flashed his car lights and honked the horn then must have rattled Dillard because Dillard lost control of his car and ran into a fence. The best friend helped the girl out of the car while the boyfriend dragged out Dillard from the driver's seat then beat the living daylights out of him. What is traceable is that I found that Mr. Dillard's lawyer filed a complaint against the boyfriend and a civil suit against the boyfriend's parents, and the girl's parents pressured the police to drop the charges against Dillard."

"I agree with Julie; it seems likely to me too; it's encouraging that you found that civil suit to back it up," I said.

CHAPTER THIRTEEN

"I discovered that Dillard was convicted of a felony in Kentucky when he was nineteen. For some reason, he didn't spend any time in prison, as far as I can tell. My guess is that his influential father pulled strings, but he's still a convicted felon and wouldn't have a legal carry permit; however, if his father always smoothed things over for him, he may consider himself above mere technicalities," Paul said.

"Did you or Julie find any connection between him and the Nashville murders?"

"He was a person of interest in one of the early cases. When I dug deeper, I found that Dillard had worked with the woman who told a friend that he had been bothering her two weeks before she disappeared, but after a railway inspector found the body of a vagrant near the tracks in a rail yard, the case was closed. It was strange because I couldn't find any connection between the homeless man and the victim. A cousin of the deceased woman's mother told Julie that the media, family, local politicians, and influential businessmen applied a great deal of pressure on the police to solve the case. When Julie asked if Mr. Dillard was one of the businessmen, the cousin told her he was one of the most insistent."

"While Mr. Dillard meddled, are you thinking he also kept his thumb on Wayne?"

"It's a real possibility and could explain why there were no unexplained disappearances for two years after that, then the year before Mr. Dillard died, two women disappeared. A farmer found the body of the first woman in a ditch near an unpaved country road three days after she disappeared; six months later, a guy who was fishing found the second body hung up in the rocks of a small river a week after the woman's disappearance. The Nashville murders continued the two-year pattern until eighteen years ago when the murders stopped. An episode of an unexplained mysteries TV show highlighted the murders a few years later and sensationalized the Ghost of Wicked Hollow."

"That must be how the Ghost of Wicked Hollow became so widely accepted in the region," I said.

"That's what Julie said," Paul chuckled. "She wants to leave Nashville and go to Knoxville. She has friends there and will be close enough to talk to people but not close enough to draw Wayne Dillard's attention. I told her I hated the idea, and she told me it's what the Gray Lady would do. You're a bad influence, Maggie Ewing."

I snickered. "What about the causes of death for Mr. and Mrs. Dillard?"

"I didn't get anywhere, but Julie found an old high school friend of Mrs. Dillard who is a retired nurse. Julie expects to hear something from her in the next few days."

"I'm in awe of Julie; she finds the most interesting people."

"She told me she's the Best Friend Lady because everybody says she reminds them of their best friend as they tell her all kinds of things."

"What about Dean Sanchez?" I asked.

"All I've found so far is that he was in Nashville on brief assignments to advise on some of their more difficult crime scene investigations. None of the murders that we're interested in seem to have difficult crime scenes, but he was in Nashville around the time of all the disappearances. That's as far as I've gotten. Glenn said he may have found a few things. We're getting together tomorrow for lunch, so we can compare notes. We can't talk in the office, for obvious reasons. One of us will call you after lunch if he has anything."

"I haven't made much progress, and I'm really annoyed because I feel stuck. I'd planned to go to the main library today, but Kate left. I feel like a plane that's been grounded by fog: all gassed up and on the runway but can't get the green light. If the fog lifts a little, I'll go to the campus library and lurk while I rub elbows with the assassins."

Paul chuckled. "Excellent plan; I always knew the prospect of lurking with assassins would cheer you up. Almost forgot that I've got one more very juicy item for you. A photographer filed a DCMA takedown notice with your blogger's service provider. The DCMA was a law passed in 1998 to provide a "safe harbor" for a service provider for hosting content that contains a copyright infringement. Because the service provider immediately took down the blog site, they could not be sued, which is their safe harbor. Your blogger did not take the pictures or write the descriptions; she violated the copyrights by passing them off as her own work."

"Were all of the pictures and text plagiarized?"

"Probably, but the service provider doesn't care because if they get into the vetting business, they've lost their safe harbor defense. The penalties for violation are very severe and the damage to their reputation is irreparable."

"What a stinker," I said.

"Thought you'd be interested."

After we hung up, my phone rang almost immediately.

"Hello, Gray Lady. This is Lily at the campus library, and your portfolio of photos that we ordered for you is here. You can pick it up anytime."

"That's great news. I'll be there in just a few minutes."

"You don't have to come right away; tomorrow's fine. It's cold, and the fog is still heavy. Oh my, I just realized the fog doesn't matter to you, does it?"

I smiled. "The cold matters to me, but you're right: the fog doesn't bother me."

I put on my sweatshirt, my new warm coat, and gloves then grabbed my jo.

"Ready, Palace Guard?"

Palace Guard frowned then pointed to my hands.

I sighed. "Your point is well-taken: I haven't practiced with gloves. Brr. I hate this, but you're right."

I pulled off my gloves and dropped them on the table then made a fist with my left hand and tugged my sleeve cuff over my fist.

"I can reach my knife, but I won't be able to reach my pistol with my coat on."

Palace Guard pointed to the oversized pockets on the sides. I unzipped my coat and removed my waistband holster then slipped it and my pistol into my pocket.

"This is perfect. There's even a small strip of elastic that will hold my holster inside the pocket. I'll bet it's there to keep tools from slipping out. I love this coat. Now can I go?"

Palace Guard motioned the elaborate *After You* wave that Spike did while I was struggling with physical therapy, and I laughed as we hurried toward the library.

The campus sounded eerily hollow and dead without the noise from the highway and the conversations of passersby, and the cold felt even more intensely frigid with the missing signs of humanity.

When I opened the library door, the warmth and the hum of activity was a stark contrast to the bleak outdoors.

Lily-blob met me before I reached her desk. "I always forget how small our campus is. Nice to see you. I have the portfolio for you right here. I put it in a large manilla envelope to protect it from the dampness. Are you going to stay a while?"

I smiled. "I'll go straight home. I don't think I could deal with warming up then going back out in that cold again."

She walked with me to the door. "Call me if you have any questions about any of the photos, and let me know if there is anything else I can order for you."

"Thank you so much. I'll definitely call if I have any questions."

When Palace Guard and I stepped outside, the icy air took away my breath.

After we were inside the apartment, I leaned against the door. "That was not my brightest idea. I was going to call Mary Leigh to see if she wanted to get together, but neither one of us has any business going out in this weather."

I hung up my coat. "I'd like some hot tea. Could you help me?"

Palace Guard's eyes narrowed, and he wrinkled his nose and shuddered.

I sighed. *I should have known American tea would be an anathema.*

"What about warming up some of the hot chocolate that Larry made?"

Palace Guard pointed to the refrigerator then shook his head.

I sighed. "We don't have any."

Palace Guard nodded.

My phone buzzed. "A text from Della. 'See you tomorrow, sweet girl. Stay safe.'"

I filled a cup with warm water from the kitchen faucet, stirred in a little honey, and dropped in a tea bag before I and carried my cup to the table. When Palace Guard stared at me, I said, "I'm pretending it's a cup of very hot tea."

Spike did his wacky dance, and I laughed and did my version of his wacky dance while I held onto my jo for balance; Palace Guard laughed and applauded when we finished, and Spike and I bowed.

My phone rang, and when I answered, Mary Leigh asked, "Are you as bored as I am? I started to walk over to your apartment, but I made a terrible mistake and opened the door to see if it was really cold. Take my word for it; it's cold out there."

"I believe you. I don't even want to know what the temperature is."

"My friend has bailed on me; she claimed she's afraid Sally might feel left out if she had coffee with me, so now I have another idea. She told me that you're a celebrity, and she knows this because Sally's husband told her that you were. I have Sally's cell number. If you text her to join you tomorrow for coffee in the office break room at nine o'clock and sign it *Gray Lady*, she'll jump at the offer because that would definitely up her stock with her little posse, and before you ask, of course, I'll be right there with you, and I promise I'll wear my bacon shirt."

"That's a terrible idea from my point of view. Text me her cell number, and I'll call you right back."

After I received the text, I repeated the number then said, "Send a text: Care to meet in the break room tomorrow at nine for coffee? Gray Lady."

I called Mary Leigh back. "I have some photos for you to look at. Maybe we can do that after Sally leaves."

"It might be simpler if we left first and went to your apartment or mine. You can claim a telecare health call or needing your nap or something. Did you hear about the student's wife who supposedly disappeared? It was a false alarm. Her mother and father picked her up, so she could attend a cousin's wedding. Her husband knew where she was, but nobody bothered to ask him; they just jumped to the conclusion that she wasn't around; therefore, she was missing. I think there are quite a few people who were very disappointed that she's okay. People are strange sometimes, don't you think?"

"It must be human nature to want to walk close to the edge of the wild side without actually being in any personal danger."

"Speaking of the wild side, would it be okay with you if Ron drives me to your apartment after supper while they study?"

"I think that's a great idea. I've got a couple of things I wish I could see that you could use your super observation powers and tell me what is there."

"Good idea. I didn't even consider there might be something I could do to help you, but it's a perfect addition for my argument of why he should drive me; see you later."

After I hung up, my phone buzzed a text. "Text from Sally: 'Nine on Saturday is better.'"

While I replied, Lucy plodded to the back door and stood with her nose at the edge of the door. "Okay, girl; we'll go outside."

I put on my new coat over my sweatshirt and grabbed my jo. When I opened the door for Lucy, Spike hung back. "Come on, Spike, we're all going to be cold together."

He shook his head. After we were outside, I asked, "Do you think it's going to snow?"

Palace Guard shook his head.

"That's too bad, except if it snowed, I'd want my cup of hot chocolate by the fireplace."

I peered beyond our back fence. "Is the fog lifting? I think I see the building behind us."

When I turned to see what Palace Guard thought, my eye widened at Spike, who wore snow boots, heavy mittens, and a one-piece snowsuit as he waddled to join Lucy. I bit my lip to keep from laughing. *I'm probably just jealous because I'd be out here in a snowsuit too, if I had one.*

"I have to go back inside. I should have looked for a wool scarf when I bought my warm coat because my face is freezing."

Palace Guard, Lucy, and Spike followed me inside, but before I took off my coat and gloves, my phone buzzed then announced, "Text from Lily: 'I have another book for you. We close at five today.'"

Lucy and Spike, minus his snow boots and snowsuit, hurried to the sofa.

I chuckled. "You don't have to go; I won't be gone long." I left my gloves on the table, and Palace Guard and I braved the fog.

As I hurried to cross the street to the library, I frowned at the sound of a speeding car that seemed to be heading our way.

"The fog magnifies sound—"

Palace Guard rapidly tapped my right arm, and I instinctively dove for the curb alongside him as I pulled my pistol then fired at the speeding car. The sound of three gunshots: two plus mine, reverberated through the fog and through my head.

One of the shots was simultaneous with mine; almost sounded like one.

The car sped away, and a familiar voice said, "Maggie, are you okay?"

My ears were ringing. *I must be hearing things.*

I opened my eye and stared at the man, not a blob, who knelt next to me. *What's my so-called father, Gary Sloan, doing here?*

"Did you shoot at me, Gary? Did I hit the driver?"

Palace Guard helped me sit up, then I slipped my pistol back into its holster.

Gary said, "I always see a shadow around you. No, I didn't shoot at you, but you probably hit the driver. I was at the corner of the library; I never saw him, but I shot at the car when I heard the shot; maybe I hit the back window. Pretty lame, but my attention was on finding you."

"My ears are ringing." I rose with the assistance of Palace Guard and the jo as I heard footsteps running toward me. *I'm in trouble. Here comes Larry.*

Larry grabbed me. "Your chin is scraped and bleeding, sweetheart. Are you okay? What happened? Why are you out here? What are you doing here, Gary?"

"I'm maintenance, but I broke my cover. I wasn't here." Gary disappeared into the fog as more footsteps ran toward us.

"Fine," I growled as I shivered from the cold. "Leave me with the dirty work."

"We heard the two shots the same time you did, Kevin, but you outran us all. Is Maggie okay?" Ron asked.

"I'll take her home, then I'll be back," Larry said.

When Larry, Palace Guard, and I reached our apartment, Larry said, "Tell me what happened."

After he helped me to the sofa, I told him about Lily's text, the speeding car, the shooter, Palace Guard's signal to dive and shoot, and Gary.

"I heard only two shots, and so did Ron," Larry said.

"My ears are still ringing from the sound of the gunshots." I yawned to clear my ears, but the ringing didn't go away. "I think Gary and I might have shot at exactly the same time. He said I probably hit the driver, but he could have hit the back window. Did you know Gary was here?" I tried to ignore the ringing, so I could hear him.

"I kind of asked Kate if the new maintenance guy worked for her, and she told me to mind my own business. I wasn't positive it was Gary Sloan until then, though. How were you able to pull out your gun?"

"You're really good at changing the subject." I showed him my pocket with the elastic to hold tools in place.

"That's slick: a real work jacket; now I want one like that. I have to go answer questions, but first I'll grab one of my old jackets. It's cold out there. I'll be back as soon as I can and brew some hot tea for you. Can I see your phone?"

"It's in the top left chest pocket of my coat."

Larry strode to the bedroom then returned with one of his jackets. After he read my phone, he exhaled and put it on the table next to me then left.

"I'm too wired to just sit here." I made my way to the dining table and sat in front of my computer. I scanned through the list of documents I had saved.

"Did I even read the documents Kate gave me about Dean's wife?"

Palace Guard nodded.

"You're right, but I must have breezed through them; I'm sure Kate gave them to me as busy work, but we know a lot more now than we did then."

After I listened to all the public real estate, census, and tax records, I listened to Kate's notes while Palace Guard read over my shoulder. "There's nothing about where Dean Sanchez was when his wife was murdered, and there's a significant gap in Kate's notes that detail the timeline of the shooting." I leaned back in my chair. "I feel like I know less, not more. I'm going to send these to Paul. Maybe he or Glenn can make sense out of them."

I added the documents as attachments to an email to Paul then sent them with an explanation: "Public records plus Kate's notes about the shooting of Dean Sanchez's wife. Appears to be gaps in the chronology of the shooting."

"What other loose ends do I have?" I asked.

Palace Guard pointed at me.

"Oh my gosh, Gary. That's who has been following some guy who has been following me. Is that it?"

Palace Guard rolled his eyes and nodded.

"Too bad Mary Leigh discouraged the group of moms from stalking him. I would have enjoyed that, if I'd only known." I snickered. "Moms stalking an undercover spy."

Palace Guard grinned.

"That kind of made my day, except this ringing in my ears is annoying. I need hot tea or better yet, a taco and a beer for my ears."

I paced until Spike and Lucy blocked my way.

"Fine, I'll sit." I sat on the sofa and listened to my ringing.

Larry came into the apartment with two blobs then sat next to me and put his arm around me. "Sweetie, the investigators have some questions for you."

Blob One asked, "Forgive me, Mrs. Ewing, but are you blind?"

Larry patted my hand. *He wants to answer.*

"My wife lost one eye then had surgery recently on her remaining eye. She currently has limited sight, but the eye surgeon assures us her sight will improve."

I like this Larry guy.

Blob One continued, "Witnesses heard two shots. We found a bullet wedged in a telephone pole about four feet from the ground."

I gasped, and Larry tightened his grip.

"My wife was on the ground next to the telephone pole when I reached her." Larry's voice was cold and hard.

Blob Two asked, "Mrs. Ewing, you're the Gray Lady, aren't you? Do you think your shot hit the driver?"

"Yes."

Blob One said, "That's the—"

Blob Two interrupted him. "We'll talk later. Can you tell me what happened?"

"I got a text from the librarian saying she had a book for me, so I hurried to the library to pick up the book."

"In the fog," Blob One said.

"The fog wouldn't matter with her limited sight," Larry said. "She's become quite proficient getting around with her cane, especially anywhere that is close to our apartment and she has visited previously like the library."

I nodded. "My hearing has become very sensitive, and I heard a speeding car as it headed toward me. When it came close and didn't seem to be slowing down, I dove for the sidewalk to get out of the street. The driver shot at me, and I returned his fire."

"The Gray Lady's reflexes and gun skills are well-known," Blob Two said. "Have you been to our gun range, Mrs. Ewing?"

"She's been training on a range with Kate Coyle, and we think her hearing will be less sensitive as her eyesight improves; but for now, the sound of gunshots is very painful for her even with hearing protection," Larry said. "She still has ringing in her ears from the two shots in front of the library."

"I'd like to take my wife to the range, but she's shy about shooting when she thinks others might be judging her," Blob Two said.

I nodded. "I understand; that was how I felt every time I went to the range until I started cleaning the rental guns."

"You cleaned rental guns? She cleans my guns all the time; she enjoys it and does a much better job than I do. Thanks, I'll tell her."

"Do you have any idea why someone tried to run you down then shot at you?" Blob One asked.

"None at all; I'm essentially on the injury list while I recuperate."

Larry accompanied Blob One and Blob Two to the door, then after they left, he said, "I'll put Kate's casserole in the oven then go pick up my things that I left in the classroom. I'm not studying tonight after supper."

"Don't be silly. Mary Leigh and I had planned for her to come here because both of us are going stir crazy. Palace Guard and Spike will be on duty."

"Casserole is in the oven. I'll talk to Ron." Larry hugged me. "When I heard the first gunshot, I was out the door because I knew somebody had shot at you." He kissed me. "When I heard the second shot, I knew you were okay, but I didn't slow down because I had to see for myself."

I returned his kiss then brushed his cheek lightly with my fingertips. "You are awesome."

He stopped at the door. "What did you name the two police officers? They didn't introduce themselves because they're used to people reading their name tags."

"Blob One and Blob Two."

Larry laughed. "I knew it." He and Palace Guard high-fived then he left.

"What was that all about?" I asked, and Palace Guard grinned then shrugged.

"This is exactly why Mary Leigh needs to come over here tonight," I grumbled. "I need to talk to someone I can understand."

I set the table with forks and plates then sat at my computer and sighed. *I'm getting used to listening to my computer, but I miss reading as fast or slowly as I like.*

When Larry returned, he pulled out the casserole from the oven, then while he dished up our food onto our plates, he said, "I talked to Ron. He told me he needs to study tonight, so he put his foot down and told Mary Leigh she absolutely was not allowed to leave their apartment."

"That was brave. What else?"

Larry chuckled. "Mary Leigh will be here after he loads their dishwasher. He told me he's certain that one of these days she'll take pity on him, so he keeps trying."

I giggled. "They do have a very unique relationship, and it definitely works for them."

"Not normal like us at all," he said.

"Yes, dear."

He spewed his sweet tea, and I snort-laughed.

He wiped his chin with his napkin. "Dang, sweetie. I have to remember you always have a follow-up zinger. That was hilarious and perfectly timed."

"Flattery will get you everywhere." I blinked my right eye to flutter my eyelashes, and he snickered.

"That bad?" I asked.

"Not saying. I'm busy eating."

After we finished eating, I cleared the table, and Larry put away the casserole and started the dishwasher then kissed me. "I'll see you later; have a great evening."

Not long after Larry left, a car pulled up in front of our apartment. Spike looked out the front window then pushed out his stomach.

I shook my head. "Thanks for letting me know Mary Leigh is here. Great impression, but you're lucky that she can't see you."

Palace Guard nodded, and Spike put his hands around his own neck then fell to the floor.

I was still giggling when I opened the front door, and Mary Leigh-blob rushed inside. "Mr. Bossy Hubs told me I couldn't get out of the car until you opened the door because you might think I was a killer. I told him you wouldn't open the door until you knew it was me, not the killer. We agreed to continue the conversation tomorrow, so he could go study. What's funny?"

"I was imagining you and Ron were having that exact discussion."

"Fine, you can tell me later. Shall I make us some tea? I brought scones and some fancy teas that my mom gave me. Mom made the scones then froze them. They'll be like fresh after I warm them a bit. You can pick a tea, and I'll brew the same tea for both of us."

"A real tea party; that sounds like fun. I heard back from Sally; we're rescheduled to Saturday at nine."

While she warmed the scones in the oven and steeped our tea, Mary Leigh said, "I'm certain your shooter will be identified very quickly. The moms' group ignored my advice and decided to stalk the new maintenance man starting tomorrow. They are on a crusade to save young women from the Ghost of Wicked Hollow. They were going to start today, but after much discussion, and I'll spare you the details, they decided to postpone. If your shooter is the maintenance man, he's a goner because the mom posse will be on his trail."

"But only during daylight hours and if the weather isn't too cold, foggy, or rainy," I added.

Mary Leigh giggled. "You are so right; furthermore, he has to stay on campus because none of the moms have cars, and he can't go too far from the apartment buildings because some of the moms are directionally challenged and would get lost on campus."

I chuckled. "Do you feel safe now? I do."

"Of course, and in fact, I think the entire mom club is safe because while they are stalking the maintenance man, he'll probably be trying to figure out what on earth they are doing. What about you? Do you have any interesting news other than being the target of a drive-by shooter?"

"I've got a portfolio of Noreen Weber's photographs; I need you to look at them and tell me what you see." I pointed at the large manila envelope on the table.

"That is definitely interesting." She put a cup of tea and a small plate with a scone in front of me then opened the envelope with the photos inside.

CHAPTER FOURTEEN

"At a first glance, all of them are pictures of farmland, a forest, or mountains in the background," Mary Leigh said as we sipped our tea and munched scones. "Starting with the first one, it's a man with his back to the camera. He's hiking on a trail near the top of a hill, and there are more rolling hills in the background; off to his left is a stand of trees. Hmm." She picked up the photo. "There's a woman standing in the trees; she's very difficult to see. Do you have a magnifying glass?"

"No, but it sounds like something I should have."

"I have one but not with me. I'll go through the rest, but I'd like to look at the man and the woman closer with a magnifying glass."

After she looked at the next photo, Mary Leigh said, "There's a man and a woman here too. The man is too far away to identify, and the woman is hidden from his view."

When she finished examining all the photos, she said, "I'm not positive it's the same man in every photo. If it isn't, the second man has the same build as the first. I'm kind of sad because there's not a tall, lean, distinguished looking man in any of the photos. I was hoping we had uncovered evidence of the maintenance man and would be rock stars because we solved the case. There are four photos with no women in them, but I'd like to look at them again when I can see the detail more closely; I'm fairly certain I saw shadows that could be a person. Give me your phone, and I'll snap photos of the pictures, so you can return the portfolio to the library whenever you like."

I bit my lip. *The phone pictures won't have the same level of clarity, but Mary Leigh wants to help.*

"It almost sounds like the woman is stalking the man," I said as Mary Leigh snapped pictures.

"Or two men," Mary Leigh added. "Why would Noreen Weber take pictures like that, or are they staged for a class she was teaching?"

Mary Leigh-blob spread out the photos. "It looks like the same woman in every photo with two people, and I don't see any other figures…"

She set aside two photos. "There might be a third person in these two, or maybe my eyes are getting tired." She picked up the envelope and slid all the photos back inside.

"More tea? Are you going for the rustic look with your hair, or would you like for me to brush it out for you?"

"Rustic kind of fits me, but I'd love to have it brushed. I try to do it myself, but so far, I haven't figured out the magic words to get the tangles out. Be right back."

I hurried to the bathroom and grabbed my hairbrush. While Mary Leigh brushed out the tangles, she said, "I love your curls; mine is so straight. Do you think it's possible the maintenance man shot at you? Can an attractive, older men be both a villain and a heartthrob for a group of young moms? If Ron knew what they have planned, he'd tell me I would have to turn the moms in." Mary Leigh growled in her best gangster voice, "I ain't no snitch unless them coppers make it worth my while."

I laughed at her terrible impression, and she laughed at me.

"We certainly are easily entertained. Have you noticed that?" she asked. "Want to split a scone? I brought a third one in case we needed to celebrate something."

"Sounds great. Let's celebrate no fog tomorrow, so the local stalkers can skulk away."

Palace Guard shook his head, and I waved my hand in dismissal.

"Warm weather and no fog," Mary Leigh said. "I don't think that is tomorrow's forecast, but it would be nice. Maybe we could spy on the moms that are stalking the maintenance guy to be sure they don't get out of line. We'd be performing like a public service, despite what the naysayers might call it."

"We'd definitely get two husbands riled up, wouldn't we? I always wanted to be a spy, and I spent my entire elementary career perfecting my spying skills."

"I spent my entire elementary career trying to learn to tie my shoes," Mary Leigh said. "Never did master that."

I chuckled. "I hear Larry; he'll be here in less than a minute."

"Will he notice your hair?"

"He will, but he'll weigh his options before he says anything."

When a car pulled in front of the apartment, I said, "A car just parked out front. They'll come in together in a few minutes. What time is it?"

"Wow, it's a little after ten. This has been a fantastic evening. Thanks, Gray Lady."

When I opened the front door, Ron hurried to help Mary Leigh into the car, and Larry ran inside.

"We got a lot done. What about you?" he asked after he closed and locked the door.

"It was great. Mary Leigh brought different kinds of tea and scones."

"Your hair is beautiful." He brushed a stray tendril away from my face then leaned down and nibbled on my ear as he whispered, "You are the most beautiful woman in the world, and I'm the luckiest man because you're my wife."

I smiled. "Flattery will get you everywhere."

I blinked my eye to flutter my eyelashes and squealed when Larry swooped me up and carried me to the bedroom. "That's my crazy, sexy Maggie."

* * *

When I woke the next morning, I listened to the sound of water, then Larry turned off the shower, and I hurried to jump into the shower while the water was still hot.

"Good morning, sweetie. The sky is clear, it's cold outside, and Lucy hates Spike and me." He kissed the top of my head. "Take your shower then come have coffee with me, and I'll comb out the tangles in your wet hair. Be careful when you wash your face; your chin has a decent abrasion from the curb."

After I showered and dressed, I hurried with my jo to the dining table.

"Your coffee is at your place at the table. I love your emerald-green striped shirt, but you have it on backwards."

"How did I do that?" I felt the neck. "Ah. It's a tricky one: there's no tag, which I appreciate except I must use the tag to find the back." I took off my shirt, and Larry whistled.

"Cut it out. I can't concentrate if I'm busy laughing at your inappropriate whistles. Is this right?" I smoothed down the front of the shirt. *Feels right to me.*

"I don't know. Do it again."

I crossed my arms and tried to glare at him, and he laughed.

"Yes, it's right. Fried egg and half a cinnamon raisin bagel sound good to you? What's your plan for today?"

I sat at the table and sipped my coffee. "Ow, hot. Fried egg and half a bagel are perfect. Della is coming to see me today, and I'm looking forward to it."

"Will she stay long enough to have dinner with us? I understand there are a lot of really great restaurants that I'm sure we'd enjoy, and we could go early before the crowds show up, or if the noise potential worries you, I could bring takeout here. That actually might be better because you and Della would have privacy, except for me, Palace Guard, Spike, and Lucy."

I snorted. "That's just the usual around here. I'll let you know whether she's staying."

"I was distracted last night when I came home and forgot to tell you about Lily's phone. It's all your fault, sexy Maggie. I was completely blameless."

I giggled. "Right, you were just your usual innocent, lecherous, bystander self."

Larry chuckled. "I'm glad you're so understanding. Here's your breakfast, sweetie."

While we ate, Larry said, "Lily didn't send the text. She leaves her phone at the main desk, but she couldn't find it when the investigator asked her where it was. They found it in the men's restroom on top of the paper towel dispenser. There's no way that she could have accidentally left it there because she doesn't go into the men's restroom, and I'm not even sure she could reach the top of the paper towel dispenser. The night janitor takes care of the restroom supplies."

"I'm not surprised she didn't send the text." I took another bite of my bagel.

"I'm not either, but she was extremely upset. I'm sure she'll keep her phone with her from now on."

"Anyone who knew of Lily's habit of leaving her phone at the main desk, which includes anyone who has attended or taught classes here or who was a regular visitor to the library, would know where to find her phone."

"Exactly." Larry cleared our plates. "What are your plans for lunch? Should I make a sandwich for you? How's the ringing?"

"Still annoying. I don't have any plans, but I can make my own with Palace Guard's guidance."

"No sharp knives." He kissed me before he left.

I shrugged. "At least I have a few kitchen privileges."

I hurried to the bedroom and made the bed. After I finished, it felt only a little lumpy. *Better than nothing.*

As I headed to the table to turn on my computer, my phone rang.

"Sorry I didn't call you last night," Glenn said. "Jennifer's radar must be on high alert because she didn't leave me alone for more than a minute. Ella picked her up this morning because they had planned a shopping trip for office supplies. How are you doing? I heard about the shooter."

"I'm fine; Larry told me I have an abrasion on my chin, but it doesn't bother me, so it must not be much."

"Good. It took a lot of digging, but I discovered that Dean Sanchez is on indefinite leave without pay from the GBI during an investigation; however, there is no formal or informal record of any investigation, although my contact thinks the FBI may have an undercover contractor working on something."

"That's interesting. No record of it though?"

Wonder if the contractor is Gary.

"No, the only records he found were three domestic violence complaints that Sanchez's wife filed, but after he attended counseling and anger management training after each of the first two complaints, she withdrew them. She filed a third complaint before she was murdered, but it was archived after her death."

"How can he be teaching here?"

"I asked that too. Sanchez has a contract for the part time instructor position with the University of Tennessee, but it hasn't been renewed after this term ends."

"Larry says he's a good instructor," I said.

"That may well be, although I'd give anything if you or I could sit in on one of his classes. He may be dropping hints because he's so much smarter than everyone else."

"Hmm." *Maybe I can find a way…*

"Maggie, don't you dare," Glenn growled.

"Dare what?" I asked.

"You know exactly what. If he's as dangerous as you and I think, you'd only be drawing his attention if you were in his classroom."

"I wouldn't be in his classroom, but maybe he'd like to speak to a group of wives about personal safety, and I know the perfect person to set it up."

Glenn sighed. "That's a totally harebrained idea, but I can see that it would certainly appeal to his ego. I'm putting my foot down and telling you don't do it, but don't forget about the audio button on your jo."

I rolled my eye. "I'll let you know if we get anything set up. Did you find anything else?"

"That's it. I still don't feel like I have anything that would impress Kate."

"Kate invited us to go to dinner with Dean and her last night, but he suddenly bailed. Kate seemed disappointed that some part of her plan fell through, but she certainly wasn't heartbroken. It was very odd."

"That makes me feel better," Glenn said.

After we hung up, I called Mary Leigh.

"Hey there, Gray Lady. Did you call to give me stalking orders?"

I giggled. "I love talking to you. I have no way to predict what you're going to say. I've been thinking—"

"Of course, you have," Mary Leigh interrupted. "Let me guess: you were thinking that we need ski pants to go with our new warm coats because it's so cold. I wish I'd thought of that. I wonder if they make maternity ski pants."

I blinked. "We'll need to check into that. I thought it would be a great idea if one of the instructors could speak to the wives about personal safety. Do you think—"

"I know exactly what you were going to say, and Bud's wife is the perfect person to line something up. We could do a morning coffee meeting, and you could teach me how to make cinnamon rolls. I'll call her right away and get right back to you when we have a day and time. The sooner the better, right? Can you tell how excited I was that you called? I've been waiting to hear our plan."

"You're brilliant. Let me know when everything's arranged."

After we hung up, Palace Guard scowled.

"Mary Leigh was super excited, could you tell? It will be fine. I'm not directly involved, and we don't even know who Bud's wife will ask to speak to the wives, but I'll bet Dean Sanchez will show up, even if he isn't the speaker."

Lucy whined as she nosed the back door, and Spike had his snowsuit on.

"Let me wrap up, and I'll go outside too."

I put on my new coat and gloves then pulled up my hood before I opened the back door. The icy air took away my breath as the three of us went outside. *Mary Leigh's idea of ski pants might not be so bad.*

I listened for the usual sounds of the dogs and the birds, but the neighborhood was quiet.

Not foggy, but it's too cold for anyone to be out.

I scanned the yard then peered at the small puddle near the fence. *Why does it look so shiny?* I made my way across the yard then tapped the puddle with my jo and frowned at the crunch as my jo broke the thick sheet of ice. *I hope the roads aren't icy.*

When I turned around, Lucy and Spike stood at the back door, and I hurried to go back inside with them.

After I put my gloves into my pocket and hung up my coat, my phone buzzed then repeated a message. "Text from Della: 'I'll bring lunch.'"

"Do we have any tablecloths or nice placemats? Maybe Ella and Jennifer bought some, but I don't know where they'd be. It would be fun for the table to be kind of fancy when Della gets here with our lunch."

Palace Guard held up his index finger.

"Okay, I can wait a minute."

He returned then guided me to my bedroom closet. After I faced Larry's side of the closet and looked up, cloth tumbled down from the back of the top shelf and knocked me off balance.

I squealed, and Lucy scrambled to the bedroom.

"Sorry, Lucy, I was surprised by an avalanche." I picked up the pile of linens from the floor and laid it on the bed then sorted the items by size.

"I need four placemats and four napkins." I picked four of the items that I had sorted into the size small pile and four from the pile I had sorted as medium. I pointed to my two new piles. "Napkins and placemats?" I asked.

Palace Guard rolled his eyes then nodded.

"They don't have to match." I carried my selections to the dining table and placed the four medium sized items on the table; after I smoothed out the smaller items, I semi-folded, semi-rolled them into four different versions of nicely folded napkins then set each one next to the left side of a placemat.

I opened my laptop and scrolled through my files as I listened for a book that sounded interesting.

"What time is it?"

Palace Guard held up one finger.

"Della should have been here by now."

I sat on the sofa then paced the great room from one end to the other until I wore myself out. I stopped at the front window and peered outside at the occasional passerby and the occasional vehicles, all cars, that crept on the road past the apartment.

"I don't know why I'm so jumpy except I don't know why Della's late. What time is it now?"

Palace Guard held up two fingers.

I groaned. "Seriously?"

Palace Guard patted my arm then pointed at the refrigerator.

"I'll wait for Della. She said she'd bring lunch."

I lay down on the floor and pretended to do yoga; Lucy lay next to me and licked my face.

I giggled. "I'm fine."

I tried to push her away, but she persisted until I got off the floor.

When I saw Spike was next to Lucy on the floor, I growled, "You told her to do that, didn't you?"

Spike grinned, and I flounced to the window. *Still no Della.*

My phone rang. *Unknown number.* I shrugged and answered it.

"It's Grandma D, honey. I hit an icy spot in the road after a son of a sea biscuit yahoo rammed the rear of my beautiful truck. I bailed before it went over the ledge and into a deep ravine. You know what I always say, look for the failures, not the successes; I'll call again when I can steal another phone for a minute or two. Don't go telling the family; they get too riled up." She hung up.

I sat in stunned silence until Palace Guard patted my shoulder.

"You heard? She called herself Grandma D and said not to tell the family, so she obviously doesn't want it to get around that she survived the crash, but what did she mean when she said, *Look for the failures, not the successes?*"

I paced from the front window around the sofa then back to the window to think. As I stared out the window, I exhaled. "We're looking at a string of murders over a twenty-plus-year span. What's a success, and what's a failure?"

I strolled to the dining table and sat. "I need to look at the failures, so what's a failure in a murder?"

I tapped my fingers on the table and frowned. "Someone tried to kill Della, but they failed."

I glanced at Spike, and he motioned his hand in circles: *again.*

"The murderer failed; we have a survivor."

Palace Guard grinned and nodded his head.

My eyes widened. "We need to be looking for survivors, not victims of the murderer. I'm calling Paul. I'll bet Della has somebody in mind, but until I hear from her again, Paul and Julie can look too."

When I called Paul, he asked, "Are you okay?"

"I'm fine; why?"

"Oh, I don't know. Somebody shot at you yesterday, so just thought I'd ask."

"We've been really focused on researching the killer's victims. Are there any survivors?"

"Well, thanks a lot, little miss Gray Lady. You've just made me feel like an old man for not thinking of that. Can I tell Julie it was my brilliant idea? Never mind, she'll know it was yours." He chuckled and hung up.

"Paul's going to put Julie on it." I held up my hand, and Palace Guard and Spike smacked it.

I smiled when my phone rang. *Mary Leigh.*

"Bud's wife arranged for Dean Sanchez to speak to the newly-formed Wives' Group tomorrow at nine on the topic of personal safety. It will be a coffee, and I offered to bring cinnamon rolls. Do we make them tonight?"

"Yes, then all you'll need to do is bake them in the morning, so they will be warm."

"Ooo. Warm, homemade cinnamon rolls. We'll be hot stuff in the Wives' Club, except we already are. Bud's wife told me we're charter members."

"Do we know Bud's wife's name?"

"Nope, unless you do, but if we have name tags tomorrow, I can tell you. I'd suggest them, but I'm sure she's already thought of that. I'm trying to decide if I want to wear my new Edgar Allan Poe maternity shirt that Mom sent me. It's heather gray with a black raven on it and says *Nevermore.*"

I giggled. "Love it. You have another option: you could save it for Saturday when we meet with Sally."

"Tempting, but I think of my Bacon shirt as my Sally shirt, but that might not work because Ron might have to help me pull it on then cut it off after I get home. This baby is outgrowing my Bacon shirt. Mom sent me another shirt that is cream colored with an embroidered pumpkin patch and the text is embroidered in yellow and orange script: *Don't Eat Pumpkin Seeds.*"

I snort-laughed. "Now I know exactly where you get your remarkable sense of humor. Have Ron drop you off after supper, and we'll make cinnamon rolls then while they rise—"

"I can look at the photos. Sounds like a plan; I'll bring my magnifying glass."

After we hung up, I sent Glenn a text: "Wives meeting tomorrow at nine with speaker."

I received a reply almost immediately. "Text from Glenn: 'I'll share with the away team.'"

I sent a text to Larry: "D delayed. Don't need takeout."

"He might not see that until the end of his class, but that's okay." I opened the refrigerator door. "I can put the casserole into the oven then turn it on. That's not dangerous."

Palace Guard hovered while I pulled out the casserole then put it into the cold oven. I frowned at the stove dials then pointed. "Is this one for the oven?"

He shook his head then tapped my arm to move over one more dial. I turned the dial then checked with Palace Guard, and he nodded.

"Thanks for helping me feel useful. I've hated that everything has fallen on Larry." I set plates on our placemats and forks on the napkins. "No reason we can't be fancy for the two of us."

When Larry pulled his truck into our parking spot, I smiled. "I can't wait to see if he's angry or happy."

Spike grinned his shark smile then scowled.

"You're betting angry? Bet's on; I'll take happy."

Palace Guard shook his head then furrowed his brow and turned down the corners of his mouth. "You bet sad? Fine."

Larry rushed into the house, grabbed me into a bear hug, and buried his face in my hair. "Mmm. You smell so good."

He raised his head and sniffed. "Did you put our casserole into the oven?"

I nodded and held my breath, and he laughed. "You concocted a plan, and Palace Guard helped."

"How did you know?"

"Palace Guard and Spike are frowning at me. What was the bet?"

"I have no idea what you're talking about." I glanced at Spike who scowled, and Palace Guard's sad face.

"You're busted, Crazy Lady; thank you for not making a salad."

After we ate, Mary Leigh and Ron arrived, then Larry and Ron left to walk to the library.

"I brought my magnifying glass." Mary Leigh set her backpack on the table.

I stared at Mary Leigh who looked more like a young, pregnant woman with straight, black hair than a blob. "You've lost most of your blobness. You're as short as I am."

"That's so exciting. Do you see the real me, or am I skinny like you?" Her mouth twitched into a small smile, and she bit her lip to hide it.

"I'm seeing a bit of your facial expressions, and you're skinny as long as you don't turn sideways."

Mary Leigh laughed. "I asked for that, didn't I? Where's the photos? Let's put me to work."

"Let's start with the cinnamon rolls, then while the dough rises, we can shift to the photos. Are you ready for your baking lesson?"

"Yes, let's do this."

Mary Leigh set up my mixer on the counter and all the ingredients on the table. "Am I ready to measure and mix?"

I told her how much to add of each ingredient, and she carefully measured and added as she followed my step-by-step directions.

After she had mixed and kneaded the dough in the mixer, she placed the dough in an oiled bowl and covered it with a towel.

"While that's rising, we'll work on the portfolio."

Mary Leigh sat at the table and pulled out the photos from the portfolio, and I pressed the middle pearl for a video with audio on the back of my jo.

CHAPTER FIFTEEN

Mary Leigh said, "I'll organize them by the number of people in the photo. I'll start with the ones that don't have any figures to see if someone is actually there."

Mary Leigh stopped shuffling the pictures. "These two look like the photos that Sally had on her blog."

"Seriously?" Palace Guard leaned closer and peered at the pictures.

"I'm pretty sure. If they are, I hope Sally had the good sense to get written permission from Noreen Weber to use them on her blog."

As she sorted the pictures, I asked, "Are there any dates? Do we know when Noreen Weber took these?"

"Good thought." Mary Leigh turned over the first photo. "Unfortunately, nothing on the back except the initials NW."

She examined the first photo with her magnifying glass. "It's very faint, but I see a figure farther away than most of the other shots. It may be partially obscured by a thicket."

She flipped the photo upside down and continued to examine it closely. "I thought a different perspective would help, but I can't tell whether it's a man or a woman, and there's no nearby reference of a tree or anything that could help with height. My magnifying glass is pretty good, but it's not as good as the very expensive ones are."

Mary Leigh described the people she saw in each photo. When she finished examining each one, she leaned back in the chair to stretch her back. "The two men are very similar in build; they are never together, but one of them is in every photo. There was not a third man after all, just small, scrubby trees. There is only one woman, and she is slender and tall. She appears to be older from her posture because she has a slight difference in the height of her shoulder blades and an increased front to back curve to her upper spine, but I can't guess how old."

I stared at her.

"Sorry, my occupational therapist side took over."

"No, that's great. I'm not sure how many people would have even noticed."

"The terrain where they are hiking is rough and would normally be difficult for an older woman, but she isn't showing any signs of distress. In fact, she's probably in much better condition that the two men who are at least twenty-five years younger than she is, judging from their stance. One of them appears to be steadying himself with a nearby tree when he stops. The other man bends slightly forward with his hands on his upper thighs, which indicates to me that he needs to pause to catch his breath."

"They couldn't follow her," I said.

"Exactly."

"Do they have any idea they are being followed by two women?"

"You're right; it's easy to forget about the photographer, Noreen, isn't it? There are no photos with the men looking back, but the photographer may not have wanted to chance a shot like that. My guess is that neither man considered there might be someone following him, but I can't point to anything to support my supposition."

I clicked the bottom pearl on my jo to turn off the video.

"Back to baking: our dough is ready for the next step."

"Good." Mary Leigh slid the photos back into the portfolio then washed her hands.

After she rolled out the dough and spread it with softened butter, Mary Leigh mixed the cinnamon and brown sugar and spread it over the butter then pressed the sweet mixture into the butter with the back of a spoon.

"So far, so good. What's next?" she asked.

"Starting at a short side, roll it into a log."

"I don't know how to do that. How tight do I roll it?"

"Don't squeeze the dough but roll it tight enough that there aren't any gaps."

Mary Leigh took a big breath, and as she rolled, Palace Guard and Spike hovered. After she reached the end, she exhaled. "How's that?"

The imaginary men held up their thumbs, and I said," Perfect."

"I am so sorry I can't sip a nice glass of red wine until I'm brave enough to ask, but what's next?" she asked.

"Cut a piece of the parchment paper for the bottom of our pan."

"I can do cutouts. I was a whiz in first grade with scissors, and I never lost my stellar cutting edge." Mary Leigh giggled as she cut the paper, and I smiled.

"What's next?"

"More cutting, except this time with a knife."

"Oooo. Advanced cutting."

"Cut the log into three-inch pieces."

"Do I have to measure? I have a tape measurer in my backpack."

"Estimates are fine. The goal is kind of equal pieces of the log."

"How many pieces?"

"Probably nine. We're not making the huge batch of cinnamon rolls that I made when I worked with Kate at the diner."

"Here goes nothing."

I smiled as Mary Leigh lightly tapped the log with the back of her knife as she planned her cuts, then she sliced the log into nine equal pieces. When she finished, she set down the knife on the counter and waved her arms in the air while she squealed, "Woo-hoo!"

Spike danced his wacky dance next to her, and Palace Guard and I applauded.

Mary Leigh grinned. "I'm awesome. What's next?"

"Put the rolls into the pan then cover it with plastic wrap and put the pan into the refrigerator, then we'll collect the ingredients for the frosting you'll make in the morning. We'll put them into a small bowl."

Mary Leigh carefully lifted each cinnamon roll with a spatula and set it into the pan. "They touch, right?"

"Yes."

After she put the pan into the refrigerator, she turned on the burner under the tea kettle.

"I'm ready for the frosting ingredients."

She measured then dropped each ingredient into a small bowl as I recited the list.

After she covered the bowl, she made our tea. "Why did I never try this before? It was scary but fun."

"I'll find a recipe that's close to what we did and send it to you. You're certainly ready to go solo."

"What do I do in the morning?"

"About six-thirty, take the pan out of the refrigerator, remove the plastic, and cover the pan with a small towel to let the cinnamon rolls come to room temperature and rise a bit more. Preheat your oven to three hundred fifty and at seven-thirty, bake the rolls for about twenty to twenty-five minutes. You want them only slightly golden brown on the edges, so they will be a little underbaked in the middle. While they are baking, dump all the ingredients from our small bowl into a mixing bowl, and beat them until they are smooth. Let the cinnamon rolls cool about ten minutes, then smear the frosting on them. The rolls will still be warm, so the frosting will ooze into the cracks a bit."

"Do I move the cinnamon rolls to my fancy serving plate before I frost them?"

"Good idea. I've never done anything except serve them at a diner, but a Wives' Meeting is different than a diner."

"Ron's going to go crazy."

"Didn't think about that. The cinnamon rolls will be fairly large. Maybe it would be better if you move them to a cutting board before you frost them. Let them cool another few minutes then slice each one in half before you put them on the plate. Your middle one might be a little soft and won't be as pretty as the others after you cut it. You can give those two halves to Ron. He can take them to share or eat both of them before he leaves."

"You're a genius, Gray Lady."

"It was your idea." I smiled.

We sipped our tea, and I listened while Mary Leigh tried to decide which shirt to wear to the Wives' Meeting. After she went through the pros and cons of each shirt based on the event, weather, and her potential mood and changed her mind four times, she said, "I've decided not to decide. I'll put on a shirt in the morning and wear the other one on Saturday."

I giggled. "Good plan."

When Larry and Ron came into the apartment, Spike did his wacky dance.

Larry said, "What the…"

"Cinnamon rolls," Mary Leigh said. "You smell cinnamon rolls. They haven't been baked yet, though. I'll bake them in the morning."

"If you'll carry the pan, I'll carry the bowl with the frosting ingredients."

I opened the refrigerator and pointed; Ron picked up the pan and the bowl, and they left.

"What was the wacky dance for?" Larry asked.

"Spike was glad you came home."

Palace Guard rolled his eyes.

"What else?" Larry asked.

"Mary Leigh has a way of talking a lot, and her topic tonight was a long, exhaustive wardrobe discussion; she wore out Spike and probably Palace Guard, and you saved them."

Larry chuckled. "How about that beer and cheese? We need to talk. How's the ringing in your ears?"

"Still there. Cheese, crackers, and beer?"

After I sat on the sofa, Larry handed me a beer and set a plate of crackers and cheese on the table. I took a sip them made a cracker and cheese sandwich.

He exhaled. "One of the guys has a scanner; Tennessee state troopers found Della's truck in a ravine after someone reported tire tracks that led to the ledge overlooking the ravine. They have a recovery team planned to search the area in the morning. She must have hit a patch of ice. I'm sorry, honey."

"She called me—"

He interrupted. "I know she was coming here to see you, but I didn't want to wait until morning to tell you."

"But she—"

He interrupted again. "She was one strong woman, but she didn't survive the crash."

I smiled, and Larry's eyes widened. "That's your tiger smile. What?" he asked.

"Don't interrupt because I'm trying to tell you something. Della called me and told me her truck was rammed and crashed in a ravine.

She doesn't want anyone to know she's alive, so we aren't to say anything. She told me to look for the failures, not the successes. It took a little thought, then I understood what she meant. Paul and I have been focusing on the victims of the murderer. The victims are the murderer's successes. Your turn."

"Wow. The failures of the murderer are any that survived. Do you think Della knew someone?"

"I'm sure of it. Della told me she'd call again next time she stole a phone."

Larry took a big gulp of beer. "I thought I'd console you with a quiet, private celebration of Della's life with a beer and snacks. I think you need to console me for forgetting to listen."

I snorted. "I'm so sorry, Mr. Sexy Pants, that you're too pigheaded to listen to me."

"Ouch. I'm consoled. Did you have lunch?"

"No, I thought Della was just running late, so I waited."

"How about a grilled ham and cheese sandwich? You know, me being pigheaded and all."

I giggled. "Half a sandwich sounds good."

While he fixed our late-night snack, Larry said, "Paul's been helping you look into the Ghost of Wicked Hollow murders?"

I nodded. "I gave him the list of victims that Mother gave to me."

"Do you think the real murderer shot at you?"

"I think I've been his target, but I don't know why. I don't think he knows I'm interested in solving the murders."

"Has Paul checked the victims for any disabilities?"

"That's an easy check, but no; we didn't think about that."

"The other option is to check to see how many killers the victims have stopped." Larry chuckled as he brought me the half-sandwich.

"You cut my sandwich in half, thank you." I drained my beer.

"Want another beer?"

"No, I'm fine." I bit into my hot, melty sandwich. "Tasty."

After I finished my half sandwich, Larry said, "Do you want me to text Paul for you?"

"Wow, thank you."

Larry tapped in a text then pressed send.

"That was amazing. Do you know how long a simple text takes me? What did you say?"

"I told him you and I talked and asked if any of the victims had disabilities."

Larry's phone buzzed a text and he chuckled. "Paul said that he's glad I'm on the home team."

"So am I, Mr. Sexy Pants."

Larry tugged on my T-shirt's neckline. "Don't mind me; I'm just leering."

He checked the locks and turned off the lights before we strolled to the bedroom with our arms around each other.

* * *

I woke while it was still dark. No Larry. I grabbed jo and my bathrobe. When I opened the bedroom door, Larry was in the kitchen.

"Good morning, naked Maggie. Coffee just perked. I'll pour you a cup; I want to get a run in before I shower."

"I'm not naked. I have on my bathrobe." I flipped my hair and sipped my coffee.

"But what's under that bathrobe is my naked Maggie." He leered as he left to run, and I hurried to take my shower before he returned.

As I was drying, Larry came into the bathroom and dripped on the floor.

"You're drenched."

"It was a bad idea." He pulled off his clothes and dropped them into a sloppy wet pile while I turned on the tub water to warm up for him.

"It's cold and there was a little light shower when I went out, but I've never let a little sprinkle stop me before. When I turned around to head back, somebody opened the sky's floodgates, and the light rain turned into a deluge. The little shower was cold; the downpour froze me to the core. It was raining so hard that I was having trouble seeing and had to slow down, then Palace Guard joined me. I ran as fast as I could and didn't worry about falling because he was there. I think I understand a little better how it's possible to run full speed with Palace Guard at your side. It really was freeing."

He turned on the shower and climbed in. "Ahh. Warm water."

I went to our bedroom then returned to the bathroom with an empty clothesbasket. After I dropped the dripping clothes into the basket, I carried them to the washer and loaded them into the machine. I sighed as I stared at the dials then returned to my coffee. *I'll have to let Larry start it.*

Larry came to the kitchen and refilled our cups. "I'm glad in a perverse sort of way that I got caught in the rain. It reminded me that I need to load up rain gear and cold weather gear into my truck, so if we're sent to the field, I'll be prepared for the weather. I'm sending Ron a text. I have a feeling about today. I think we'll go out."

"We may have a quart of Jennifer's chicken soup."

"You're right." He returned from the pantry and dumped soup into a pan. "If I have this in a thermos in the truck, I'll have something warm in the field. Am I weird?"

"Yes, honey, but a smart weird. You can leave your rain and cold weather gear in your truck, and the soup won't go to waste. We can cook up some pasta and add it to the soup for supper tonight. If you have the soup for lunch, we can open a jar of chili."

"Thanks, what do you think about oatmeal for breakfast?"

"Perfect."

While we ate breakfast, Larry worked on a list of gear to store in his truck. "I'll put my gear by the front door. Shall I make you a sandwich for lunch?"

"I hear you nagging me about eating lunch. I'll make my sandwich." I rolled my eye.

"You're getting better at that eyeroll, sweetie." Larry chuckled. "I'll grab the rest of our dirty laundry then get the washer going. Anything else you can think of?"

"That's it."

"I'm worried about you walking to the meeting, but Palace Guard will go with you, I'm sure. Text me if you need me. The instructors will understand; everybody's worried, sweetie."

Larry poured the hot soup into a thermos then carried his gear out to his truck. He came inside and held me. "Sweetheart, please be safe."

After a sweet kiss, he left.

I stood by the window and watched as he pulled away from the house, then his truck disappeared in the dark and the rain.

Spike and I managed to coax Lucy outside. She nosed the back door, but I said, "Take your break, girl, then we can all go in."

She dashed out to the yard and disappeared in the rain and dark then dashed back to the door. After we were inside, she shook herself, but I was ready and dodged the spray. I grabbed a towel and rubbed her dry.

"I'm planning a normal, quiet day today." I carried the soaked, doggy-smell towel to the washer and dropped it on the floor.

When someone tapped on the front door, Palace Guard and I rushed to the window, but I had turned off the porch light, and I couldn't see anything.

I shook my head. *Not that I could see anything more than a blob, anyway.*

After Lucy stood at the front door and whined, I opened it, and Della said, "Got any coffee? I walked from the bus station."

"Oh my gosh, you're soaked. Take off your wet things in the bathroom. Take a warm shower if you like. I'll bring a cup of coffee to the bathroom for you and get you some dry clothes; I'm sure you'll be able to wear one of Larry's long-sleeved T-shirts and a pair of his sweatpants."

"Hand me a cup, and I'll take it with me. I didn't expect to get caught in a downpour, but I seem to be attracting the unexpected the past day or so."

"I'm glad you're okay. We can talk after your shower."

While Della was in the shower, I sent a text to Larry. "Grandma D is here."

When Della came out of the bathroom, she said, "That was a great idea, Maggie. I feel human again; best part about that rain was that it cleaned all the dirt off me. Any way we can toss my duds into the washer or maybe your dryer?"

"Larry started a load this morning, and I moved it to the dryer then punched and twisted buttons; it started, but I don't know if the clothes are dry yet."

"Show me your washer, and I'll get my clothes washing and check that dryer for you. Are you doing any cooking?"

"I can't see well enough to be safe with knives or the stove. Have you eaten? Do you mind cooking yourself breakfast? Our refrigerator is well-stocked."

"Bless you, darlin'. I'm so hungry, I could eat a polecat."

I snickered. "I'm not sure the refrigerator is that well-stocked."

Della carried her wet clothes to the washer and started it, then I heard the dryer going too.

"The dryer was set on fifteen minutes of air fluff; it wasn't quite enough to dry the clothes." She chuckled. "Shall I make another pot of coffee?"

"Sounds great. I'll get the coffee out for you."

"You just relax, honey. I'm a snoop from way back; I'll find what I need."

After the coffee started perking, Della said, "I found the fixin's for biscuits. It'll just take me two shakes to get them into the oven. Have you had breakfast? You can have a biscuit with butter and this homemade strawberry jam. Did you know strawberries are better for your eyesight than carrots?" I smiled at Della's hearty laugh.

While Della mixed the biscuits, I said, "I've been looking into the Ghost of Wicked Hollow murders along with a friend, Paul Vargas."

"Paul Vargas? He was a brilliant detective back in the day before his troubles. I'd heard he'd finally cleaned himself up and was working with Glenn Coyle. You've got the best."

"We've been focused on the victims for commonality or clues that could lead us to the killer. When you told me to look for the failures, not the successes, I realized we weren't thinking about the murderer's failures: the ones who got away. Paul's shifted his focus."

"I knew you'd understand. Who are your suspects?"

"Wayne Dillard and Dean Sanchez, but we don't have any compelling evidence on either one."

"That is so interesting. Noreen Weber Dillard was worried that her son was emulating the Ghost of Wicked Hollow, but at the time, I was investigating Dean Sanchez. Noreen wanted to follow her son because she was certain that he was mentally ill, and I wanted to follow Dean Sanchez because he would disappear at times that corresponded to the deaths of young women. We joined forces, and I tracked, and she photographed. Before she died, Noreen was convinced that her son had quirks, but she wasn't as certain that he was a killer. We investigated two other suspects that we quickly cleared, but at the end, we still had two suspects."

"How did Noreen die?"

"After her husband died, Noreen grieved by immersing herself in her photography. She stopped scheduling any appointments at all that weren't related to her photography, including regular dental and medical checkups for years, and the cancer grew. By the time she was too weak to continue with her photos, her cancer had metastasized; she died two months after her doctor's appointment. I've always believed she died of a broken heart."

While Della pulled out the biscuits from the oven and scrambled an egg, I put the portfolio on the table. "The Nashville Library had a collection of Noreen Weber photographs."

Della poured our coffee and put a buttered biscuit smeared with strawberry jam on a plate for me, and two biscuits and her egg on a plate for her then joined me at the table.

She shook out the photographs and glanced through them then sipped her coffee while she reviewed them more slowly. "I'll go through these with you after I finish eating. I'm in most of them."

I nodded as I bit into my heavenly, light biscuit, and butter oozed down my hand. *Should have known.*

"I'm going to a Wives' Meeting at nine at the office. It's only half a block away. Dean Sanchez is speaking to the group about personal safety."

Della snorted. "I sure wish I could go, but he'd know me right off and clam up. You be safe. He's a snake. Are you carrying?"

"Yes, ma'am. I'm good with my knife, and Kate said my shooting skills are fine. My hearing is very sensitive, so I'm not crazy about gunshots. Somebody attempted a drive-by shooting yesterday and missed me, but I think I may have winged him."

"Which side?"

I stared at Della. "Holy moly, nobody asked that. I think everybody assumed he drove past me then off campus; I know I did. If he drove away to the campus exit, he would have been shooting out the passenger's window; but I'm certain he shot from the driver's side window and across the road. The only way for him to leave would be to drive past the library again, but the road was congested with campus police and a dozen crime scene investigator students and instructors. He must have parked on campus to wait until the road cleared."

"Smart girl."

"I just need to know where Wayne Dillard was yesterday afternoon, so we can cut him loose from our suspects."

"Right. We have a lot more to talk about. Go to your meeting and listen very carefully. While you're gone, I'll order myself a drop-off rental car. I grabbed my leather bag with all my IDs and credit cards, but I must have dropped my phone in the process of my hasty exit to land on dirt not rock. I bought an over-priced, prepaid cell phone at the bus station to get by for a few days."

On the way to the office building, I stopped before I crossed the road and called Paul.

"What's up?" he asked.

"Does Wayne Dillard have an alibi for yesterday morning during the shooting?"

"I don't know whether he was scheduled to volunteer at the main library, but you finally have a question that will be easy to answer."

"After the Wives' Meeting, I'll go see Betty, if I can get a ride. If I can't, I'll call her and let you know."

"You on your way to the meeting?"

"Yes."

"We're ten-ten and listening in. That's old CB radio talk for transmission completed; Heather and I are at her old office, so we'll be listening to what you're recording."

I rolled my eye. "Do I say ten-four, good buddy?"

Paul chuckled as he hung up.

"I don't know why, but I'm worried Della will be gone when we get back," I said.

Palace Guard patted my back.

Before we reached the office building, I asked, "Do I record just audio?"

Palace Guard shook his head.

"Okay, so I'll have to sit where my jo has a clear view of Dean Sanchez, but I don't want to sit in front."

When I walked into the lobby, there were five or six blobs huddled close to the door to the meeting room. I pushed the middle pearl on my jo to begin the video. As I made my way to the door, Palace Guard tapped my arm to guide me, and I continued to the meeting room with his help.

Mary Leigh was standing near the back of the room, and I joined her.

"I'm not quite sure why everyone's hanging out in the lobby," Mary Leigh said. "Pick a table, and I'll bring you a cup of coffee. I'll get us a cinnamon roll bite after people start coming in. Ron suggested I cut the rolls into quarters because it was a group of women. He said if it was his buddies and him, I could leave them whole."

"Hmm," I muttered. "Where do I want to sit?"

Palace Guard guided me past the front row of tables, then we turned back to the second row before he stopped me at the table closest to the exit. "I think I'll be able to hear best at this table."

"I think you're right," Mary Leigh said. "Usually, nobody sits in the first row except those who wants to be recognized by the speaker as being very interested in the topic. I think all the questions will come from the first row until one person in the back row decides to dominate the discussion. Here's your coffee."

"Interesting observation; it'll be fun to see who the front-seaters are and how close your prediction is. Which shirt did you wear?" I asked.

"Pumpkin seeds. I decided it was dressy." She snickered.

"I think that's your power shirt," I said.

"Thank you; what's a power shirt?"

"Something I made up." I smiled when Mary Leigh snorted.

CHAPTER SIXTEEN

The room began filling up, and I reached into my backpack and pulled out my earplugs.

Mary Leigh patted my hand. "It's a bit loud even for me. Earplugs were a great idea."

I smiled. "They were a gift from Kate. They do a great job of toning down the noise level but still allowing me to hear conversations."

A blob marched past us and headed straight for the front table in the middle. *Has to be Sally.*

Mary Leigh grabbed my arm then leaned close and whispered, "Sally sat at a table in the first row; she chose the seat directly in front of the podium. I'm sure she's watching for the rest of her posse to join her."

"No surprise."

Mary Leigh sighed. "I'd love to touch the back of one of the chairs to see how long it would take for her to tell me the seat was taken, but my waddle is starting to slow me down. It's not worth the effort."

I glanced toward the door, and Palace Guard blocked my view. He stood close to my back and faced the door, and I smiled. *It's reassuring to have Palace Guard watching my back.*

Two more blobs joined Sally at the table.

Mary Leigh whispered, "Two of Sally's friends joined her. That's a relief to me because you would have decided we needed to sit with Sally."

I snickered. "Only to be sure she didn't move."

"See? I knew that; am I in training to be a junior Gray Lady?"

"I don't know if the world is ready for two of us." I snickered.

A blob approached our table. "Hi, I'm Lori. Oh, there's Jessie." The blob waved.

"Join us," Mary Leigh said.

"Save our seats; I want coffee, and it looks like that's where Jessie's going."

After she left, I whispered, "Lori is Bud's wife. I recognized her voice."

"Jessie must be John's wife. Let me know if you recognize her voice too. Want more coffee? I'll get us cinnamon roll bites too; I want you to tell me how wonderful they are."

After Mary Leigh left, I listened to the conversation at Sally's table.

"Dean Sanchez asked me what he should talk about to the wives' group, and I suggested personal safety," Sally said.

"You should have organized the meeting too; I expected much more at a breakfast meeting than a few pieces of cinnamon roll and a platter of melon cubes," one of the women said.

"I was going to bring scones, but the bakery closes at four o'clock. I heard they open at seven-thirty, but who wants to go out that early?" Sally asked.

"Not me; that's for sure," a third woman said. "Did you hear about the shooting yesterday?"

"My mother heard about it and wants me to come home because it's so dangerous here. She told me it was gang-related, according to the news," Sally said.

"I heard the Gray Lady was shot, but she seems fine to me," the second woman said.

"It was probably a backfire that's been blown out of proportion," the third woman said.

Lori-blob returned with Jessie-blob.

Lori sat in the third seat. "Mary Leigh was in the line behind me; I carried her plate of cinnamon bites, so she could bring the two coffees, Gray Lady."

"Lori, scoot your chair closer to Mary Leigh, and I can move this chair, so I don't have my back to the speaker," Jessie said.

"I'll move my chair and Mary Leigh's around a little farther, so we'll all have enough room to maneuver." I rose from my chair and moved it a few inches, then Palace Guard tapped my arm, and I moved it a few more.

Lori moved Mary Leigh's chair closer to me then moved to give Jessie more room.

"Perfect, thanks," Jessie said.

"Were y'all rearranging the furniture while I was gone? I'm sorry I missed that," Mary Leigh said. "So, what do y'all know about Dean Sanchez?"

"He has a reputation for being a good instructor, so I have high hopes that he'll have some practical ideas for personal safety for us. He didn't give me an outline and didn't want an overhead for slides, so I suspect this may be a topic he's presented fairly frequently in the past," Lori said.

After everyone was seated, the roar turned to conversations, then a hush fell over the room, and Dean Sanchez walked in.

He's a blob. I can't tell if there's a bandage under his shirt.

Sally's table of blobs jumped up and began applauding, and the rest of the room joined in, except for our table. Mary Leigh golf-clapped, and I bowed my head to keep from laughing. Lori strode to the front of the room, and chairs scraped as everyone took their seats.

How do I ask Mary Leigh if there's any evidence of a bandage under his shirt?

I whispered, "Tell me what he's wearing."

"A boxy, brown, corduroy jacket with brass buttons at the sleeves and a single button on the front of the jacket at the waist; it's buttoned. He's wearing a medium blue shirt with the top button unbuttoned, khakis, and brown loafers. His jacket is perfect to hide the imprint of a concealed weapon."

I rolled my eye. *Either no bandage or it's hidden by his perfect jacket.*

Palace Guard stood next to me; and held up one finger on his left hand and two fingers on his right hand then raised his eyebrows, and I nodded as I remembered the man who followed me, and the second man who followed the first. He kept the finger on his left hand raised then pointed first to it then to the blob who stood at the front of the room.

My eyes widened. *Why was Dean Sanchez stalking me?*

"Evidently our speaker for our first Wives' Group needs no introduction for many of you, but for the rest, Dean Sanchez has been an investigator for the Georgia Bureau of Investigation for the past twenty-five years."

Several women behind me gasped, and Mary Leigh elbowed me then wiggled her eyebrows as she whispered, "Old."

I smiled then whispered, "You're killing me."

Jessie smiled and nodded.

Lori continued, "He is also an instructor for the University of Tennessee and is highly regarded by his peers as an expert in the field of criminal investigation. Please join me in welcoming our first guest speaker, Dean Sanchez."

Lori led the applause then took her seat.

"Thank you, Mrs. Kingston, for the wonderful introduction. You are only too kind, and thank you, ladies, for the warm reception."

Mary Leigh pulled out a notebook and a pen from her purse and wrote in large print, "Ladies?? Can we hurt him now?"

I picked up her notebook to bring it closer to my eye but couldn't read what she had written.

When I sighed, Mary Leigh whispered, "He said, ladies, so I asked if we can hurt him now."

I tilted my head in thought. "Hmm."

Palace Guard poked my shoulder, and I resisted sticking out my tongue at him as I sighed again and shook my head, and Jessie sighed too.

Lori snorted then hissed, "Y'all behave."

Dean Sanchez began his talk with a list of all his accomplishments; I covered my yawn with my hand.

Sure am glad I can't see Lori-blob. I'll bet she glared at me.

When he finally shifted to his first point in personal safety: Be Prepared, Mary Leigh frowned.

After he announced his second point: Street Precautions, Mary Leigh pulled out her phone and tapped then scrolled and stared at her screen; she leaned close to me and whispered, "We'll talk later, but his third point will be Car Safety."

Dean finished up his discussion on street precautions then said, "Car Safety."

Mary Leigh whispered points four and five before he finished his exposition on car safety, "While Waiting for a Bus and Office Security."

Jessie coughed, I covered my mouth to stifle a laugh, and Lori snorted.

At the end of his five-point speech, Sally and her blobs rose and applauded.

"I need to stretch too, shall we?" Jessie asked.

"And that's a wrap." I pressed the bottom button on my jo to turn off the video.

We stood as Sanchez-blob waved his arms toward himself to welcome his adoring fans to come forward to fawn over him.

I rolled my eye. *I might be giving the impression that I don't like the man.*

As the press of blobs gathered around Sanchez, Lori asked, "Shall we adjourn, *Ladies*? My apartment is the closest. It's time for a charter member meeting."

Mary Leigh and I followed Lori and Jessie out of the building then to Lori's apartment; Palace Guard stayed next to me.

When we were inside and seated, Lori said, "I'll start the introductions: I consider myself a trifle overweight; my former doctor told me I was morbidly obese, and I told him he was morbidly obsessed with my weight. We mutually agreed to part ways. My mom's family is from Tennessee; I spent a lot of time with my grandmother when I was growing up and learned how to make bootleg whiskey, except Meemaw called it tonic and sold it at a good price. Mom told me Meemaw's recipe kept the family from starving in the Depression and was a family secret; if prohibition comes back, we're set."

Jessie chuckled. "I'm the only Afro-Haitian woman in the wives' group. My grandma was a highly respected Mambo, a leader of Vodou, and I spent many hours with her as a child and learned Haitian Creole from her. I try to honor her memory by wearing the traditional reds and blues, especially when I attend any function. I would have worn a skirt today if it wasn't so cold, so I wore a blue blouse with red rickrack on the front instead."

"My parents immigrated to Georgia from Thailand before I was born. My parents speak Thai at home and English in public, so I'm bilingual but prefer Thai when I'm stressed. You already know I'm pregnant and short, Gray Lady." Mary Leigh giggled. "People assume I'm from India or China. When they ask me where I'm from, I tell them Savannah. The first time someone asked me if I was Buddhist was when I was six years old, and I said I was a girl; my mom increased my allowance."

I chuckled. "My great-grandmother was Irish. My mother grew up playing with fairies, and she taught me a few songs and words in fairy. The surgeon removed my left eye after a jewel thief sprayed a strong alkaline cleanser into my eyes. Just before we came to Tennessee, the surgeon performed a second surgery on my right eye to clean out some infection and remove some scar tissue. I can see light and vague outlines of people—"

Mary Leigh interrupted, "Blobs."

I snickered. "Yes, Mary Leigh-blob is right. I call the outlines blobs. The eye experts are hopeful that my sight will improve but normal for me won't be the same as your normal eyesight."

"Well, that just stinks," Jessie said. "Except for the Mary Leigh-blob part: that is funny, and the fairy part is downright awesome."

"My eyesight deficiency gets me down sometimes but not for long."

"Anyone want coffee?" Lori asked.

"I've had my quota," Mary Leigh said.

"I didn't have a chance to tell you that your cinnamon rolls were delicious, Mary Leigh. Thank you so much for making them," Jessie said.

Mary Leigh giggled. "The cinnamon rolls were actually the Gray Lady's. I just washed my hands and did what she told me to do."

"Sounds like you're a much better instructor than that buffoon, Sanchez, Maggie," Lori said. "He really irritated me with that opening, but Mary Leigh, how did you know what his topics were?"

"I've been doing a little research on personal safety, and I found a short article provided by a big city police department with the five points that Sanchez quoted. I remembered it because it struck me as particularly inappropriate for me. When his second point was Street Safety, I knew exactly how out of his league he was. He might be a good instructor within his area of expertise, but personal safety isn't included in his toolbox of knowledge."

"I was shocked at how little of his talk related to his audience, but what's up with the adoring fans? Does anyone know?" Jessie asked.

"I have no idea," Lori said. "As soon as word got out that we were planning to host a talk on personal safety, several women, all of whom were sitting at that front-and-center table, called me and suggested Dean Sanchez. It wasn't a total loss, though; at least the four of us found our tribe."

"I have to leave," Jessie said, "but I'll host our next tribal sanity meeting at my place."

"I'll have to spend the rest of the day with my feet up; they look like watermelons," Mary Leigh grumbled as she and I left.

When Palace Guard and I neared the apartment, I abruptly stopped and stared at the car parked in our assigned parking spot.

"Do you think that could be Della's rental car? Seems awfully fast for it to have arrived."

I waited while Palace Guard checked the car; after he returned and nodded, we went into the apartment, and I stared at Della-blob who was mopping the kitchen floor.

"The floor should be dry except for this last area in the kitchen. I thought I could clean this tiny apartment while you were gone, but you came back sooner than I expected. How was Dean Sanchez?"

"Unimaginative and boring," I said.

Della chuckled. "He hasn't changed a bit. He's always had a pompous side, but I'm still convinced he's the killer. I went through all the photos. These are copies of Noreen's photos that I've already seen. She was an absolute fanatic about making copies of anything she thought was important, like photos and letters. She always signed her original photos and put NW on her copies, but she never signed her letters. I once asked her why, and she told me if I ever got a letter from her that was signed, I'd have the signature of a forgery."

She sighed. "She was a talented, strange woman, which is probably why we were friends. It took me a while to examine the pictures because I got lost wandering down memory lane. Noreen wanted to follow Wayne, but I didn't want her out in the sticks alone, and she was a bit of a sissy anyway, so she didn't mind that I tagged along. We followed Wayne for a while. She tried not to get me into too many shots at first, but we decided it didn't matter because it gave me a reminder of where the picture had been taken, so we could compare notes and talk about her photos later. I asked her if we could follow Sanchez too, so we did. The photos are of Wayne and Sanchez at different times. I numbered the pictures on the back with a pencil; 1 for Dean, and 2 for Wayne. Noreen and I always referred to them alphabetically by their first names."

"Thanks, I appreciate it. Would you have time to take me to the town library? I wouldn't mind talking to Ms. Betty in person about Wayne Dillard."

"Good idea, and I'd be interested in where Wayne Dillard was yesterday morning; I've got a little research I'd like to do. Do you have access to Larry's class schedule? If you do, I may be able to check on Dean Sanchez too."

"Sure do." I turned on my computer then logged into the class schedule before I rose from my chair and turned it over to Della.

"Dean Sanchez had two classes to teach Wednesday morning and none yesterday," Della said. "If Sanchez had been a no-show for either class on Wednesday, Larry would know, but it doesn't prove anything except he was on campus Wednesday. Too bad he didn't have any yesterday. As far as his classes are concerned, Sanchez wasn't teaching a class when you were attacked or when I was rammed."

The wind suddenly rose, and rain pelted the window.

"It's raining hard again," I said. "If you're being careful about staying incognito, how were you able to rent your car?"

Della chuckled. "All good FBI undercover folks, even the retired ones, have a few alternate IDs and credit cards; goes with the territory, darlin'. We'll probably have rain all day, off and on. We can still go to the library whenever you like. My clothes should be dry soon."

My phone buzzed a text from Larry: "We're going out to the field. Glad I prepared for the worst cuz it is."

"That's downright slick, honey. I'm amazed at the technology these days."

"It definitely makes a difference in helping me feel less isolated," I said. "After your clothes are dry, I'd like to go to the library. If Larry can brave the cold, wind, and rain of the elements while he's investigating an outdoor crime scene, I should be able to sit in a warm car to go to a warm building."

"Atta girl," Della said. "I'll check my clothes. Do you have anywhere you'd like to go to lunch?"

"I've only been to one place in town, and the food was good."

"We'll go there. I understand you have Chef Daryl's recipes; do you happen to have his Cajun gumbo recipe? Larry might enjoy that after a cold, wet day outside."

"That sounds awesome; does that mean you'll be here for supper?"

"No, after we go to the library and have lunch, I'll stop by the grocery story to pick up whatever we need for gumbo. I'll have to leave for Georgia after I get it on the stove and simmering. All you'll need to do is stir it occasionally, then Larry can make the rice when he gets home. We'll make him work for his supper," Della said.

I pulled up the recipe file on my computer; Della found the Cajun gumbo recipe and printed it then checked the refrigerator before she jotted down her shopping list.

After Della dressed in her clean clothes, she said, "There's nothing like clothes straight from the dryer to warm the soul on a cold, wet day. Wrap up warm; we'll go to the library first."

When we walked into the library, Della said, "I'd recognize Wayne Dillard anywhere; dang, he got old."

She veered off to the historical fiction section as Palace Guard and I hurried to the desk and pressed the left pearl to record audio.

"Hello, Gray Lady," Betty said. "What brings you out on this blustery day?"

"I wanted to thank you for all the audio books and chat when you have time, Ms. Betty."

"You're most welcome; let's go to my office," she said. "I never turn down an opportunity to chat."

After we sat, I turned down the offer of hot tea. "I was wondering about the library policy on concealed weapons. If there's a sign on the door, I couldn't see it."

"All our county buildings have the same policy: no knives, guns, or other weapons are allowed even if the patron has a valid concealed permit."

"That makes sense."

"Of course, we don't have a metal detector or anyone checking people as they come in the door, so we're expecting our patrons, staff, and volunteers to honor the policy. I know many don't, and I don't blame them. In fact, we host a monthly gun safety class here and encourage all our patrons to attend."

"Who teaches the class?" I asked. *I hope it isn't Dean Sanchez.*

"Our local sheriff teaches it; he wants everyone to be safe. I frequently attend the class when I'm not swamped with work because I learn something new every time."

"That's very commendable of him to be concerned about his community."

"He's one of the best we've ever had. The gun safety and yoga classes that we sponsor are our most popular classes."

"I saw Wayne Dillard here today; does he teach any classes? It seems like he must be here all the time."

"He occasionally leads a class on local history that is very well-attended. We have quite a few patrons who are history buffs, and they particularly enjoy Wayne's descriptions of old homesteads and family gravesites that he has come across and documented on the hikes he takes into the backwoods. Wayne always invites one of our elderly patrons to speak, and we're spellbound by the events they've survived. He always serves a tray of crackers and cheese and has a jar of peanut butter for the crackers at his classes. He told me he's worried some of our seniors may be skipping meals. Our patrons love him. I never miss one of Wayne's classes. He's one of our more dedicated volunteers, but he's backed off to only one or two days a week recently. He will probably be here tomorrow. We have a schedule for our volunteers. If they follow it, fine; if they don't, that's fine too."

"That's interesting. Do the volunteers let you know if they aren't going to be here?"

"That's never been a requirement. I want them to be here when they can but not feel obligated. All my volunteers are retired, and I learned long ago that they are independent cusses and would quit if coming to the library started feeling like work."

"How far back do your records go for volunteer attendance?"

Betty cackled. "Only a librarian would even think of that. You've got data in your blood too, don't you, Gray Lady? I've got twenty years' worth on my electronic spreadsheets; before that, I kept paper records, then we had a late season tornado go through one night, and it ripped off the roof. All my records and many of our books were lost or drenched. It was horrible to see, but no one was hurt, so we cleaned up, repaired the roof, and moved on. I'll copy the records to a flash drive and give it to you. It would be too tedious to email. Sit tight; it won't take me long. Are you going to write an article about libraries and volunteers? I'd be happy to beta read or even edit for you if you like."

"Thanks; I've been kicking around different ideas and doing a little research."

I pushed the right pearl and relaxed while Betty copied spreadsheets to a flash drive. After she removed the flash drive, I held out my hand.

"Here you are, dear. I had the spreadsheets in files by year, so I know you have everything. Let me know what else I can do to help you. What are your plans for the rest of the day?"

"I'm going to lunch, then I plan on a serious listening session this afternoon. I have one more book to read, and it's calling me."

"I understand that. I keep a book at the main desk that is my reward when I catch up on my daily tasks."

When I reached the desk, Palace Guard guided me to the front door, and I stopped to zip my coat. "Thanks again for the help."

I stopped on the sidewalk, and Della joined me. "I moved my rental car to a spot that couldn't be seen from the library. Pesky red rental car. I should have told them to give me a camo car. What's the address of that café?"

After I gave her the address, I asked, "What was Wayne Dillard wearing?"

"Should have told you earlier. He wore a long-sleeved white shirt with an oversized, knit sweater over it. He was talking to one of the patrons, so I didn't see any sign of favoring his left arm or side."

When we reached the café, Della said, "I sure 'nuf see why this little café isn't called a diner. Even though it looks comfortable and inviting, I can't see the local farmers gathering here for lunch."

When we went inside, there were already several tables with the customers ordering or eating.

Cassandra-blob hurried to greet us. "Gray Lady, how nice to see you again, and this is…?"

"My Grandma D; she surprised me with a visit, so I thought she'd enjoy coming here for lunch."

"You have a beautiful café," Della said.

"Thank you, it's very nice to meet you. Come right this way." The three of us followed her.

"I have a table that is perfect for you, Gray Lady. It's away from the door and other tables, so there will be less noise to disturb you."

As we sat, she asked, "Would you like coffee or hot tea?"

"Coffee for me," Della said.

"Hot tea, please."

After the owner left, I whispered, "She'll bring me a braille menu. I didn't have the heart to tell her I can't read braille."

"What a kind-hearted woman," Della said. "How can I help?"

"I'd like a side dish that isn't hard for a poorly sighted person to eat without spills."

"Gotcha. I'll scan for one, and you ask for a recommendation."

When the owner returned with our menus, my cup of hot tea, a mug, and a coffee pot, she poured coffee into the mug then said, "We'll give you a few minutes to look over the menu. Do you have any questions?"

"What would you recommend as a good side for me to go with a sandwich? I'm a little nervous about eating anything in public that might not stay on my spoon or fork or might drip on me."

"Chef makes delicious baked sweet potato chips; they'll be easy to pick up and eat and won't be greasy on your fingers. Perfect for you, Gray Lady."

After Cassandra left our table, Della whispered, "I can't find that on the menu, honey. You really are a VIP here, and thanks for introducing me as Grandma D; under the circumstances, it would have been rude to avoid saying my name."

When our server-blob arrived, she said, "Our specials today are vegetable soup with homemade rolls, chili with cornbread, and a grilled ham and double cheese with roasted potato wedges. Both the vegetable soup and chili can also be ordered as sides with any sandwich. Did you have any questions, or are you ready to order?"

Della groaned, and I smiled. "What kind of cheese with the grilled ham and double cheese?"

"It's your choice; we have Swiss, sharp cheddar, pepper jack, and Monterey."

"I'd like half of a grilled ham and double Swiss cheese sandwich and a side of sweet potato chips."

"Yes, ma'am."

"I'll have a grilled ham and cheese with Monterey and pepper jack, and a side of chili."

"Yes, ma'am. I'll put your order right in. Chef said to tell you to save room for dessert." She refilled Della's coffee then left.

"I need to get some certain guy fired or in the slammer, so I can take his job and eat here every day," Della said.

I giggled. "At least you have lofty standards for your motives."

A heavy squall of rain and wind blew in, and a group of four squealed as they hurried inside and brought a new level of noise to the café with them.

"What a downpour," one of the newcomer-blobs said.

I reached into my backpack for my earplugs and inserted them.

"Those look fancy. Do they work well?" Della asked.

"Kate gave them to me because noise bothers me so much. I can hear conversations, but the loud noises are muffled."

Della lowered her voice. "I'm glad you have something that helps you deal with that squawking. They're giving me a headache, and my hearing is shot."

Our server came to our table with another cup of tea. "We thought you'd like more hot tea, Gray Lady. This is peach tea; we hope it chases away any chills for you."

I held onto my hot cup to warm my hands, then the server brought our food.

"The chili smells wonderful."

I bit into my sandwich then tried a sweet potato chip. "This is perfect for a cold day. I think the sweet potato chip has a little spicy heat to it. It's really good."

After we finished eating, the server whisked away our dishes then returned with two plates with slices of pie. "This is Chef's famous chocolate pecan Tennessee bourbon pie. Enjoy."

When Della took a bite, she said, "I'm getting myself put on the instructor list first thing after I get home. Can you believe this pie?"

I was too busy eating to answer.

Della snagged the bill before I could. After she paid, she said, "Thank goodness it's raining because I know you'd insist that we run to town."

I hid my smile behind my hand, and Palace Guard grinned. "Not funny," I mouthed behind Della's back.

"Yes, it was, and you thought so too because you smiled," Della said.

I pulled up my hood before we hurried to the red car. Palace Guard helped me in while Della jumped in to start the engine.

After she parked as closely as she could at the grocery store, Della said, "I'll leave the engine running to keep you from freezing. I won't be long."

Della dashed for the entrance, and I pushed the button to lock all the doors.

"Dean Sanchez forgot to mention it's important to lock the car doors if the engine's running, and no one is in the driver's seat," I said then pushed the pearl on the left side of my jo.

"Wayne Dillard was at the library, so I asked about him. He was wearing a long-sleeved white shirt with an oversized, knit sweater over it. He was talking to one of the patrons, so he didn't give any indication of favoring his left arm or side. Palace Guard identified the man who has been following me: it's Dean Sanchez." I pushed the pearl on the right.

I unlocked the doors when Della splashed across the parking lot as she hurried to the car during a lull in the downpour.

After she pulled out of the parking lot, she said, "I'm going to have to stuff my poor boots with paper to dry them out. We'll heat up that little apartment with the aroma of spicy gumbo to knock out the wet boot smell."

After we were inside the apartment, Della stuffed her boots with packing paper that Ella had neatly folded and placed on a top shelf of the pantry then emptied her grocery sack.

"What can I do?" I asked.

"Keep me company while I cook," she said. "I'll get the roux going first then chop the celery, onion, and fresh parsley leaves then slice the okra."

"I don't think I've ever tried okra. Everybody says it's slimy."

"It is if it's not cooked right." Della stirred the roux in the large stew pot. "I found smoked sausage stuffed with jalapenos and cheddar cheese. It might not be exactly what Chef Daryl had in mind, but I'm sure he'd approve."

"I think he would too."

CHAPTER SEVENTEEN

"Next up is chicken then the sausage." Della continued to stir the roux while she diced the chicken then browned it and added it to the sliced okra in the bowl. After she sliced and browned the sausage and added it to the chicken, she set the bowl with the okra and the meat in the refrigerator.

"After I add the vegetables, chicken stock, and some spices to the roux, I'll set a timer for one hour; at the end of the hour, you stir in the meat and okra and set a timer on your phone for another hour. Let the pot simmer uncovered and stir once in a while. If you hear it bubbling, turn down the heat."

"Wow; that's easy."

"It really is. The hardest part of the recipe is making the roux because it takes thirty to forty-five minutes of constant stirring until it develops a silky chestnut color. The rest of the recipe is easy: stir occasionally then after an hour, add something and repeat."

"I could stir the roux, but I'd need someone else to tell me when it was the right color."

"Won't be long until you'll be able to see; I can feel it in my bones. My boots are mostly dry; they can finish drying while I drive. Depending on the traffic, I'll be in Atlanta before dark."

I put two Jennifer cookies into a sack. "Here are some cookies for the road."

"You are a sweetheart. Now remember, let me know if you have any more questions about Noreen, Sanchez, or Wayne. I'm checking in with the GBI in Atlanta, and I may be back this way in a couple of weeks, but you can call or text me anytime."

After Della left, I inserted the flash drive then dropped the files on the shared cloud drive Heather set up for me. I pressed the left pearl on my jo and said, "files are on Gray."

As I clicked the right pearl, my phone buzzed a text from Paul. "Got them."

My phone rang and announced the caller, "Campus Library."

"Happy Friday, Gray Lady, this is Lily. How are you doing?"

"Just fine; I'm staying warm, which is my goal for today."

Lily tittered. "A very worthy goal. I believe I'll put it on my list too. My friend at the Nashville library called me; she came across some letters that Noreen Weber Dillard wrote but never mailed. She thought you might be interested in the letters because she found some references to the photos. I told her to send them on. Are you interested? I should get them on Monday or Tuesday."

"I'm very interested."

"I'll call you when I get them. My friend is planning to visit me next month and wants me to arrange for the three of us to go to lunch, if you're interested and available."

"I'd love it. Did she know Olivia Chandler Edwards too? I'd love to hear more about Olivia sometime."

"She did. We could spend an entire afternoon telling you of our escapades. We always said Olivia brought out our wild side, but she claimed she was only the innocent bystander." Lily chuckled. "We should include Ms. Betty too; her stories are always amazing, and her stories about Olivia are very insightful. I'll talk to you early next week. Be safe."

After we hung up, Palace Guard raised his eyebrows.

"Interesting news, isn't it? I'm excited to learn more about Olivia."

I rose to go to the stove, and Palace Guard stayed by my side. When I stirred the gumbo, Spike crowded close and inhaled, so I inhaled too.

"Mmm. This smells good; it definitely reminds me of Chef Daryl's kitchen."

I returned to my computer to check the schedules for classes that Dean Sanchez had taught then banged my fist on the table. "I can't read the schedules, and I don't know enough about how to search by listening. I hate not being able to read." I slammed my computer shut and crossed my arms to pout.

Palace Guard tapped my shoulder then pointed at Spike, who stood with his feet wide apart and his stomach pushed out. When he patted his stomach, I laughed. "You guys win. Why be crabby when I could be creative? I'll see how Mary Leigh is feeling."

When Mary Leigh answered her phone, I asked, "How are you doing?"

"Much better, but don't tell my doctor because when she told me to put my feet up once in a while, I didn't realize she meant it literally. I thought she was saying to take it easy or relax once in a while. Do you have a job for me? Can we hurt Dean Sanchez now?"

I smiled. "Yep, you're better. I need to know when Dean Sanchez taught classes over the past five years. I have access to research it through Larry's class schedule, but I became really frustrated when I tried to research by listening."

"That's wonderful; oh, that didn't sound right. I didn't mean it's wonderful that you can't read or that you were frustrated. You can't read, and I can't listen; no, that sounds negative. You listen; I'll read. Got it."

She hung up, and I laughed. "Mary Leigh hung up on me, and she's on it."

I held up my hand, and Spike and Palace Guard smacked it.

"Sounds like the rain's stopped; we should probably go out while we can."

When I put on my heavy coat, Lucy trotted to the back door then the four of us went outside. A wind gust blew cold air down the neck of my coat in the back, and I took off my gloves to button the top button. I shivered as I put on my gloves to thaw my fingers. I frowned at the engine sound of a car that crept toward our apartment. Palace Guard disappeared around the corner, and I listened while the car continued past ours and stopped at another apartment farther down the row. When a car door slammed, he returned, and I exhaled.

"Am I being too paranoid?"

Palace Guard shook his head.

When Lucy headed toward the back door, I hurried to open the door for her. "I agree, girl; it's time to warm up."

After we were inside, I stirred the gumbo. "I probably don't need to stir it as often as I have, but it's a great excuse to stand near the warm stove."

When the timer went off, I jumped. "I forgot about the timer." Palace Guard pointed to a button on the stove; when I pushed it the beep stopped.

"Thanks." I emptied the bowl with the meat and okra into the pot and stirred then said, "Set timer for sixty minutes."

I grabbed my phone and kicked off my boots before I sat on the sofa with my feet up. "Mary Leigh had the right idea. I was wearing out."

My phone buzzed a text then said, "From Larry: Back from field. Wet and cold. It was great."

Spike did his wacky dance, and Palace Guard and I laughed. "Larry's a natural, isn't he? Only a die-hard crime scene investigator would say it was great being out in weather like this."

My phone rang and announced, "Call from Mary Leigh."

"Hi, that was fast," I said.

"Don't give me that much credit. Did you hear from Kevin? Ron was obviously in his element today. My interpretation is that they played in the mud and pretended it was work. One of the moms in my moms' group asked if anyone wanted half a carrot cake. She'll order up to three cakes. What did you have planned for supper? I was thinking of taking out the lasagna that Mom made from the freezer, but it's too big for the two of us. We love leftovers, but by the fourth day, we're tired of it. Want to come here for supper?"

"Why don't you come here and bring your cake? I have gumbo simmering on the stove and have been stirring it all afternoon."

"You made gumbo? Does Kevin know? Now, I understand why he worries about leaving you alone; you're scaring me."

I chuckled. "I didn't go reckless on you; an old friend of the family stopped by to see me and made a big pot of gumbo before she left. It's been my job to stir it every hour or so, and I'm not sure, but it feels like there's enough for at least four more meals."

"Did your mom ask her to check up on you? My mom has done the exact same thing; in fact, I suspect one of my aunts will show up any time now. Did she tell you she just happened to stop by on her way to Cleveland? That's what one of my aunts from Atlanta said one time after Ron and I were newlyweds and living in Savannah." She giggled. "I'm glad my sense of geography isn't as bad as hers. We'll come have gumbo and bring cake after Ron cleans off that mud and thaws out with a hot shower. We'll see you around five thirty or six."

After we hung up, I said, "Mary Leigh is bringing carrot cake for dessert. It sounds like a celebration of sorts, and maybe it is. First week of crime scene investigation and new friends. I love how Larry always finds his guys."

When my phone rang again, it announced, "Phone call from Mother."

I rolled my eye. "Hello, Mother. How are you and Sarge doing?"

When she started speaking, I held the phone away from my ear because her voice was so loud. *She must not be wearing her hearing aids.*

"Margaret, We're in Utah. Big D wants to buy a small cattle ranch and raise beef and yak, so we're going to work at one of his friend's ranch for a month. Actually, he's going to work on the ranch, and I'm going to take pottery lessons. They've got an RV hookup for us, so we can sleep in our own bed. We'll have meals with the family, and I'll be getting cooking lessons while I help with the meals. Did you ever think I'd be living on a cattle ranch in Utah?"

"Actually, Mother—"

"I know; neither did I. We're having grilled yak steak and mashed potatoes for dinner tonight. It's a good thing Big D and I love potatoes because they're served at almost every meal. I'll learn how to make potato rolls tomorrow. How are you and Larry doing?"

"We're fine; Larry likes his classes, and we have new friends here."

"That's nice; I'm glad you're finally making friends, Margaret, because you were always such a loner."

She hung up, and I chuckled.

"I can always count on Mother to hang up on me; sounds like she and Sarge are enjoying life, doesn't it? I never thought of Mother as a good cook or an adventuresome eater, but I probably never paid attention to what she cooked. I ate a small portion of everything that was put in front of me then dashed away from the table to work on my latest spy research."

I leaned back and closed my eyes but opened them when Lucy nosed me. Spike grinned as he stood next to Lucy, and Palace Guard smiled.

"You guys got Lucy to wake me up?" I grumbled.

Palace Guard made a stirring motion with his hand.

"Sorry, I woke up cranky."

When Spike grinned and elbowed Palace Guard, I rolled my eye.

"Okay I have a correction: sorry Lucy woke up cranky." I snickered. "Thanks for waking me up; I'd feel awful if I let the gumbo stick to the pot and burn."

I stirred the gumbo and scraped the bottom of the pot, just in case. "Good news: nothing stuck. What time is it?"

Palace Guard held up five fingers.

"Larry should be home any time, now." I shivered with excitement when I heard his truck roll down the road and park at our apartment.

When Larry came into the apartment, he rushed to me and grabbed me into his bear hug, and I snuggled against him as he whispered, "I missed you, sweetie."

"I'm glad you're home." I wrapped my arms around him.

When he shivered, I said, "Get into a warm shower before you become hypothermic."

"Will do, just as soon as you tell me what I smell," Larry nibbled on my ear then kissed my neck.

I giggled and reflexively raised my shoulder to protect my neck from being tickled. "It's gumbo, Mr. Sexy Pants; I'm glad you're home. You're freezing me; get in the shower."

"Yes, ma'am." Larry kissed me then patted my bottom before he headed to the bathroom.

After his shower, Larry came out of the bedroom; he had changed to a red plaid flannel shirt and clean jeans, and I smiled. *My man belongs in the woods.*

"Della made the gumbo before she left, but I've been in charge of stirring it," I said. "I invited Mary Leigh and Ron to eat with us."

Larry strode to the stove and peered into the pot. "Our apartment smells like Chef Daryl's kitchen; it must be one of Chef Daryl's recipes. What do I do?"

"After Mary Leigh and Ron arrive, we can start the rice. Mary Leigh's bringing carrot cake for dessert."

"That sounds great, so tell me what I need to know about your day," Larry said.

"Mother and Sarge are in Utah and will be living on a cattle ranch for a month. Sarge wants to buy a small cattle ranch and raise beef and yak."

Larry laughed. "There is no way I could have guessed that."

I giggled. "I thought they were in Arizona."

"What about your progress on the Ghost of Wicked Hollow?"

I sighed. "It's hard not to think that the killer really is a ghost. He's been very elusive for at least twenty years from my point of view. Della and Noreen Dillard tracked both Dean Sanchez and Wayne Dillard. Della was certain that Dean Sanchez was the killer, and Noreen was worried that Wayne was. I have copies of some of the photos that Noreen took of both men, and Della is in most of them. Unfortunately, they never came to a point where they could prove the innocence or guilt of either man."

"What was your impression of Dean Sanchez from the morning's discussion on personal safety?"

"He's pompous and clueless when it comes to personal safety."

Larry snorted. "I take it he won't be invited back by the Wives' Group to speak again."

"He has a small group of avid supporters, but you're right. Mary Leigh wants to hurt him, and I'm still mulling it over."

Palace Guard scowled, and Larry chuckled. "Please don't unless Palace Guard gives you the okay."

Palace Guard smirked, and I scowled, but before I could complain, Ron knocked at the door.

As he strode to the door, Larry said, "There's more, isn't there?"

"Yes."

When they came inside, Mary Leigh and I sat together on the sofa while Ron set the carrot cake in the refrigerator, and Larry started the rice.

"Your apartment smells amazing. I think this baby likes gumbo, he gave me a hard kick when we came inside," Mary Leigh said.

"Your mom would have a fit if you have a baby with a taste for Cajun food," Ron said.

"It's spicy and a rice dish; we may be able to squeak that past her. Dad will help; he'll tell her at least it isn't a cheeseburger."

While we ate, Larry and Ron talked about the afternoon, argued about their conclusions, and continued their discussion while Ron served the carrot cake.

Mary Leigh and I moved to the sofa while Ron cleared dishes, and Larry loaded the dishwasher and divided the leftover gumbo into two-serving portions in a container to freeze, a container to be warmed up for tomorrow night's supper, and a bowl for Ron and Mary Leigh to take home.

While Larry finished putting away the containers and bowl with Ron's help, I whispered, "Wait for it."

Larry strode to the sofa and asked, "Sweetie, would you mind if Ron and I spend a little time at the library this evening? We've got a few things we need to research before tomorrow's study group."

"That's fine. Mary Leigh and I have a few things to catch up on too."

After they left, Mary Leigh giggled. "How did you know?"

"I'm an extremely astute wife, in addition to the fact that they did rock, paper, scissors to decide who would ask if they could go to the library."

"I've been bursting to tell you that I finished checking Dean Sanchez's schedule. Five years ago, he taught one class the first term then nothing the rest of the year, and that has been the pattern every year. Another instructor teaches the same class the entire year, so Dean Sanchez may be filling in at the first of every year when the number of students is greater."

"He may well be the source of his reputation for being a wonderful instructor," I said.

"Yes, and the new students don't care because they're grateful to be here and are taking advantage of the library and other resources to expand their knowledge."

"That really makes sense, especially with their willingness to share what they've learned with each other."

"I have a spread sheet with the dates and times of Sanchez's classes for the past five years. It wasn't hard to pull together at all. I sent it to you. This digging into details is fun. What else have you got?"

"That's an easy answer: I don't know."

"If you need a little time to analyze what you have, I'll be happy to put up my feet and rest my eyes."

"I need a little break time too; I'd love to listen to a book that I'm about halfway through. I'll let you know if I come up with any ideas."

After I rose, Mary Leigh-blob put up her feet, and before I reached my computer, her even, slow breathing became a light snore. I smiled as I put on my headphones then found the email from Mary

Leigh and forwarded the spreadsheet to Paul with a note that included what Mary Leigh had said.

Paul replied, "Good work; very helpful. I have some names of attempted kidnapping victims. There are only a few, and they don't quite meet our pattern. I'll send them to you."

I listened to his email again while Palace Guard read over my shoulder.

"How do we find any unreported, unsuccessful kidnapping attempts?" I whispered as I removed my headset.

Palace Guard frowned then shrugged.

I put on my headset and said, "How to estimate unreported kidnapping attempts."

I rolled my eye as I listened to all the irrelevant articles my search browser recommended in its unsuccessful attempt to find anything about how to estimate unreported kidnapping attempts. I shook my head. *How ironic.*

I was ready to quit until I came to an article written by a private security consultant that discussed a specific topic of unreported kidnappings: kidnap for ransom and release. Palace Guard had wandered away, but I motioned for him to read as the consultant discussed personal safety and how to avoid being a target.

At the end of the article, I removed my headset. "The most interesting point that caught my attention was that the consultant said almost all of the kidnap for ransom cases occurred outside because the kidnapper studies their routines. We may have some useful information about our unreported failed kidnappings by looking at the successful kidnappings that we do know about."

Palace Guard nodded.

"Paul's going to retire after we're done, isn't he?"

Palace Guard grinned as I picked up my phone and sent a text to Paul. "Where are the victims that we do know about kidnapped? Indoors or outdoors?"

My phone buzzed a text. "From Paul: where do you come up with this stuff? On it."

I snickered, and Palace Guard nodded.

We can at least get a better idea of whether our kidnapper has a preference, and it might give us a better hint of his personality.

I stretched and turned off my computer before I sat in the soft chair and closed my eyes as I listened to Mary Leigh's soft snore.

I woke when I heard Larry's voice as he strolled across the street to our apartment. "I'm glad we cleared up that ambiguity before tomorrow's study session," he said. "We just saved ourselves from listening to two hours of arguing among the guys."

He unlocked the door, and I was waiting for him. I grabbed him into a hug and whispered, "You've been ambushed."

He laughed, and Mary Leigh woke up. "What did I miss? What's funny?"

Ron chuckled. "I think you missed an ambush. It was so fast, I almost missed it myself." Ron joined Mary Leigh on the sofa as she sat up. "It was a brilliant idea to research tonight before the study session tomorrow. There were too many open-ended questions that could have derailed us if we hadn't spent a little time to nail down the details. Ready to go home, honey?"

Mary Leigh yawned. "It must be past my bedtime."

Ron nodded as he helped her with her coat. Larry gave him the bowl of gumbo, then Ron and Mary Leigh left.

"What time is it?" I asked as I moved to the sofa.

"You were smart to wait until after they left to ask: it's eight thirty," Larry said.

"I thought it might be a little early when Ron didn't say anything."

"How would you like a beer or hot tea with crackers and cheese? You can tell me the rest of what you haven't told me yet."

"Hot tea sounds good. While you were studying, I tried to research unreported kidnapping attempts."

Larry turned on the kettle. "Because unreported kidnapping attempts could be the killer's failures."

"Yes, but I didn't find anything except an excellent article by a private security consultant on kidnapping for ransom. I hadn't stopped to think how many types of kidnapping there are."

Larry chuckled while he brewed my tea. "Only my sweetie would be excited to learn about the different types of kidnapping."

I smirked. "And only my Mr. Sexy Pants would know that I was."

"True, so tell me what you really learned."

"Most kidnappings for ransom occur outside, so I've asked Paul to check where the victims were kidnapped."

Larry handed me my cup of tea and set the plate of cheese and crackers on the table. "I'm really dry; I'll have a glass of water. Can rain dehydrate a person?"

"I wouldn't think so, but I'm sure the cold and wind could."

Larry sat next to me. "If all the victims were kidnapped while they were outside, we'll finally have a pattern for the killer. He's stalking them to learn their routine, then he's picking his best time and place to snatch them."

I nodded. "If most of them were taken while indoors, then their kidnapper was at least an acquaintance."

Larry leaned closer to me and kissed me. "Sometimes I feel like my sexy, naked Maggie is also my private tutor. You are absolutely brilliant."

"What's your plan for tomorrow?"

"Our Saturday study session is at nine. Since Ron and I are prepared, we don't have to go in early. We may want to do that every Friday evening after supper."

"Whatever you need to do is great with me, but you know that."

I kissed him, and he stroked my hair and kissed my eye. "You'll be well soon, but meanwhile, you are still a force. I love you, sweetie."

One tear after another rolled down my face. "It's hard sometimes to deal with not being able to see. I love you so much; I can't imagine what I'd do without you."

Larry brushed away my tears then took me into his arms and rocked me while I cried. "I know, honey; I know."

* * *

I woke the next morning in Larry's arms and snuggled closer.

"Good morning, cutie," Larry said.

I giggled. "You're still in bed with me; what a nice surprise. Is it cold?"

"It sure is. I was going to get up to make coffee, but you held me down."

"I'm a terrible person." I buried my face in his chest.

"And a terrible influence to boot." He chuckled as he rubbed my back. "I'll be brave and get the coffee going. You can stay here where it's warm, and I'll bring you a cup. We need an automatic coffee maker that I can set up the night before."

"Sounds like a shopping trip to me."

After Larry dressed and left the bedroom, I stepped into my slippers and grabbed my jo then stopped at our closet to dress. When I hurried to the kitchen, the coffee was perking.

"Coffee will be ready soon, sweetie. I thought you'd stay in bed."

"It got cold when you left."

"Blueberry pancakes okay for breakfast?"

"Oh, yes."

Lucy padded to the back door and nosed the door. "I'll let you out, Lucy, but I'm staying inside," I said.

When I opened the door, Spike followed Lucy. I watched them while Lucy took her bio break then hurried to the back door. When I opened it, she dashed inside with Spike behind her. "You're a good man, Spike."

Spike blushed, but I pretended not to notice as I dished up Lucy's food and put it on her mat for her.

When Larry's phone rang, he answered it then frowned. "I thought we said nine o'clock."

He listened then glanced at me. "I can be there after we've eaten breakfast."

CHAPTER EIGHTEEN

After he hung up, Larry said, "One of the guys wants to start early. He's struggling with the material. We've all got areas where we're weak, but he can't seem to get a grasp on any of it. I haven't quite figured out if it's because it's over his head or if he's stressed. What do you think about going with me to listen to him? Your insight will help me determine how I can help him."

"I'd be happy to go with you."

After Larry made our pancakes, he buttered mine and cut it into small pieces for me then drizzled syrup over it in a slow stream to let it soak in.

While we ate, Larry told me what he knew about the man we'd be meeting at the library. "He's been in law enforcement for three years, so he's not a rookie, but he's still pretty new. He's been married less than a year. He said his wife is shy; she didn't come to the meet and greet with him, and she didn't attend the Wives' Group yesterday."

"Do my shirt and my eyepatch match?" I asked.

"No, but they usually don't; do you want me to find the patch that matches your shirt?"

"No, I don't want to look too fashion conscious."

"You definitely have that covered, sweetie."

"Good. I'll be ready to go in five minutes; no, make it ten. I didn't brush my hair."

"Get ready, then I'll brush your hair."

On our way to the library, I asked, "Did I meet...what's the name of the guy we're going to help?"

"Justin; I don't think you met him at the meet and greet. He didn't stay very long."

"I've got an idea. You can ask me how I'm doing after you and Justin talk for a while. If I say I'm okay, then Justin's okay. If I tell you I'm wearing out, he's not doing so great, and I can tell you why."

"That's great, and if I forget?" Larry asked.

"You're on your own." I giggled.

When we were in the library, Larry found Justin. "This is my wife, Maggie. She's going to join us, if you don't mind."

"That's fine; nice to meet you, Maggie."

I smiled. "You too."

The three of us sat at a table, and I listened while Justin asked Larry questions. Justin was initially a little hesitant, but as their discussion continued, he warmed up.

After Larry and Justin solved one of the problems that Justin said stumped him, Larry looked at his notes and said, "Glad we went through that; I had it wrong."

I kicked Larry under the table; when he glared at me, I smiled, and his eyes widened.

"Are you doing okay, sweetie?"

"I'm fine."

"Maggie, my wife is here too. I know she'd love to meet you."

I glanced at Larry, who shrugged.

"That sounds great. I'd like to meet her too."

Justin-blob left then returned. "Maggie, this is my wife, Tonya."

I held out my hand. "Nice to meet you, Tonya."

Her handshake was firm, and I smiled.

"I have a table to myself. Would you like to join me?" she asked.

Palace Guard and Larry stared at her.

"That sounds great. Can I take your elbow?"

"Of course."

She helped me find her blob-elbow, then we strolled to a small table around a corner. She pulled out a chair. "You could sit here, if you like."

I touched the chair back then sat, and she sat across the table from me.

"My sweet Justin tells everyone that I'm shy. I have been nervous lately because I have had this feeling that someone is following me, but I actually am extremely hard of hearing and wear hearing aids. It's hard for me to make friends because I can't bear to be in crowds; the noise is more than I can handle, but if I turn down my hearing aids, I can't hear what anyone is saying."

"Wow, I can't take the noise of crowds very long either, but it's because my hearing has become so sensitive since I lost my sight."

"Really? I've been hearing impaired since birth. When did you lose your sight?"

I told her about being attacked and the surgeries.

"I've never thought about it before, but I'm not sure which impairment is worse," Tonya said. "Being impaired but never knowing any difference or becoming impaired and knowing what you're missing."

"That's an interesting question. Worthy of a beer and feet up discussion, don't you think?"

Tonya giggled. "Preferably in front of a fireplace with our husbands cooking dinner."

I smiled. "Now that's a picture I could focus on."

"I didn't have many friends when I was a kid; only an imaginary dragon, and she was my best friend; she still comes around once in a while, but she really is shy. Is the Palace Guard next to you your imaginary friend?"

I looked at Palace Guard, and he gaped at Tonya.

"I'm sorry; should I not have said anything?" Tonya asked.

"We were just surprised because not very many people can see him."

"Their loss." Tonya smiled, and Palace Guard beamed.

"You're right; he's my imaginary friend."

"Justin can see my Kiki; can Kevin see your Palace Guard?"

"Yes, he can. Do you have any idea how strange this conversation is?"

"Yes, and it's also why I don't have many friends. When someone talks to me in a rude way, Kiki pretends she is wounded by their words and reels then drops to the floor and plays dead; unfortunately, I laugh."

I giggled, and Palace Guard grinned. "I'm afraid I'd laugh too."

"Here you are." Lily came to our table. "Kevin told me you were here. We had a little mix-up in our communication; Nashville sent the letters to me by email, not postal mail, as I expected. I'll forward them to you right away. It's a good day to be inside and read letters, isn't it?"

"Yes, ma'am; thank you so much," I said.

After Lily left, I said, "Guess I'll need to go home to my computer. Would you like to go along? It will be terribly boring because I'll put on my headset and listen to the letters with my text to speech software."

Tonya snickered. "Are you sure? I can't think of anything more wonderful than reading a book while a friend listens to letters."

"Let's check in with our men then go."

"You don't need to take my arm, do you?"

"Nope." I held my jo in front of me, and Palace Guard tapped my arm.

"Awesome." Tonya followed us.

I stopped at the table where Larry worked. "Tonya and I are going to the apartment, so she can read in a quiet place, and I can check my email."

Larry smiled. "Good."

After we were in the apartment, Tonya-blob stopped at the door. "What a pretty dog. Another imaginary man, Maggie?"

I glanced at Spike who stared at Tonya with his mouth open.

"That's Spike. Spike, Tonya can see you and Palace Guard; I think it's because she had an imaginary dragon when she was a child, and she still sees her dragon. It's like she has an eye for imaginary."

Spike nodded.

"Do you have any more imaginary men, Maggie?" Tonya asked.

"No, just the two."

"I just have Kiki, but she's more than enough." Tonya sat on the sofa, and Lucy and Spike joined her.

I signed onto my email then listened to Noreen's letters while Palace Guard read over my shoulder.

I peered at Tonya who was engrossed in her book before I said softly, "Noreen told Della that she found a failure that cleared #1 before she talked about the plans for a new café in town. Could that be Cassandra?"

Palace Guard nodded.

I turned off my computer and called the café. "Hi, it's Maggie. Is the offer still open to come by before you open?"

Cassandra laughed. "What's wrong, Gray Lady? That diner grease in your bloodstream bothering you?"

I chuckled. "You know it."

"Of course, come see us. Do you have transportation? I could send someone for you if you like."

"I think I could find a ride."

"Tonya," I said, but Tonya didn't answer.

I moved to the soft chair then spoke in a loud, clear voice. "Tonya."

"I was really immersed. Have you been trying to get my attention for a while?"

I smiled. "Not at all. I need to go to a café in town to talk to a friend. Shall I walk with you back to the library?"

"How are you going to get there? Were you going to call a cab?"

"My friend offered to have someone come get me."

"Do you mind if I tag along? I'm perfectly safe to drive, and Justin and Kevin will be busy until lunch."

I furrowed my brow. "Are you sure? I hate to cause you to change your Saturday plans."

Tonya giggled. "What plans could I have?"

"If you're sure…"

"I'll send Justin a text, then we can go to my apartment and pick up my purse. Palace Guard will go with us too, right?"

I nodded.

As we walked to her apartment, she asked, "Does Spike usually stay with Lucy? He seems like a kind-hearted man."

I snorted, and Palace Guard rolled his eyes.

"Wrong first impression?" she giggled.

"He taught me to fight dirty and to cheat, but he does have a soft spot in his heart for Lucy."

"Do I turn down my hearing aids while we're there?"

"There shouldn't be too much background noise, so I think you can leave them on normal conversation. We're going to Cassandra's Café. I can tell you the address."

"I know exactly where it is; I memorized the local area streets and businesses. Justin thought I was being silly, but he didn't say anything. I like to know where I am, and where I'm going; I rely very heavily on my sight."

After we were in the car, Tonya sighed. "The worst part of only one car for me is trying to get this seat close enough to reach the pedals; the worst part for Justin is when I forget to put the seat back for him."

On our way, I said, "Ms. Cassandra is sensitive to disabilities. She has a braille menu and seated me away from the crowd, so the noise wouldn't bother me," I said.

"Wow. That's really rare."

When we reached the café, Tonya parked in front, then Palace Guard guided me up the curb to the café. I tapped on the door, and Cassandra-blob opened it. "This is such a treat. Welcome, Gray Lady and …" Cassandra gasped.

"Cassandra, this is my friend, Tonya."

"Nice to meet you, Tonya." Cassandra spoke in a clear voice.

She noticed Tonya's hearing aids.

"You too, Ms. Cassandra. This is the most beautiful café I have ever seen."

"Thank you. Would you like a tour of the kitchen? Chef will be happy to explain how it's set up for efficiency."

"I'd love it," Tonya said. "I might need Chef to speak slowly, though, so I can understand."

"We'll see what Chef can do." Cassandra chuckled.

Odd thing to say.

I walked with Tonya as we followed Cassandra to the kitchen. When we stepped inside, Chef-blob raised her hands in front of her and said, "Welcome."

Tonya gasped and moved her hands. "You signed. Thank you. How did you know?"

Chef-blob pointed to her ear, and Tonya laughed.

"Shall we leave these two chatterboxes?" Cassandra twittered.

After we were in the dining room, I said, "Now I understand why you were so excited to see Tonya. She told me she has a hard time making friends because of her hearing impairment, but she and Chef bonded instantly."

"Exactly as I had hoped when I saw Tonya. Chef doesn't make friends easily either and for the same reason as Tonya. Chef prefers to hide in her kitchen."

"Coffee?" Cassandra poured two cups then we sat together at a table. "Tell me why you really wanted to see me."

"Am I that transparent?" I asked.

"No, but I've been a Gray Lady student for years. You don't do anything casually."

I nodded. "I have letters that Noreen Weber wrote. She mentioned that one of the failures of a murderer that she was tracking was related to a new café in town."

"That's an odd concept. The failure of a murderer."

"It is, isn't it? I'd never thought of it until someone who knew Noreen Weber well told me to look for the failures not the successes."

"The failure of a murderer would be a survivor," Cassandra said softly.

"Yes, and I also came across the phrase unreported kidnappings in reference to ransoms, but why wouldn't other types of kidnappings also be unreported?"

"Especially in the case of a failure," Cassandra added.

"Yes."

"I said I've followed your career but to see your brilliance in action is almost terrifying."

"Scares me too sometimes," I said.

"I did get a little overdramatic there, didn't I?" Cassandra said, and we giggled.

"You're right. I was one of the murderer's failures. I'm really sorry I can't tell you who he was, but I can tell you that he took me to a shack in the hills not too far from here near a road. I can give you the GPS coordinates because I've driven past it many times. I've been trying to get up the nerve to burn it down, but the idea of getting close to it is terrifying." She exhaled.

"He grabbed me when I went on my regular evening walk and tossed me into his trunk. After we were out of town on a secluded back road, he pulled me out of the trunk, and I screamed and tried to fight him; I even bit him when he put his hand over my mouth. He knocked me down and beat me while he screamed at me for being depressed and ranted that my fiancé would commit suicide because of me. I tried to protect my head with my arms, so I never got a good look at him."

"Were you engaged?"

"At the time, yes. When I woke up, I had tape over my eyes, and my wrists and ankles were tied. I heard rats..." Cassandra's voice wavered. "I was terrified, but I kept hoping the rats would chew the ropes, and I would be loose. Crazy, I know. I scooted around the floor and found a nail sticking out. I tried to hook the nail to cut or pull away the ropes, but I pulled the nail out."

Cassandra rose and refilled our coffee then paced to the front of the café and back. After she resumed her seat, she said, "This part is gross. I became sick at my stomach and vomited. I rolled through the vomit over and over and finally slicked up my arms and wrists enough to slip out of the ropes that were around my wrists. I ripped the tape off my eyes then crawled and slid out of the shack into the woods before I freed my legs. I had no idea where I was, but I had to get away from the shack. For all I know, I walked around it all night. When the sun came up, I was so overcome that I survived the night, that I ran wildly and blindly then collapsed. When I woke, I was next to a stream. The weather was mild, thank goodness. I washed myself the best I could in the stream. I was terrified the killer would find me, but I was terrified to move because he might find me. I lay motionless in the bushes for what seemed like hours."

She paced again, and I rose from my chair. Palace Guard patted my shoulder.

"Sorry, I'm making you nervous too," Cassandra said. "Noreen Weber found me and took me to her cabin. I showered; she fed me then drove me to my home. No one knew I'd been gone all night except my fiancé, and he became enraged because he was positive I'd gone to a bar and had been out all night on a last fling before our wedding. I broke the engagement and threw him out. I've always been grateful for seeing what a jerk he was before we were married. After that, I spent two years hunting for that shack to destroy it. When I finally found it..." Cassandra sighed. "I'll text the coordinates to you."

"What a terrifying story. You must have suffered from the trauma for years."

"I adjusted on the outside, but on the inside, I was always on hyperalert and always will be until the killer is stopped."

"Thank you. I know it has to be hard to talk about, even now."

"Yes; I wish I could tell you something about the killer that could help you."

"What did he taste like? When you bit him, what did he taste like?"

"I started to say salty because he was sweaty, but it was not quite salty; it was kind of sweet."

"What did he smell like?" I asked.

"Sour-sweet."

"Were his hands soft or rough?"

"Soft. I hadn't thought about any of these things. If you'd asked if I could describe him, I would have said no."

"Who else did you tell about your ordeal besides Noreen?"

"Nobody."

"Wrong," I said.

"Fine, smarty pants, who did I tell?" Cassandra's voice rose in volume.

I leaned back and smiled.

Cassandra grumbled, "You're no fun. I can't argue with a smiling, sight-impaired woman. You have the unfair advantage of being the Gray Lady."

"You were saying?" I asked.

"I'm trying to maintain my composure. You're not helping." Cassandra cleared her throat. "I told a woman who said she was undercover and was investigating the killer. She told me she overheard my ex-fiancé brag in a bar that he dumped me because I'd been out all night and looked awful when I came home. She didn't ask the questions that you did, but she told me no one would ever know I'd said anything."

"She told you the truth. There are absolutely no records of you or your attack."

"She was killed."

I shook my head. "I'm sorry; I really appreciate your help because I'm going to stop the killer."

"I believe you. Shall we interrupt Tonya and Chef? I have a feeling they could go all day, and I'd have a café full of sad, starving people."

I chuckled. "Let's go in together; there is safety in numbers."

When we went into the kitchen, the Tonya and Chef blobs seemed to deflate when they saw us, and I bit my lip to keep from laughing.

On our way back to our apartments, Tonya said, "I could have stayed there all day. Chef had so many interesting stories about learning her craft with a hearing deficiency. She has hearing aids, but she never wears them to work. She said it helps her to focus on cooking, and everyone knows she can't hear them, so they don't bother her."

"I'm having trouble thinking of what might be the downside," I said.

Tonya giggled. "Absolutely."

"Where are you going to park?"

"I'll drop you off then park the car at home before I go back to the library."

"Park your car, then we can walk together to the library. I'll need to let Larry know I'm back."

"Is he a worrier? Justin's a worrier. Thank you so much for this morning, Maggie. I had a wonderful time."

"I'm sorry the Wives' Club is too much for you, but I understand completely. Maybe a smaller group might work out better for you."

"Maybe; I'll have to think about it."

After Tonya parked, she said, "Just a second. I want to grab a warmer coat."

While she was gone, I pulled out my phone and sent a text to Della. "Was #1's wife undercover?"

When Tonya returned, she said, "This coat is much warmer. It's the one that I wear when I go for my walk every evening."

"What color is it?" I asked and held my breath.

"It's maroon. What's your favorite color?" she asked.

Too bad it's not more muted. Maroon is too easy to see.

"Gray," I said, and she laughed.

"Why did I ask? I knew that," she said as we strolled to the library.

When we stepped inside, the warmth was a stark contrast to the cold outside. Larry was heads down at a table as he and three blobs pored over their notes. One of the blobs jumped up and hurried to Tonya. "Are you doing okay?"

"I'm fine. I had a wonderful morning. We can talk later; you study, and I'll read."

Justin-blob hurried back to his seat, and Tonya said, "Thanks again, Gray Lady. You've shown me how to open doors."

"Good."

Larry looked up at the sound of my voice and hurried to me. When he reached me, he hugged me. "Hi. honey. Everything okay?"

"Great. We're going home. See you later."

Larry kissed me, then Palace Guard and I went back to the apartment.

I took off my coat and kicked off my boots. "Really productive morning," I said. "I think I'll call Ms. Betty."

Palace Guard narrowed his eyes.

"I'm just going to ask an innocent question."

CHAPTER NINETEEN

I picked up my phone and called the library. "Hello, Ms. Betty. I was reading some old procedures and remembered a patron at the library when I worked with Olivia who was a diabetic. If he missed lunch, he'd crash. Olivia always packed an extra sandwich in case he went into a slump, so I started doing it too, but I never saw anything in our procedures that required us to do something like that. Do your procedures address anything like that?"

"Not really, but Wayne knows all our patrons and their medical complaints and keeps tabs of the diabetics and our heart patrons."

"Was Olivia diabetic?"

"I'm not sure; I do know she was prediabetic when she was younger, so she may have been. I can see where being diabetic would have made her more sensitive to the needs of other diabetics."

"That's an interesting observation. Do you think Wayne might be diabetic?"

"I've never thought about it before, but he might be."

"It was just a thought because the lack of any guidance in our old procedures struck me."

Ms. Betty twittered. "Now I'll need to research signs and symptoms of a diabetic emergency and the recommended initial treatment for lay persons. I'll see you next week."

After we hung up, I said, "I'm definitely suspicious of Wayne Dillard. I can see where he might think I'd become depressed because of my eye, so I would be on his list of victims, wouldn't I?"

Palace Guard nodded, and Spike put his hands over his ears.

"Oh, you're right; Tonya might be another potential victim with her hearing deficit, and her regular evening walk in her same jacket would definitely make her an easy target."

I picked up my phone and sent a text to Larry. "Please ask Justin to go with Tonya on her walks."

Larry replied, "Will do."

I sighed. "I wish I could have some hot tea."

I found the pitcher of sweet tea in the refrigerator and put a small glass in the sink before I poured sweet tea mostly into the glass. After I returned the pitcher to the refrigerator, I picked up the glass and spilled a little in the sink. I stood at the sink and took a long drink of tea then set my glass back down.

I rinsed and dried my hands as my phone buzzed a text from Cassandra with the coordinates.

"Good. Let's check to see how deep in the woods the shack is." I pulled up the map on my computer and asked for directions from our apartment to the coordinates for the shack.

"The shack is only about three miles from the campus. We could easily walk there in forty-five minutes, couldn't we?"

Palace Guard nodded.

"I'm a little surprised at how close the shack is to the campus. For some reason, I expected it to be farther away from town." I sighed. "Noreen's letter is the only evidence we have that might clear Dean, so right now, we still have two potential suspects."

My phone buzzed a text from Grandma D. "Your logic is impeccable even though we're not privy to a confirmation."

Palace Guard stared at me when I pumped my fist. "Yes!"

"Dean's wife was undercover. She wouldn't have been investigating her husband, though. I think she was investigating Dillard."

Palace Guard raised an eyebrow.

"Okay, you're skeptical; I admit I have no proof, but I'm sure I'm right." I flipped my hair. "After all, my logic is impeccable."

Palace Guard rolled his eyes as Larry came into the apartment.

"Are you two in the middle of an argument? The weather is warming up to almost mild. How would you like to go to the dog park after lunch? There's a trail to run; maybe Palace Guard could give me a workout."

"Fresh air sounds great as long as it isn't too cold."

Palace Guard and Spike nodded.

While Larry made sandwiches, Paul called me.

"Glenn and I finally feel like we're getting some traction. We set up a matrix with Dean's courses, Wayne's volunteer schedule, and the known victims, or to use our new terminology, the killer's successes and found a fallacy in our data. The dates we have for the successes are when the victim was found not when the victim was kidnapped."

"Wow; how can that be traction?"

"We do have the date reported missing for most of the victims, so we also have a small group of unreported successes, which doesn't really help us with unreported failures as far as we can see. I'm glad you understand all this because it sounds a little goofy when I say it aloud. On your question of indoors or outdoors, so far it appears that outdoors is the winner for successful abductions."

"So, you've matched the date the kidnapping was reported with Dean's and Wayne's schedules."

"Yes we did, but we also added the day before the family reported the abduction as a second possible kidnapping date and discovered that Dean was scheduled to teach during three of the kidnapping dates during the last five years, at least according to the class schedule, which assumes that he hadn't found a substitute. We found two schedule conflicts for Wayne to have been the kidnapper according to Ms. Betty's records for volunteer attendance. Our next step is to find the estimated time of day of the kidnappings. If the woman disappeared in the evening, for example, then any schedule conflicts for that day didn't matter."

"Y'all are awesome."

"We're just taking the data you give us and organizing it. We're your eyes until your sight improves." He chuckled. "Then you'll do in an hour what took two old men three days."

I smiled. "I really appreciate it."

"Our next step is to follow up on time of day for the kidnappings. I'll be getting back to you."

After we hung up, Larry said, "Lunch is ready. That was Paul? I only caught part of what he was saying."

While we ate, I explained the process Paul and Glenn followed and their results so far.

"Those two have so much knowledge. Too bad we can't get them to be instructors here."

I snickered. "I think they're having too much fun to be corralled into a classroom."

Larry shook his head. "You're right, but I'm going to call them with some of the problems that have us stumped to get their ideas." Larry narrowed his eyes. "Maybe after we get back from the dog park, we could talk about the one we're struggling with. You're the one that should be teaching these classes. Which reminds me: why is Justin struggling?"

"The material is not over his head; he's having trouble with stress. He's really worried about Tonya. How was he after Tonya and I left?"

"I thought he'd warmed up to us, but now I understand why his stress level dropped." Larry shook his head. "I should have realized that. I was terrified when you were in the hospital after the explosion."

He pulled me into a protective hug. "Little did I know that was only the beginning." He chuckled as he kissed the top of my head. "Guess I can't share that with Justin. It's not very reassuring at all, is it?"

After he released me, he smiled. "Let's go to the dog park for a normal afternoon."

"Do I need my heavy coat?" I asked as I pulled on my ballcap.

"Don't think so. Wear your sweatshirt and your lightweight jacket. The layers will keep you plenty warm."

When we reached the dog park, Lucy ignored the younger and more energetic dogs that chased each other or the balls that their owners threw for them; instead, she and Spike investigated a hole she'd found at a far corner.

Before Larry and Palace Guard headed for the trail, I said, "I want to run with you too. I brought my running shoes."

"Should have known," Larry grumbled. "Same drill as before? Palace Guard and I run with you, then Palace Guard runs back with you before he catches up with me and runs my legs off?"

Palace Guard stood next to me in his running shorts and shoes as he bounced on his toes and grinned.

I snickered and pulled out my running shoes. After I put them on, I did a light stretch then walked to the beginning of the trail and back. "Okay, I'm ready."

I started out more slowly than I expected, but after I warmed up a bit, my speed increased a little. When I was ready to stretch my legs and run, Palace Guard put up his hand, and Larry said, "Time to go back."

"I was ready to hit my old pace." I glared at the two men who stood next to each other on the trail and blocked my way like a wall.

"Fine." I turned back and ran as fast as I could. I heard Palace Guard behind me, and I pushed to run faster. When I reached the bench where I'd left my boots, I stopped and raised my arms in victory. After Palace Guard smacked my hand with a high-five then left to catch up with Larry, I collapsed on the bench and leaned forward to put my hands on my thighs as I struggled to breathe.

When I finally caught my breath and straightened up, Spike punched my arm then chased Lucy as she ran after a squirrel.

I rubbed my arm where Spike punched me. *Spike knows how hard I worked.*

I relaxed a few minutes more then jogged to join Lucy and Spike. *Feels good. I'm getting there.*

When a sudden gust of cold wind swooped down from the north, we hurried to the truck. I opened the door for Lucy then climbed into the passenger's seat. "Brr. I'm glad Larry left the truck unlocked."

Larry and Palace Guard ran full speed to the truck, and Larry jumped in and turned on the engine. "That was an abrupt blast of frigid air. The forecast was for colder temperatures tonight, but I didn't expect the front to hit us so early. We're supposed to get fog tonight too; I can't think of a better night to have hot chocolate and cuddle in front of the fireplace. We need a fireplace in our next house."

"Agreed," I said, and the men nodded.

After we were home, Lucy and I rushed inside as Larry and the men followed us. Larry changed out of his running shorts to jeans and a warm shirt, and Spike changed to a buffalo plaid flannel shirt and a wool cap with earflaps.

"I need a cap like Spike's," I said.

"Does look warm, doesn't it? I'll have to see what I can find online."

While Larry made our hot chocolate and stirred the leftover gumbo, I sat on the sofa with Lucy and rubbed her face. "Do I have any long johns? My knees are aching from the cold." I pulled the afghan over my legs.

"I don't think so; I'll add long johns for both of us. We'll be ready for this cold weather in a couple of weeks."

I snickered. "Just in time for the spring warm up."

"You got it, sweetie. Come to the table for your hot chocolate and cookies."

"Cookies? We still have cookies left?"

"I found a second stash that Jennifer had hidden under the large bag of broccoli in the freezer," Larry said.

While I drank my hot chocolate and Larry put the lid on the pot of rice to cook, I asked, "How did your study session go?"

"We still have a couple of questions that need work. Okay if I run them past you tomorrow?"

"That would be fun."

"I thought so too. How many cookies do you want after supper?"

"I want two, but I have a feeling I can eat only one because Jennifer's cookies are huge."

Larry stirred the gumbo. "Gumbo is perfect for a cold, damp, windy night," he said.

When the gumbo was hot, and the rice had cooked, Larry served up our food in bowls.

"I don't know if I have any long-ago Cajun relatives, but it sure feels like I've got Cajun blood flowing through my veins tonight," Larry said.

"Me too."

"Dat makes sense, sha," Larry said in his best Chef Daryl Cajun accent, and I laughed.

"Pretty good impression, wasn't it?" Larry asked.

"Yes, dear," I said, and Larry laughed.

Larry cleared our dishes after we ate and put our leftovers in the refrigerator. "This will be perfect for tomorrow's lunch. Do you want more hot chocolate with your cookie?"

"I'd love a cup of hot tea," I said.

Larry turned on the kettle, then as he dropped my tea bag into the hot water in my cup, his phone rang.

"I'll be right there. Who's organizing? Call Ron. I'll be right there."

"I need to go." Larry hurried to the bedroom then returned with his backpack.

"What's going on?"

"While Justin was in the shower, Tonya told him she was going out to get her gloves out of the car, so they wouldn't be cold in the morning; he told her to wait." Larry exhaled. "When he got out of the shower, she wasn't there; Justin thought she'd decided to take her walk after all but when he couldn't find her, he realized he needed help; he's calling Ron. I'll keep you posted."

"Larry, wait," I said, but he was gone.

"We know where she is, Palace Guard. Let's go."

Palace Guard shook his head and pointed at Spike's shirt then at me.

"I need to layer. Got it."

I hurried to the bedroom and pulled off my jeans, put on my pajama bottoms for a layer under my jeans then pulled on my jeans. I put on a sweater over my long-sleeved T-shirt and tucked in the sweater, so I could pull my pistol out of its holster before I put on my heavy coat. "I don't have a warm cap; I'll just wear my ballcap."

I grabbed my backpack and my jo. "Ready?" I asked.

When Palace Guard and Spike went outside with me, I moaned. "Oh no, fog."

Palace Guard tapped my arm, and I ran tentatively through the fog at first then warmed up and gained the confidence to run at my full speed.

Thirty minutes. If I can keep up my pace, we'll be there in thirty minutes. Hang on, Tonya. We're coming.

When we were getting close, Palace Guard called a halt. At first, I was irritated, then I realized how hard I was breathing. As I slowed my breathing, I realized that Spike had run with us. I exhaled slowly then nodded; we ran at a pace that was comfortable for me. Palace

Guard stopped me in a stand of trees, then Spike disappeared into the fog. When he returned, Palace Guard guided me. *We must be following Spike; I am definitely walking blind.*

When I stepped into the shack, the smell of blood and burned flesh took away my breath. I heard quiet grunts of labored breathing, and Palace Guard guided me to kneel next to a blob; it was Tonya-blob. I hummed a fairy tune as I touched her. She didn't have on a coat, her skin was cold, and her breaths were ragged. *At least she's breathing.*

When I struggled to remove my coat to put over her, Palace Guard helped me. Spike knelt next to me and put his face close to hers, then he disappeared. My hands began shaking from the cold, but I continued to hum.

"Maggie?" she whispered. "Are you here? I hear a song. Is it you, Maggie? He told me he'd kill me then Justin if I made a sound. He pulled out my hearing aids and put tape over my eyes then taped my hands and legs." Tonya sobbed. "He beat me; I think I have some broken ribs because it's hard to breathe. When I heard him scream and smelled burning flesh, I knew Kiki burned him; he ran away from her, but I know he's coming back to kill me."

When I reached for my knife to cut the tape away from her hands and feet, Palace Guard tapped my arm to rise and step away from Tonya.

"No, no, don't go. I don't care if you're a dream or imaginary, stay with me."

When I heard the rising panic in her voice, I hummed a short tune, and she sighed, "Ahh; thank you."

After I stood in the spot that Palace Guard selected for me, he tapped my left hand to be ready to throw my knife, and I pulled it from its holster and held it at my side.

I remained motionless at the sound of footsteps as they drew closer then stopped.

"Well, if this isn't my lucky day; two for one. Can't get any better than that," Wayne said.

I smiled as I waited for Palace Guard to toss the rock, and when it hit the wooden floor of the shack, my knife flew through the air as a shot rang out.

Cringe later. I drew my pistol, and Palace Guard adjusted my aim then tapped for me to shoot; I pulled the trigger then maintained my shooting stance as I waited for Palace Guard's next tap.

When a truck skidded as it sped down the lane toward the shack then slid to a stop, its headlights lit up the shack, and Palace Guard tapped my shoulder to stand down.

"Maggie!" Larry shouted. "Don't shoot me!"

"What is it? Who's there? I heard shots." Tonya's voice rose in terror as she tried to move away from the door.

I knelt next to her and stroked her cheek as I hummed; Larry rushed into the shack and lifted me up from the floor. "Are you okay? Is Tonya okay?"

He held onto me and whispered, "I had to step over Wayne Dillard to get in here. Good shot, girl. Please don't ever run off like that again."

Justin rushed into the shack. "Tonya, are you okay? Where are your hearing aids?"

"Wayne Dillard threw them away," I said. "Tonya's ribs may be broken."

"One side of Wayne's face is burned. How did that happen?" Larry asked.

I shrugged then whispered, "Tell you later."

"Oh man, pulling off this tape from her eyes is awful," Justin said.

"Let me," I said.

"Thanks, I'll cut the tape that's around her legs and wrists," Justin said.

Another car pulled in near the shack, and its flashing blue lights flooded the area.

"Be right back." Larry strode out of the shack to greet the latest arrivals.

I sat on the floor next to Tonya and hummed a fairy tune as I slowly lifted off the tape from her eyes.

Tonya inhaled then groaned. "Breathing deep was a bad move on my part. Thanks, Maggie. Not being able to see or hear was terrifying. Did you know Kiki's on your right shoulder?"

I touched my right shoulder and felt tiny talons.

"Hi, Kiki. Thanks for the help."

I felt a flutter on my ear that tickled, and I giggled.

"She gave you a dragon kiss," Tonya said.

"Thank you, Kiki; it was nice," I said.

Larry returned and threw Lucy's dog blanket from his truck around my shoulders then helped me up. As we walked together to his truck, he asked, "Did you know you left your phone in the truck?"

"I didn't know that. I was cold when we got back from the dog park; I guess I was in a hurry to get inside." I shook my head. "I never would have found it."

"You got a text from Della. She said number one was under arrest for embezzlement and fraud, and he was surprised because he thought you were investigating him. Do you know what that means?"

I snickered. "It means that Kate nabbed her man."

"Dean Sanchez? So, she was investigating him when we thought he was her boyfriend? That's really sneaky."

"That's our Kate." My teeth chattered, and I shivered. "Oh my gosh, you left the engine running; the truck will be warm."

"I didn't expect you to give your coat to Tonya, but I thought you'd be cold."

"I thought I'd never be warm again." I shuddered as Larry helped me into the truck where Palace Guard and Spike waited in the back seat.

Larry slid into his seat. "Are you hurt at all, sweetheart?"

"Not at all. How did you get here so fast? I thought Spike went for help when he disappeared into the fog, but I wasn't sure how long it would take for him to find you."

"When Spike came to get me, he put his hand over one eye then covered his ears, so I knew you'd found Tonya. I yelled at Justin to follow me, and Spike jumped into my truck and pointed. Justin didn't hear me, but when he saw me tear out, he was on my tail; I called for law enforcement and an ambulance on the way."

"I knew Spike would think of something."

"I want to hear everything, but first, how did Wayne's face get burned."

"The dragon."

"Maybe I don't want to hear everything after all. Let's go home; Lucy's probably worried."

After we reached the apartment, I sat on the sofa, and Larry wrapped me in a blanket then fixed a cup of hot tea for me and opened a beer for himself. "Let me know when you want a beer; I thought you'd rather warm up first." He put his arm around me and took a big sip. "Okay. Now I'm ready to hear everything. Start with the dragon that burned Dillard."

"It's actually very simple. Tonya's imaginary dragon from her childhood stayed with her. Wayne Dillard was beating Tonya with his fists and broke her ribs; Kiki blasted him with flames to save Tonya."

"A giant dragon was in that little shack?"

"Kiki is a miniature dragon. She sat on my shoulder while I took off the tape from Tonya's eyes and gave me a kiss."

"Did you see the dragon?" Larry asked.

I giggled, Palace Guard rolled his eyes, and Spike did his wacky dance.

"You want some cheese and crackers? Wasn't that a graceful change of subject to cover up my amazingly clueless question? Better yet, why don't I warm up some leftover gumbo? I can warm up enough to fill a couple of mugs for us."

"That sounds good," I said.

"Why wasn't there any tape across Tonya's mouth?" Larry asked while he stirred the gumbo and added a little more chicken broth.

"Dillard told her he'd kill her and her husband if she made a sound. I think the purpose was to add to her terror."

"I'm not sure I know the whole story on Dean Sanchez." Larry brought two large mugs of gumbo and a plate of crackers and cheese and put them on the table in front of the sofa. "I forgot to tell you that Gary jumped into the car with Justin and was at the shack. If Dillard wasn't already dead, I think it would have been a toss-up over who nudged him over the edge, me or Gary."

I shook my head. "I'll never understand Gary. Speaking of Sanchez and Gary, Gary was investigating him for Kate. If you already knew that, I apologize. Dean's wife was investigating Dillard and must have gotten close because he shot her."

Larry's phone buzzed a text. "Justin said the doctors are still evaluating Tonya, but all they've found so far are three broken ribs. He said thanks."

I spooned up a bite of gumbo and blew on it then popped it into my mouth. "Mmm. This is great."

"Did you and Paul have enough evidence to convict Dillard?" Larry asked.

"We were close. You'd have to ask Paul how solid it was because that's not my area of expertise. We can go through it sometime when you feel like it."

"Blue lights are coming our way," Larry said.

I picked up his beer and took a big swig. "I'm off duty. I learned that from you."

Larry kissed me. "You're amazing, sha."

ACKNOWLEDGEMENTS

Huge thanks to my husband for his awesome advice and for his patience when I tell him something funny that Maggie said.

Thanks to the fabulous cooks and bakers in my family. You are an inspiration for Maggie. Thanks to my editor who is an absolute genius and my daughter and daughters-in-law, the original Mom Force.

Thank you for reading. *You keep reading; I'll keep writing!*

What to read next?

SLIP FROM SIGHT, BOOK 6
MAGGIE SLOAN THRILLER

Runaway girls. Calculating charmers. Human trafficking. Maggie sees the link; the kingpin sees her as an easy kill.

Maggie's on the trail of a human trafficking organization that she believes includes a ring of kidnappers and charismatic men that lure vulnerable women to a remote "resort." When friends die in their efforts to uncover the criminals, Maggie steps up her game; as she closes in, the mastermind is confident she'll step into his trap and die.

Subscribe: to the newsletter!

Look for the Subscribe button on www.judithabarrett.com

ABOUT THE AUTHOR

Judith A. Barrett is an award-winning author of mystery, crime, and survival science fiction novels with action, adventure, and a touch of supernatural to spark the reader's imagination. Her unusual main characters are brilliant, talented, and down-to-earth folks who solve difficult problems and stop killers. Her novels are based in small towns and rural areas in south Georgia and north Florida with sojourns to other southern US states.

Judith lives in rural Georgia on a small farm with her husband and two dogs. When she's not busy writing, Judith is still busy working on the farm, hiking with her husband and dogs, or watching the beautiful sunsets from her porch.

Website   www.judithabarrett.com

Barrett Book Shop www.BarrettBookShop.com

Subscribe to the eNewsletter via her website

Let's keep in touch!

www.ingramcontent.com/pod-product-compliance
Lightning Source LLC
Chambersburg PA
CBHW030352030726
47497CB00002B/302